THE KEPT MAN

ALSO BY JAMI ATTENBERG

Instant Love

THE KEPT MAN

Jami Attenberg

RIVERHEAD BOOKS

a member of Penguin Group (USA) Inc.

New York

2007

RIVERHEAD BOOKS
Published by the Penguin Group
Penguin Group (USA) Inc., 375 Hudson Street, New York, New York 10014, USA ·
Penguin Group (Canada), 90 Eglinton Avenue East, Suite 700, Toronto, Ontario
M4P 2Y3, Canada (a division of Pearson Penguin Canada Inc.) · Penguin Books Ltd,
80 Strand, London WC2R 0RL, England · Penguin Ireland, 25 St Stephen's Green,
Dublin 2, Ireland (a division of Penguin Books Ltd) · Penguin Group (Australia),
250 Camberwell Road, Camberwell, Victoria 3124, Australia (a division of Pearson
Australia Group Pty Ltd) · Penguin Books India Pvt Ltd, 11 Community Centre,
Panchsheel Park, New Delhi—110 017, India · Penguin Group (NZ), 67 Apollo Drive,
Rosedale, North Shore 0632, New Zealand (a division of Pearson New
Zealand Ltd) · Penguin Books (South Africa) (Pty) Ltd, 24 Sturdee Avenue,
Rosebank, Johannesburg 2196, South Africa

Penguin Books Ltd, Registered Offices:
80 Strand, London WC2R 0RL, England

Copyright © 2007 by Jami Attenberg

Published simultaneously in Canada

An excerpt of *The Kept Man* appeared, in a different form, in *Spork* magazine.

Library of Congress Cataloging-in-Publication Data

Attenberg, Jami.
The kept man / Jami Attenberg.
p.   cm.
ISBN 978-1-59448-952-5
1. Painters—Fiction. 2. Invalids—Fiction. 3. Arts—Themes, motives—Fiction.
4. Family secrets—Fiction. 5. Psychological fiction. 6. Domestic fiction. I. Title.
PS3601.T784K47 2007   2007017392
813'.6—dc22

Printed in the United States of America
1   3   5   7   9   10   8   6   4   2

Book design by Amanda Dewey

THE KEPT MAN

Prologue

I have been waiting for my husband to die for six years. Martin has been in a coma ever since he knocked his head—*hard*, of course, it's not as though he just bumped it one day and then was (almost) gone forever—in his studio. First there was an aneurysm, an explosion of sorts in his brain, and then he fell from the ladder he was standing on, fifteen feet up in the air, knocking his head on a painting, another one next to it, the edge of an easel, and finally landing solidly on a paint can, a serene blue oil, that tipped over and spilled forth, mixing with the blood that began to ripple from his head, so when I found him— oh yes, I found him, when I came back from my morning walk on the waterfront, maybe an hour after the fall, but don't worry, if I had gotten home earlier it wouldn't have made a difference, the doctors have told me, he was completely fucked on impact— I at first thought he was merely sleeping in a sea of paint, a mix gone bad. (Purple? He hated purple.) It wouldn't have been the first time he had napped on the floor of his studio. He spent nights there sometimes, instead of walking through one doorway, and then another, into our bed.

But then I saw the easel, and the second painting—an impressive piece depicting a woman bearing a strong resemblance to his mother in her younger days; the woman holds a cross made of garish red bulbs, the kind that might line the stage at a strip club, and she has the same peaceful, creepy look, the glazed smile and eyes, and the gray hues in uncomfortable places, that permeated so many of Martin's paintings—which had collapsed on its back on the floor. He wasn't careless like that. All of his work was neatly organized in stacks by year and then subject matter and then title as if at any moment someone might want to catalogue his work, which in fact several someones have since he entered—entered, like through a door, that's the only way to explain it, in one door, though never out the other—his coma.

I kneeled in my summer skirt, yellow, I remember, like a sour lemon candy, my bare knees impressing an outline in the paint next to him, and I touched his head, and I tried to turn him but he was heavy and I said, "Martin," and he said nothing, and then I said his name again, but louder, and still nothing, and then I slapped him and he didn't move, and then I said, "Martin Martin Martin." There was the ambulance, and a lot of noise, and me and Martin in the hospital, paint on his face, paint on my knees, the two of us the weirdest people in the room, as usual, only this time I didn't have anyone to talk to but myself.

Then came six years of waiting, all different kinds of waiting. Waiting for the doctors and test results and the final word (even though nothing has ever been final, really) is a different kind of waiting than waiting in the hospital lobby for the car service to take me back to Brooklyn at the end of the night, wrapped in a soft, small blanket stolen from his room. Waiting for phone calls to be returned from his parents, who start praying the minute you tell them, or his best friend, who can't stop cursing, is different from waiting for phone calls from a lawyer, who is all business and zero hope, or an anxious owner of a small art gallery whose whole life will be transformed. Waiting for visiting hours to start is different from waiting for visiting hours to end. Waiting for the nurse to give him his medicine is different from waiting for the pharmacist to bring yours; the pills that help you sleep through the night. Waiting for him to get accepted into the first nursing home, the first one that will take him, anyone, please, take him, is different from waiting for the second nursing home (the one that wins awards, the one that people whisper about and pray for, like a dream come true this place, they say) to open their doors to him. Waiting for the first doctor is different from waiting for the latest doctor, the one who will tell you what you already know. Waiting for Martin to wake up is a different kind of waiting than waiting for him to die.

Wake up. Die. Wait.

PART ONE

1.

It's spring today, at last, as I search for a decent laundromat in Williamsburg. Turquoise-blue cloudless skies, the remnants of last night's rain huddled in the gutters. I leave my apartment, take a left, and head to Bedford Avenue, past a man huddled on the ground with a plastic bag, his dog idling nearby, past the Brooklyn Brewery, past the cool record store I have no use for anymore but always wish I did. On Bedford I find all the old-timers are still in existence, the ones with the grubby floors, painful fluorescent lights that amplify pore size, the depressing clang of Spanish music mixed with the tumble of battered underpants against ancient machines. A roommate-wanted flier taped to the window, next to an offer for guitar lessons. You can fax here, and make copies, too. Open late. A gumball machine raises pathetic quarters for charity. It seems impossible to imagine that the machines in these particular environments would be capable of effectively cleaning my clothes. They could beat the stains down into a state of submission, but they would never kill them.

Still on Bedford, I walk south, my sack of laundry on my back, past the new crop of restaurants: a gourmet pizza place that spits out the scent of homegrown herbs, a new bagel joint to vie with the old one farther down Bedford, and across the street, a fancy Chinese place with an ornate front, and a sign that promises a back garden. And so many clothing stores and furniture stores and stores of just *crap*, the kind of stuff you think you need but you don't, like hand-blown glass candleholders and purses made of hemp and body salts imported from Costa Rica. When I moved here to be with Martin years ago, there was nothing but delis and pizza joints around, and a couple of Polish butchers. I'm happy the Greenpoint Tavern is still there, the grubby old Polish bar that serves beer out of styrofoam cups. Looking at all of this change makes me feel like I need a beer, and I almost would have gone in had it not been eleven a.m.

I walk the waterfront, usually, when I leave my apartment. If I leave my apartment. I prefer the quiet thunder of trucks to the buzz of hipster kids on Bedford. The sound of wheels on gravel, hurling into potholes. A dusty mass of chopped-up street against the dirt-covered sides of the trucks. (I think about that dirty kid from the Peanuts cartoon—Pigpen—as I pass through it. Always a dark cloud following him.) But there are days when I am forced to interact with the world, days when my carefully constructed universe fails me. Like when my washing machine breaks—a churn, a spit of metal against metal, and then it was all over—and I'm too broke to call a repairman. I so want to be an elegant woman, delicately mourning her husband high up in a loft. But even Jackie O needed clean drawers.

As I approach Metropolitan, I see two punks, clothes gray with dirt, black pants, black combat boots, a T-shirt with "Fuck You" scrawled on it in Magic Marker on one of them, the other in a shirt, shredded but somehow still whole, defiantly battling rag status. They're squatting against a brick wall covered with graffiti, not wild, hell-raising graffiti, but commissioned-by-the-community graffiti, blocks of wall real estate carefully delegated to top vandals in order to keep them out of trouble.

I feel a flush of warmth for the punks, these remnants of years past, when things in the neighborhood were a lot messier. They hold out their hands to me, and the one in the "Fuck You" T-shirt says, "Want to buy me a beer?"

"Sure," I say. I drop my bag of laundry on the ground, shove my hand in my pocket, pull out a dollar bill and drop it in his hand. I owe them already for playing their part in my life. It's like this every time I leave the house. I always feel like people are grouped together in bunches, and then they take action, they perform just for me. I never feel like I'm a participant in my surroundings. I'm just standing and watching, outside myself, outside the world, looking in somehow.

"Thanks ma'am," he says. He has pretty, focused blue eyes. The pupils are like stones.

"You have much luck?" I say.

"Some days," he says. "Mostly it's a bunch of fucking cheap-ass yuppies." He looks at me in my neat blue jeans and the ridiculous pink cashmere sweater Martin had given me for Christmas one year, my short black hair held tidy with a barrette. "No offense," he says.

On the corner two young women, lithe in short skirts and high boots, embrace goodbye, and the other punk yells, "Can I have a hug too?" The women turn to find the voice, and then give faint smiles, separate, walk in opposite directions.

He pokes his friend. "You see that? They were this close to doing it."

"It's better at night," he continues. "When everyone's shit-faced." He shrugs. "But it's not like I have anything better to do today."

That, I understood.

I lean down, pick up my laundry bag, and hoist it on my shoulder.

"You want to hang out?" he says. "We could party or something. If you've got some more money, I've got a number." He pats his pocket.

"Laundry day," I say.

"Laundry. Yeah. I need to do some of that sometime."

I laugh, he laughs, I start walking. I know better than to waste my time worrying, or even lingering.

At the corner, I scan the horizon. A few blocks ahead on the right, past the YMCA, is a laundromat that also offers postal services. To my right, a construction zone. And to my left, there it is, a massive, shiny, new laundromat. I hate myself a little bit for wanting the new, feel disloyal in some way to my old neighborhood, but this was not a six-dollar microbrew versus Budweiser in a styrofoam cup, these were my clothes, the last vestiges of identity I had left. If I can still look good, just a little bit, I can hold on a bit longer, for me, for Martin.

I walk a half block and stand in front of it, face the high glass windows, the warehouse-like quality. There are easily one hundred machines in there, a Galaga videogame, an Internet workstation, and a seating area with standard Ikea-issue furniture: a pale wooden table and chairs, plus a gray couch that looked like it would be comfortable enough. The laundromat is empty of people, but the machines—all spectacular metallic whirls—are in motion. I can almost feel the vibrations from where I stand, the water, the bubbles, the force of furious cleansing.

I enter, drop my bag to the floor, and start dragging it toward the aisles. The square-tiled floors are new, still bright and pristine. Techno music filters overhead, the thump weaving with the rhythm of the washing machines. A dance club for washing machines. Waiter, where's my cocktail? How delightful and preposterous. *This* is a place where I can clean my clothes.

At the front counter a young Asian man, hairless and short, with swiftly moving tiny hands, stands with an older, missile-shaped woman. She has dark skin and plucked eyebrows. She is shaking her hands at the cash register and her voice, cigarette-scratched and low, is tired.

"Not my fault," I hear her say.

I pick an aisle—Right? Left? No, dead center—and head down it, my bag sliding behind me, a giant slug.

Ordinarily I enjoy doing laundry. It gives me a sense of accomplishment. I can make a whole day revolve around it. Reds in one load, yellows in another. A white load with lots of bleach, a load of delicates. All other colors go together, and then one more load for anything denim-related: jeans, skirts, a jacket, and one of Martin's old work shirts I sleep in sometimes, flecks of paint forever a part of the fabric. When you have your own washer and dryer and nothing but time, the possibilities are endless. But out in the world, at the laundromat, it is in and out, get going, no time to waste. Efficiency. Speed. Exactitude.

And so: quarters, soap, start.

I shuffle back to the front seating area, take the couch, feet up and underneath me. I pick up a *Village Voice* sitting next to me. There's a band on the cover, an intense bunch of older men, haggard eyes, messy hair. The man in the center is wearing dark nerdy glasses and he is smiling. They are the next big thing, the cover tells me. The best band you don't know about yet. Be careful what you wish for, I think.

The front door opens, and three men enter, a stream of yellow sun behind them so bright that it pinches at my eyes. One is holding a notebook and a coffee, one is pushing a stroller with one hand and holding a coffee in the other, and the third just has a coffee. They are laughing, they are smiling. They are all friends, I think. I am immediately jealous because I have no friends anymore, at least not friends like that. Stroll around town friends. Grab a beer and shoot the shit friends. Do your laundry together friends. You know: fun.

No, I have friends who are mostly no fun at all, even when it feels like we're supposed to be having a good time. I have Alice, Martin's art dealer, an extremely tart British woman—just thinking about her makes me want to suck in my cheeks—who tends to my financial needs and occasionally rewards me with art-world gossip and vague compliments about my loyalty. I'm relatively certain neither one of us likes the other. And I have Davis, Martin's best friend, a combustible Tennessean who likes to moon about old times with me, occasionally holding me too close for too long. There are strings with both of them, attached from so many parts of my body that I feel like a marionette when I'm around them. These are not the kind of friends I need, but these are the kind of friends I have.

The one with the notebook sees me on the couch and hesitates, looks at me like I'm in the wrong place—What are you doing on my couch?—then sits down on the chair diagonal from me. The other two ignore me, the man with the carriage seats himself on the far end of the couch, and the third man rests in the chair across from me, which he promptly shifts to face the other two. I open the *Voice* and try to ignore them, too. But it's impossible: the man across from me looks like a movie star, slender and tight all over, from his chest to his narrow waist and hips—his clothes look like they could slip off his body, and indeed his pants hang precariously low on his hips—he is a precise line, but not unbending or uninviting, just well sculpted, and then his head is big, it seems to come into focus more than anything else, as if the thin lines of his body are directing me to look at that face, a mysterious mixture of ethnicities—the hue of his skin seems Middle Eastern, the wide blue eyes are Norwegian or Swedish, the shape of his nose, Roman, off a statue in one of those hidden rooms at the Met where they keep the crumbly old pieces, and the smooth skin that should belong to a woman, as if he has never had to shave a day in his life, and then finally his jaw, set perfectly, the final piece of a jigsaw puzzle clasped into place. The man with the baby—a girl, I think, she is in pink, I can see her bootied feet kicking from where I sit—reminds me of the men in Martin's family, solid westerners, with his stocky chest, a mountain of a frame, and his blond beard, gray in small patches, matching the gray in his temples, a big mess of hair all over, on his chest, too, I could see it coming up through his shirt, small curls, darker than the hair on his head. The man with the notebook is wearing glasses identical to those of the man on the cover of the *Voice*, and he has thick muttonchop sideburns that my eyes follow up to his sharp, dark hair, a wicked curl hanging over his forehead and down to his eyes, which are golden brown and seem gentle, but I don't believe it, his lips are fixed too wryly for any sort of sincerity, and I realize I like looking at his face because I don't know what is going on there at all, ah, but then there's the rest of him: tall, so tall, with long legs, and I imagine there are muscles underneath his jeans, finely honed like an expensive knife set, all in place, just like his arms, those I can see, they are tan and the upper parts bulge out of his shirt, short-sleeved, button-down, loose, and his feet are long, too, long toes stretching out from blue flip-flops, and from the neck down he is just one long perfect line.

Looking at them is like when Martin used to take my picture at night up on the roof of our building with one of his rickety old cameras: a pop, a flash, I'm blinded, and then I can see. I am suddenly hungry to know them, to know everything about them. I have not wanted to know anyone new in a very long time.

The man with the notebook leans forward, alert, his dark, thick sideburns casting an intense look on his face, and speaks:

"Okay, so my wife's kid brother, he's living in Texas the last ten years. Austin. He works in technology, got in at the right time, got out at the right time, started over at the right time, and made a bunch of money. Stinking rich. Like everyone else in my wife's family."

The movie star across from me rolls his eyes at his friend. A supportive eye roll.

"He goes away for vacation last winter. Skiing, somewhere in Montana. Like out near Yellowstone, this little fly-fishing town out there. It's where they filmed *A River Runs Through It* or something. He asked us if we wanted to come but Lily wouldn't go for it. I thought it sounded like fun, but she wanted a tan instead. Anyway, so he goes out there with a few of his buddies, and they tear it up, skiing all day, drinking all night. Bunch of rich tech guys pretending like they're cowboys, something they can't be in their hometown because the real cowboys in Texas have got their number. They hang out with the locals, who apparently are total freaks, just a bunch of hardcore drunks. Eccentrics. He gets into really intense conversations with these locals about nothing at all. Suddenly he finds meaning in small things he never thought about before. The mountains. The trees. The snow. The sunrise and the sunset. Fish. You gotta be here for fly-fishing season, they tell him. You can't miss it. You have to see the sun hit the fish right after you catch it. Some guy gives him this whole speech about the colors of the fish, they're sitting there drinking whiskey one night, and he just listens to him roll, and, he told me, it was like the guy was singing practically."

"Rainbow trout," says the man with the baby carriage. He has stopped rocking it. The sun glints in his hair and beard.

"So the vacation's over, he heads back to Austin. He starts fly-fishing, gets really into it. He stops working on the weekends, spends all his time out on the lake there. Lake Buchanan. He joins this club, starts hanging out with these old fishing guys, drinking on the weekends, like he did in Montana. Basically he begins to re-create his Montana experience in Texas. Reframes his life."

I remember a time when Martin took off, alone, for his family's cabin in Washington, near the Oregon border. He didn't want to come back, either.

"And nobody gets it," says the movie star. That skin, so shiny and clean and tan.

"Nobody gets it. His girlfriend doesn't get it. His friends get it a little bit, but they were in Montana on *vacation*. You go, you have your fun, you leave it all behind. And then you go back to work. But even though he's fishing, he's having his fun, he can't see the colors on the fish, it's not like he imagined. He starts to think about how maybe the fish are different in Montana, maybe Texas fish aren't as good as the Montana fish. Maybe he needs to go back to Montana. Maybe the fishing is better there."

The baby coos. The washing machines whirl. The techno music drops, then rises.

"He called us last night. He's in Montana. Not only is he in Montana, he's not coming back. At least not anytime soon. He's checked into some cheap motel, he found a job waiting tables, he found the guy who gave him the whole fly-fishing closer to God speech, still sitting in the same place at the same bar he goes to every night, and said to him, 'Teach me everything you know.' And the guy said, 'Sure.' So that's what he's doing now. In Montana."

The other two men nod. The baby makes another noise, this one a little more aggressive, and her father pulls her out of the carriage and onto his lap. He begins to bounce her.

"Lily's freaking out. The whole family is. The phone was ringing off the hook last night. I say, let the man go to Montana. But, you know, nobody cares what I think."

The three men sit quietly for a moment. I flip to the personal ads at the back of the *Voice*. Transsexual escorts. Body work. Call now.

"I camped there for a week," says the man with the baby. "One summer in college. I saw shooting stars every night. I stopped counting them, there were so many." He dips his daughter down, hand behind her neck for support, then swings her back up again. She is delighted. He does it again. "You like stars, don't you, little girl? Don't you?"

"I wouldn't go to Montana," says the movie star. "I'd go to a tropical island somewhere, work at some beach bar. Con tourists out of their money. Live in a fucking straw hut."

"I couldn't imagine leaving," says the man with the baby. He puts his face close to hers, and she reaches out a tiny hand and touches his nose. "You have my nose," he says. "It's all yours."

"Well, I'm thinking about leaving my wife for her brother right about now," says the storyteller, and then they all laugh really hard, too hard, because it was funny, and it wasn't. "I swear I'd kill someone just to get an apartment in the city," he says. "I'm over Brooklyn."

I tap my hand on the couch.

"I would just get in a car and go," I say. It surprises me that I'm speaking; most of my words get trapped in my head and never make it out of my mouth, especially with strangers. And yet I knew I had to talk to them. They were shining so brightly in front of me. If I was going to be out in the world on this sunny spring day, I was going to take full advantage of it. "I don't know if I would ever stop."

They each turn to me, but differently. The movie star looks me up and down, lingers as long as he likes. The man with the baby gives me a quick glance, takes in as much as he can handle, which I guess isn't much, then returns his attention to his baby. The storyteller smacks his notebook on his leg a few times, looks me in the eye, and he seems a little dead in there, but also alive. He is stuck just like everyone else.

"You running from something?" he says. I feel a thrill run through my body, tiny knives against the inside of my skin.

"I just want to know what it's like out there," I said, and it was true. I didn't know what I was missing, but I knew I was missing something. People say that New York is the capital of the world. They say that anything you want or need you can get anytime in New York. They say that it can change your life forever, this city. That the world will open up before you once you move here. I say New York is an island, and it is just as easy to hide here as anywhere else.

We introduce ourselves. Mal with the notebook. Scott with the baby, whose name is Nina. Tony with the movie-star head. Antonio, he says. But Tony is fine.

Me, I'm Jarvis, Jarvis Miller. Yes, it is a strange name for a woman. It's a family name. A great-uncle.

They tell me they come here every Tuesday to do their laundry, that they're in a little club.

"What kind of club?" I say.

"The Kept Man Club," says Mal. He smiles wide. His smile is like a truck. He just hit me with a truck, I think. "We all stay at home while our wives work. We are bon vivants."

"Living the good life in a laundromat," I say.

"Hey fuck you, Mal, I have a job," says Tony. "I'm a real estate agent." He pulls his wallet out of his pocket and hands me a card, gives me a winning smile, those exotic lips stretching up over gleaming teeth. "If you're ever looking. But really I'm an actor. I am *always* going out on auditions." Is that a small flash of nerves? The bravado fallen to the floor, hustling time around his feet. Whatever it was, it quickly dissipates.

"I believe you," I say.

"Raising a child is a lot of work," says Scott. "It's a full-time job."

Mal looks at me, with that big grin. "Right, we all have jobs. I'm a writer. I am writing a novel. Look at me write."

"I'm looking," I say.

"Actually, I'm almost done with it," he says.

"What's it about?" I say.

"It's about sponging off your wife," he says. He gulps a laugh and no one looks at him. "Nah, it's about music. Being in a band. What else would I write about?"

"Your father," says Scott.

"Who's your father?" I say.

Mal says the name of a once popular and now famously corrupt senator. I had read the newspapers like everyone else. I knew Mal had an illegitimate brother in suburban Maryland. (The mother had worked for Mal's father as his press secretary.) Whatever money the family once had was probably gone, what with the sexual harassment and paternity suits. And yet he still gets a significant number of write-in votes every election from his Delaware constituency, even ten years after he was kicked out of office.

"Fuck that," says Mal.

"You know, everyone likes music," I offer.

"Mal used to be in a band," says Scott. "They were famous."

"Almost famous," says Mal.

"What about you?" says Tony. "What's your story?" He snaps at me. I don't think he likes me, but he's not the one I'm worried about.

I take a deep breath. Behind Tony, through the glass window, the punks walk by on the street, heads down and close, conspiring. I am tempted to wave.

"My husband has been in a coma for six years," I say. "So I'm just . . . waiting, I guess."

It is always a grim moment when I tell people who I am. My poor, sick husband has become my identity, and while I don't blame people for not being able to look beyond it, I sure wish they would. Of course I don't tell them that the value of my husband's artwork quadrupled after his accident—the art world loves tragedy—and the only reason why I'm in a laundromat is because my washer broke and I'm between checks right now, I'm waiting for the Australians, or the South Africans, or someone from some country far away, to ante up for another Martin Miller original. You better hurry up. There aren't that many paintings left, and I've got news for you, there won't be any more after they're gone.

"Jesus," says Tony. He feels like an asshole, I can tell. From now on he's going to be very nice to me.

"It's okay," I say. "It's really really okay. I am okay." And of course there is a catch in my throat, the coma catch, and of course there is a rim of water in my eyes now, and of course it is not okay.

Scott puts his hands on his daughter's face. She looks spectacularly soft. "Well, you can wait with us if you want," he says. "Every Tuesday, we're here. Waiting."

"Definitely," says Mal, and I see a full flood of life in his eyes. "The only thing is—you can't tell our wives anything we talk about."

"This is a safe space," says Tony, and he moves his hands in the shape of a circle until they meet.

"I swear I won't. I swear on my life," I say, and I mean it, and they know it, Scott and Tony solemnly nodding, and Mal making a little bit of a grossed-out face.

I realize that besides nurses and doctors and lawyers they are the first new people I've met in years. Maybe they're not the kind of friends I should be making, but these are the friends I want to have.

2.

I am walking in a daze down Bedford, replaying every moment of the afternoon. Go home, go back, and think about what just happened; think about the three handsome men, and their charms, no matter that the charms are transparent, just appreciate that they're working, appreciate the fact that you've been charmed after so many years of seeing nothing but the past, and a man in a hospital bed.

I drag the bag of laundry behind me on the ground. I am wondering how I will wait a whole week to see these men again. And then I remember, I should be good at waiting by now.

SIX YEARS OF Martin in a coma, some of them were longer than others. The first two years seemed short because everything happened quickly and repeatedly, like an asteroid attack in one of those seventies space flicks, the unstoppable assault of unique life-forms, real people and real problems, so terribly foreign to a woman like me. Two years, snap, gone. There was a newness to all of it, and I was invited to so many parties then, this mysterious half-widow of the brilliant Martin Miller, poor thing, let's call her, shall we? Let's have her over. Let's see how she's doing. Let's give her a nice night out. People will want to know how she is doing. How he is doing.

And I went because that was all I knew how to do, go to parties, that's all I had been doing for a decade, and I had always been so good at it. But then I was never the party guest they anticipated, I acted fucked-up because *my husband was in a coma*. My antics were not even interesting in a performance-art kind of way, no Courtney Love hugging the punk hippies around the candle-strewn memorials, and then a year later bouncing back to flash her designer-clad augmented breasts at anyone who would look. I would cry in the bathroom, but everyone knew, she's crying again. I would talk too much about him, for hours straight, clinging to their hands, a child's grip in a crowd. I would make awful faces when people asked me how I was doing, and then I wasn't even pretty anymore, the final layer of tolerability removed. So I stopped getting invited to parties.

Some of them were jealous, too, these artists who suck up emotion from everyone around them and spit it out on the canvas like babies regurgitating mother's milk. I think they were jealous because my suffering was *authentic*, while the only thing they had to complain about was the occasional broken heart or bad review. I guess I could stop it if I wanted to, but there were a dozen reasons why I didn't, not the least of which was that then I would be that woman who pulled the plug on her husband. And for six years I haven't wanted to be that woman.

The end of 2001 took forever. Forever. It was the only time I felt the same as everyone else. The city seemed leveled; we were all equally sad. I felt relieved that I wasn't alone anymore, and then guilty for that relief. After the attacks, people went broke all around me, and I became useful to them again. It was not enough that the city was mourning, but now so many were unemployed or unable to sell their work. People who had disappeared from my life reappeared only long enough to ask me for help. They'd all come to my loft, *I'm checking up on you*, but then what did I have to report anyway, so we'd talk about them, about their problems. It was sometimes exhausting, but mostly exhilarating. Out there in the world, people had needs; it was tantalizing to let myself believe I was no longer alone in my suffering. Poor, starving artists. So I gave them money to cover their rent, help save the gallery/loft/studio. I wasn't asking for them to repay me—I could barely leave my apartment—and they weren't getting in line to track me down either. After a few feeble attempts at payments, *I'm going to do the right thing by you, don't worry*, those people, too, would fade into the graffiti that lines the streets of Williamsburg, and along with them the brief, sweet, urgent feeling I had experienced in their need.

And then the last few years I've settled into it, this waiting game. I installed a wireless Internet connection in my house, and a washer and dryer, too: two steps to ensure I never need leave my house unless absolutely necessary. I contemplated suicide once. I tried doing volunteer work—Davis would give my number out to people for a few years, telling them I had a lot of time on my hands; I think he just wanted to get me out of the house—but I'd eventually lose interest, probably because I wasn't able to make any serious emotional connections with anyone. I have just been too numb for too long. Now I just write them checks: Planned Parenthood, a homeless shelter, a high-end thrift store that benefits an AIDS organization ("I thought at least you might have fun with all the clothes," said Davis sadly), and the Brooklyn Botanical Gardens, where I had one awkward night selling raffle tickets at a fund-raising event. All the shiny yuppies in cocktail attire searching for love amidst foliage drove me to a crying fit in the bathroom. They never asked me back.

Mostly I have made my life the business of Martin. Being with him was the best choice I ever made, and I've never found another way to spend my time that made me as happy. Occasionally I spend time on the Internet, searching for his name. There are more than a few fans out there, people who have made tribute websites, and every so often I find someone writing about their excitement at discovering his work. I saw that a student at Brown had written her thesis on him last year, and that touched me in a strange way. It was sweet, but also it seemed so final: his work encapsulated in one neat document.

It seems an impossible idea, too, capturing his work when no one knows where it all is anymore. Davis had set to work cataloguing it after Martin first fell into the coma, but about six months later Alice grabbed much of Martin's work from his other studio, the one over on North Third. (He used it at night when he didn't want to wake me. He had terrible aches at times, all over his body, that kept him up all night, and the only thing that soothed him was to paint.) I had seen this studio only a few times—a small, open space with one big window and a sagging futon on one side, with hundreds of paintings stacked on the other side—and I had no intention of contending with the mess. I was so tired then—I was at the hospital every day, all day long—that I just told them to sort it out between themselves, and Alice moved in for the kill. So Davis has some, Alice has a lot of it, I have whatever was in the loft, and then in Europe there are various gallery owners who have been resistant to sending me back his work. The excuses are myriad: they can't find it, it's too expensive to ship, it was a gift, we have a contract, on and on. I hired another lawyer, wrote another check, and prayed that someday everything would be in one place.

I keep selling off his work to keep the Martin Miller machine going. I sold off twenty of his paintings for an average of $50,000 each to pay his medical bills and my rent. They were from the series he did on the kids of Bedford Avenue. The pretty ones he picked up on the street and brought home in the afternoons. Polish girls and punks and art students and Dominicans. I cooked them lunch, and then he took their pictures, which he used later as the basis for the paintings. Sometimes they sat for him for a little while, occasionally a few returned. They weren't my favorite paintings of his—I preferred the portraits he did of his intimates—but they did get him some attention, that first burst, a little write-up of his show in the *Times*, he sold three of them, enough to cover rent for the next six months. All of his subjects came to the opening. That was a night. That was a party. I close my eyes and it's as if someone has tattooed an image of the party guests inside of them: a bunch of underage kids, some wearing thrift store dresses, others in tight jeans or torn jeans or baggy jeans hanging off their asses, getting drunk on bottled beer, and the

Polish girls, the tall ones in lots of eyeliner, every one of them getting hit on by Martin's best friend Davis. And the gallery owner, Alice, with her short, butchy hair and assured British voice, in the corner, talking to very important people, yet somehow hovering over Martin at the same time. It was like she had a third eye. And there was Martin, long, limber legs, the foundation to that chest, which heaved like a bull's, so much power in it, from his torso to his arms, one with black bars tattooed across it, remnants from his youth spent in punk bands, all of it topped off by this solid, handsome face—Can a jaw be charismatic? With its permanent stubble and masculine jut, it seemed to have a personality of its own—and his dark, focused eyes that tracked you, tracked everything, made sure you were paying attention; and he is trying to have very serious and very important conversations while keeping an eye out for all of them, the kids, his friends, and me. I'm there too, in a black cocktail dress with a strap across one shoulder (I got it for four dollars at the Goodwill), hosting, being very delightful and very carefree, drinking warm red wine out of paper cups, spilling it a little bit on my legs so that later on when Martin and I were in bed and he was kissing me all over, Martin said, "You taste like wine." And then he kissed me more.

Oh, Martin. Everything wraps around back to him. I can't say what I've been doing without him because it always returns back to what I did with him. One foot out the door, one foot in.

I did sell those paintings, though. I kissed them goodbye, as much as it hurt. One less piece of Martin in my possession. I've already lost the most important part of him, but there are still hundreds of tiny pieces left to sell, 325 to be exact.

It makes me sick to think about it, but the longer Martin lives, the more they're all worth. But then when he dies, look out, buddy. Hoo boy. Lucky me.

Lucky, lucky me.

NOW I'VE TURNED ON EIGHTH, a nice street where it seems like nice people live quietly. The laundry bag thumps behind me. I am planning imaginary outings with my new friends. Hop the Q train to Coney Island when it gets hot out, and dip our feet in the dirty Atlantic. We can rent a car and drive upstate, a day trip, a hike in the woods. A weekend in Atlantic City, gambling away our laundry money. Cotton candy on the boardwalk at midnight.

And then I remember: they have wives of their own, they have lives of their own, and there won't be any out-of-town trips with these men.

And besides, I have my own man waiting for me. How could I ever, ever forget?

3.

The day after I meet the men in the laundromat I visit Martin at the Beverly Home. I go every Wednesday. So I can get through the week. So I can ruin my week. It's a strange necessity, to feel this pain.

I take a car there because otherwise I'd have to take a complicated series of subways and buses, and I like to look my best for my husband, not show up all sweaty with the smell of other people. I've recently moved him to a new nursing home in Queens, one that we had been on the waiting list for since the first week after his accident. I never liked the smell of the last home. It seems like it shouldn't be that hard to make a place smell nice, but in fact it is; the last home smelled like death, it was a place one would go to die rather than to live. He has a sunny room at the Beverly Home, and it's a mixed-use facility, part assisted living, part long-term care, and they even have a day-care center for kids attached, and I want him to be surrounded with life. I thought it might be encouraging to him. To me. When I moved him this time, I was a different woman than the one who had checked him into the first home; I was more experienced, but also wearier and more cynical. It struck me, certainly as it had a million times before, but this time somehow differently, that he really wasn't going to come out of this. That I could spend the next fifty years shuffling him to a more comfortable bed, and all he would do is continue to sleep. It didn't mean I had an answer, it just meant that I realized more than ever that there was a problem.

I call my regular driver, Missy, one of two female cabdrivers in my neighborhood, a sharp little woman who always wears her hair in a ponytail, and curses only occasionally. (Her real name is Maritza but she insists I call her Missy because she says she likes having a different work identity. I think it's just because I don't know how to pronounce her real name correctly, though I've certainly tried.) Missy's been driving a cab since she was twenty-five. Her uncle owns the car-service company, and he helped her get started. She lives on the south side of Williamsburg with her mother, sister, and four-year-old daughter, Mira, whom her mother watches during the day. At night they switch off, and her mother works an evening shift as a prep cook at a family-owned restaurant. ("My mother's hands have smelled like peppers for as long as I can remember," Missy told me once.) The father of her child has lived in Florida for the last year, and good riddance I say. He led this secret life as a collection man of sorts for an escort agency—she refuses to say the word "pimp"—and when she found out, she had a nervous breakdown; she lost twenty pounds and had to pay a visit to the emergency room with heart palpitations. She's better now, though, and it's good to know that she's okay. I missed her when she was gone.

For the last three months, her grandmother—who lives down the block from her, right next door, practically—has been dying of cancer, and family members from across the country and Puerto Rico have been streaming in to pay their respects, many landing in her apartment for weeks at a time. "They're rowdy," she complains. "The noise, the cigarettes, they're drinking every night." I have offered her my apartment many times—it is for selfish reasons, too, as I am of course incredibly lonely—but she always refuses. "You can see the Manhattan skyline," I say, but she just shakes her head, her pretty gold earrings dangling.

It impresses me, this network of family members, how they support one another, with work, with money, with any sort of emotional crisis. She can just pick up the phone whenever she needs anything, and they all know they can do the same with her. When Martin had his accident, his parents came out from Seattle for a month, bringing with them an intense outburst of prayer and priests, but I haven't seen them since, unless you count their well-defined visages on their annual Christmas card, set against one of Martin's father's massive paintings of the Virgin Mary on their living room wall. There's Meryl in taupe, always in some shade of brown, with a big Christmas pin—sometimes Santa, sometimes a Christmas tree, in the last few years a bejeweled cross—attached to her chest, her gray hair combed and curled around her ears and chin, her precious features carved and doll-like, only lines around her eyes and hair revealing her age. She and Martin share the same crinkle around the corners of the eyes, but in her the sense of humor is absent, replaced instead by exhaustion. And there is her round belly, puffier every year, stretching the fabric of her pleats, always those pleats, ill-advised, unfortunate, and inevitable. (It is unfair, but I always compared her to my own mother, so careful about her appearance, her hand-sewn clothes, even the clothes she bought at the thrift store, which she redesigned in some way or at the very least tailored for a precise fit. Meryl made me miss my mother, who died when I was just a child, so dreadfully. There is nothing Meryl wanted to do more than nurture me—she craved taking care of others—but she was no substitute for a mother like mine.)

And Calvin, he of the gifted-mimicry brushstrokes—Martin always felt he had a talent that was wasted on repeated interpretations of various historical figures which he distributes regularly to friends and family (there are five of the paintings stacked close together in our bathroom; my favorite is of George Washington crossing the Delaware, his flag waving proudly against the wind)—Calvin, with his same military haircut, a full head of gray spikes, clean-shaven save for the one year with a beard, the year when he had the tumor in his neck removed. Still tall and forceful, burly and strong, in one of his colorful plaid shirts, down-to-earth, rich in a reliable homey warmth that made him a leader in the military for twenty years and then later a successful farm-supply entrepreneur up and down the West Coast. And Martin is all over him, or was anyway, the firmness, the powerful jaw, the sturdy energy. Every year when I get the card I stare at it for a long time. It seems like between the two of them I could get some answers, but I'm not sure what my questions are.

I know also that they visit him a few times a year—I'm alerted by the staff at the nursing home that they're coming, so that we can conveniently avoid each other—and I know that they check on his health by calling his doctors regularly. Beyond that, they are absent from our lives, which is, I guess, as it should be, for we are unusual, and they are not.

MISSY ARRIVES AT NOON, as always, the classic-rock station whimpering in the background (Missy loves her some Mick Jagger), lowered to enable our conversation. I do not always like to talk—sometimes I can only listen—because some days are harder than others, but today I feel like my whole world could open up.

"How's your grandmother doing?" I ask her. After years of listening to the minutiae of Martin's physical state, I think Missy is slightly thrilled to share her own dramatic health-care moments.

"You know, not too good, Jarvis. The doctors, they're saying there's not much they can do for her now. They say we're wasting our money."

"It's not a waste," I say. Because this is what I have to believe.

"They didn't say it like that exactly, but I got their meaning."

Her fingernails are immaculate on the steering wheel, lacquered and pink and shiny. There is a small rhinestone embossed in one, near the tip of the nail, and a carefully articulated red swirl across the base of it. The headset to her cell phone is unplugged, as usual—she says she likes to concentrate on me—and the cord dangles down her shoulder, rippling whenever she turns the steering wheel.

"What do you think?" I say.

"I think she is going to die." Hands firm on the steering wheel.

We are silent for a while until we approach the ramp to the BQE.

"So we're moving her home," she says. "This weekend. Back to her place. I gotta go clean it out tomorrow."

"Are you hiring a nurse?"

"My cousin Sandra is a nurse. She says between all of us we can work it out, you know, take care of her." A sigh shifts from her body. "We don't even know how long she's going to live, you know what I'm saying?"

"Right, right," I say.

"It could be two days, it could be two weeks."

"I wish I could help somehow," I say.

"Help I got plenty of," she says. "If you want to call it that. Last night I swear Freddy drank a whole case of beer during the Yankees game. He's yelling, he's screaming, then when it's over he decides now's the time to teach Mira how to salsa. He was yelling at me, 'Don't you teach this girl anything?' Like I'm a bad mother or something. And then he tripped over the coffee table, fell into the couch." She lets out a loud, extended laugh. "Oh shit, it was so funny. I almost peed my pants."

I am so jealous of her, of the people she has, it hurts my teeth. I have almost no extended family, although I surely could have used some in this life. My father had an estranged relationship with his parents: his father was a control-freak small-town sheriff in North Carolina who bounced from county to county, corruption charges trailing him wherever he went; his mother, a quiet woman who looked twenty years older than she was her entire life, meekly followed, because, as she once told my father, who would she be without her

husband? He used to make my father clean the carpets with a
fine-tooth comb and then tiptoe around the edges to get out of
the room. If he messed up, he'd get a kick in the rear. Same
went for painting the trim on the porch of every new home they
moved into, the weekly detailing of my grandfather's extensive
vintage automobile and motorcycle collection, and all the
other little chores my father grew up doing, till finally he got
out of there, went east to art school on scholarship, and never
looked back. At least until one Christmas.

I can't remember exactly when it was—but I know my mother
was still alive, so I couldn't have been older than five or six—my
grandfather sent my father a package. I remember sitting with
my parents when they opened it: there was a Bible, and there was
a letter, which my father read to himself. He let out a low whistle,
and then handed it to my mother, who read it and started laughing. (She had the loveliest laugh, high and sweet and silly, as if
she had never learned how to laugh like a grown-up, just found a
style she liked as a child and stuck with it.) Then he cracked open
the Bible, and taped to the front page was a five-dollar bill. My
mother laughed even harder, but I think my father was shaken.
Every year after that, my grandfather did the same thing: Bible,
note, five-dollar bill. My father stacked them neatly in the
garage and told my brothers and me not to go near them. They
were still stacked there the day I moved out and headed off to art
school myself.

My mother's parents, too, were lost to her. My grandmother
died of breast cancer right after my mother started college,
when her father was already on his fifth wife, his second hotel
chain, and his first horse ranch in Brazil. My mother and her
sister loathed him, and had never taken a penny from him.

(She once archly called her father "carnivorous," and my mother was not prone to arch tones.) So it was just the three women, their own little family, for a long time. We saw my aunt a few times a year when my mother was still alive—she would drive up with her kids from Bethlehem, Pennsylvania—but less so after she died and my father discovered a previously untapped talent for destroying relationships. She was a fiercely competent woman who was busy raising her own three children, two boys, one girl, just like our family, and barely getting by herself. After my dad started drinking, I used to fantasize what it would be like if I was one of Aunt Patty's kids. I bet Aunt Patty would read me a bedtime story without slurring her words, I would think. I bet Aunt Patty smells nice all the time. But, sadly, there was no room at that inn. She sends me a family newsletter every January. *Ethan's wife is pregnant again, Natalie's a Captain now in the Air Force, Pierce is almost done with grad school. He plans on teaching.* It's nice to hear good news, but I know I'm just a name on a mailing list to her.

"What about you?" says Missy.

"What about me?"

"How you doing this week?"

I tap my finger on the door handle, roll down the window. Warehouses to the right, a threatening chunk of gray storm clouds hover above them. I roll the window back up again. I prefer the tint. I want to be misled.

"I met some people," I say.

"You did? That's great, girl. You need to get out of that house more. You're too young to be a—"

"Widow?" I say.

Silence again. I think about the word for a while. I picture an old lady with a scarf covering her head at a funeral, muttering prayers, working herself up into a state, until finally she hurls herself on a casket as it's lowered into the ground. A crowd of people watching her flail, shaking their heads. Who will pull her up? No one wants to touch her.

We are three exits away from the nursing home. It is greener here, less industrial. Off in the distance I see a thick gray puff of smoke chug into the sky. There must be a fire. Maybe Martin's nursing home is on fire. Maybe by the time I get there he'll be gone.

I release something within myself, a moment of peace secures itself in my chest, and then I feel the inevitable disgust at my thoughts. Why do I think like that sometimes?

"So tell me about them," says Missy. "The people you met."

So I tell her about Mal, and Tony, and Scott, about their rich wives, and their good looks, and their wistful conversations.

Missy considers what I've told her for a bit. She brushes her hands, palms flat, against the steering wheel. She turns off onto Martin's exit. Finally she says, "Not for nothing, Jarvis, but where I come from, we'd call these guys *maricones*."

"What does that mean?" I say.

"It means they're pussies," she says.

4.

The Beverly Home is on a hill in Queens, and set so that when you look out the window you can see the tops of buildings for miles, until of course you dead-end at office buildings, housing projects, and luxury condos—it was hard to tell if they were in Manhattan or Long Island City, they were far away, and in New York height can translate to a lot of things. I prefer it to the last place, and I hope he does, too, though I don't know what that would mean.

I wave at the receptionist at the front desk—her name tag says "Linda J." and I imagine several other Lindas running around, distinguished only by their last initial—and she greets me back with "Good morning, Mrs. Miller." This is one of the few places where I am known that way. Well, this is one of the few places I am known.

Down the hall, through the assisted-living unit with its mauve walls and paintings of seashells and seashores and seagulls, elderly men and women are sitting out in singles and pairs, heading to another bingo game or art class, coffee in the cafeteria, a walk through the gardens. They have an award-winning rose garden, tended to by one of the residents, Philo, a retired pharmacist from upstate who transplanted his entire garden with him when he moved into the home.

As I heard it from one of the nurses—Linda S.? Linda T.?—he had moved here with his wife, Patricia, five years ago, and they were model tenants. She would sew, he would garden, and their children and grandchildren would visit them every week-end. Tour guides would introduce prospective residents to the couple, so idyllic and healthy were their lives. And then six months ago Patricia had a heart attack, and in a day she was gone forever. Since then Philo has deteriorated; he's lost weight, his hair has thinned dramatically, and his mental faculties have diminished. He walks around listlessly holding a garden hoe, telling anyone who will listen about how his great-grandfather had brought it from Norway. "One hundred years old," he told me once. His belt is too big for him, and the tops of his pants spill out where it's cinched. "I had to replace the wood a couple times, but this metal's one hundred years old." He slapped the metal base of it gently.

"That's amazing," I said. "You going to work in the garden?"

He hesitated, stared off down the hall, as if waiting for a command. "Yes. Well. I'm going to get some coffee." He brightened. "You're beautiful," he said.

"Why, thank you, kind sir." I flirted with all the residents when given the chance, to make them feel better. To make me feel better.

And then he had strolled off, dragging the hoe behind him, the metal nibbling at the carpeting.

Today Philo is already sitting in the cafeteria—it smells like old hot dogs, there is often a whiff of old hot dogs—when I walk through toward Martin's unit. As I pass by the puddings, brown, yellow, white, all with a neat dollop of whipped cream on top, Philo waves at me. There are three watches on his arm, laced over his flannel shirt, which is buttoned neatly to the top. I wave back.

A quick walk through the hallway bordering the ICU—green seafoam walls with yellow trim—and I'm almost there. There's always so much pain, it makes me shudder. I avert my eyes from any open doors, cut through quickly to the stairwell, walk up three flights. I hear a dog yap down the hall, and then a nurse's aide in an unflattering pink smock strolls by with a Yorkshire terrier, tongue panting happily. They have a menagerie of animals at the home to cheer up the residents, keep them active and engaged. There's a sunny aviary on the fourth floor with cages of parakeets and one dominating parrot, a rotating shift of dogs that are brought in from the local shelter, and about half a dozen cats, at least that's how many I've seen, that have infiltrated every crevice of the home, much as the nurses have tried to keep them out of their locker rooms, or say, the Alzheimer's unit.

On Martin's floor I am struck as always by the yellow walls, so bright and cheerful, and the stunning black-and-white photographs displayed on them. The photos were taken by Sylvie Porter, a legendary photographer now in her eighties and a resident of the home. Her husband lived on the unit for a few years, and she donated the works when she followed him here, although she has a reportedly beautiful studio—artwork dripping from the walls—in the assisted-living section. The photos were previously unreleased, and I always think how unfortunate it is they are on the walls of a place where no one gets to see them but a few straggling relatives and nurses.

In the series, she had somehow followed a cat—white, or perhaps yellow, it's difficult to tell since the photos are black-and-white—through the streets of the East Village in what looked to be the late sixties. In each frame the cat makes an appearance, sometimes his whole body, sometimes just a leg or an ear or a tail, as he weaves through the crowds of hippies and freaks who had taken over that part of the city at the time. What's most remarkable about all of them is that the sun, a burning flash of light, is always exactly opposite the cat in the frame, so that when viewed next to each other it's almost a flip-book effect—all that changes is the story in the middle. It's as if the cat knew exactly what he was doing, though logic dictates Porter was the one in control. At first, I didn't notice how each photo connected to the next, but after six months of staring at the photos it finally became clear to me that she had mastered something very special.

I was certain I had never seen these photos before, and had looked through all of Martin's collections of her work several times at home, and searched online as well. It seemed to be our little secret, shared only by me and Martin and the rest of the comatose.

I pass the other rooms, full of young and old alike—the only place in the home where you'll find someone under the age of sixty in a bed. There's a sixteen-year-old girl named Amanda who fell from a water tower while she was tagging graffiti for the first time. There is still hope for her recovery. I sometimes see her parents in the chapel, huddled with intensity. There's twenty-nine-year-old Ira, a rich boy from the Upper East Side, who was involved in some sort of financial scandal with his parents' money. He tried to shoot himself in the head and somehow failed, or failed just enough, anyway, and he's been asleep for two years now. It seems unfair to me, that they continue to keep him alive, because he so badly wanted to die. And there is Judith Keener, now forty years old, who is the most famous patient, or was for a while, anyway. She was the subject of a few court cases in the 1990s—her sister sued to keep her on life support, while her husband, a dark-haired businessman with a shady past involving offshore something or other, sued to take her off; her sister won, and the husband hasn't been seen again, though he still pays the bills—and sometimes you still see a reporter trying to talk to a nurse, only to get swatted away by security. Judith was a cokehead, as well as a diabetic, a brilliant combination of death wish and death sentence. She bled from her nose and her mouth for six hours before anyone found her.

The rest of the patients are old, and I do not mean to disregard them, but I wonder if it is the same kind of shame.

And then, at last, there is Martin Miller, room 325. The door is shut. I push it open and a cat, a sleek yellow puff of air, runs out past me. It smells like disinfectant and a lingering trace of a nurse's perfume or hand lotion, no trace of human waste or illness. I know the room usually gets cleaned before I get there, so I can have a good time with my husband. A good time.

I do what I always do with when I visit Martin. (First I lock the door. I am allowed two hours of a locked door. At two hours they come to check him. They knock, and then they unlock.) I kiss his forehead, I stroke his chin with my fingertips, lingering on the cleft. He is gaunt, cheeks sucked in, colorless. I always think of the pictures of prisoners in a concentration camp that they showed me in high school during history class: the starvation, the almost-lifelessness, the souls drained.

I squeeze his hand to see if he will squeeze back, and then let go when he doesn't. I slip off my shoes and slide them under his hospital bed. I fold back his blanket, make it crisp, smooth out the wrinkles. Then I sit on the bed, angle my legs up and over next to him, slide them under the blanket. Legs next to legs, flat and motionless. I pull his arm around me, I nestle in tight, and then I go to sleep with my husband.

I DREAM OF MARTIN and me in our home, sitting on the black leather couch in the living room, the one that sinks when you sit in it. We're holding hands, and a yellow cat—is it the one I saw earlier? This one is brighter, he is radiating yellow—is pacing between us, up and over our laps, rubbing his head up against us as he passes. His coat is spectacular. It is glowing and golden like the sun. We don't stop to pet him, though, we're just holding hands, holding tightly, relaxing into the couch until suddenly we're sinking, and then we're so far down we can't get up, and there are just our legs dangling from the edge and our arms sticking up and out and over and we are not waving for help, we are not fighting it one bit, we are just being sucked away.

When I wake up I feel like I have stopped breathing and I take a gasp of air. Martin's monitor beeps gently. We're all still here. We're all still alive.

5.

It takes me a day to recover each time I see Martin. Either that, or I choose to take a day to recover. It's an indulgence, I know, depression. A safe harbor for those of us who can't put up a fight, cannot raise our hands in firm fists and say, I am going to try and handle all of this bullshit. Who can we blame first? Were our mothers uncaring and distant? Were our fathers self-obsessed and cruel? Were we poked and prodded on the playground by mean little children who had uncaring and cruel parents of their own? Who can we blame last? Or perhaps it is merely neurons, not firing enough or maybe firing too much, conspiring against joy, or at least complacency. Whatever the reason, I am now a member of that club, the one that requires nothing to join; less than nothing, an *absence* of something. Survival skills. Self-love. Inspiration.

So I wake up late, close to noon, and I stay under the covers for another hour, a pillow over my head, a blanket over that, and not a fingertip nor a tiptoe touches air. All I see is the white of the blanket, and the blue of its trim. It is down and puffy. I fondle the grooves of it, and for a moment I feel sort of sexy. Now is the time to try once again where I usually fail. If only I could think about someone besides Martin maybe it might eventually work, but I cannot think of a man, not a one, who could take his place in my mind.

I put my hand first on my breast, feel the heft of it, and then stretch my thumb and index finger out, around it, and then finally rub my palm across my nipple. Martin at the beach, dripping and smiling. Too sweet. Martin standing above me, touching my hair while I suck on him. "You like that? Tell me you like sucking my cock." Too rough. I make him silent, I focus on the face he is making, how good he feels. "You make me feel good, baby." I want to make him feel good. This seems safe, him standing, me kneeling, and I slip two fingers on the other hand down to my stomach, and work my way down. "You're so beautiful," he says. "You're so pretty when you're unfaithful," he says, and now there is a Pixies soundtrack to my fantasy. But of course I was never unfaithful, I am fine. He laughs. I suck away, I rub myself. He rolls his head back, eyes shut, mouth open, a groan, and I am rubbing faster. And then he is not moving, his eyes are still shut, and he is quiet, he is asleep, and I am sucking off a comatose man, and I start to cry. Goddammit. Every time.

Get out of this bed before you kill yourself, Jarvis.

So it's early afternoon now, and I've got the whole day ahead of me to drive myself mad with my pathetic, self-indulgent rituals. Where do I begin? Which trip, which memory lane?

There is an entire closet of old clothes to smell, the shirts with the holes in the sleeves and the sweat stains in the armpits, the work pants with the paint stains and the faded outlines of pens and brushes in the pockets, the vintage suits—you loved that Valentino we found in a thrift store in Hoboken of all places—the crisp button-down white oxford shirts, the crazy ties with all the patterns, the normal ties—"high tea" ties, you called them—the blue jeans, softer by the year, the V-neck sweaters, slightly pilled, the elbows stretched out in just one wear after washing but I had never washed them again, a Naked Raygun T-shirt, his favorite, and I start with that, I bury my head into it, I rub it on my cheeks, my chin, my forehead and I *breathe*.

I WASN'T ALWAYS SAD. Before Martin, before everything, I was much tougher. A troublemaker, a shit-starter, a jaded practical joker; flip through a deck of cards and you'd find me peering out between the queen and ten, eyes high and wide, deathly white skin, and dark, red lips curved around a devious smile. Short dresses that needed to be buttoned and tied in awkward locations. Black bra showing through flimsy material. Wobbly high heels. *Glamorous*.

"Why would such a pretty girl want to look so ugly?" Martin asked me soon after he first met me, but he laughed and bought me dinner anyway. I felt unstoppable.

That was at first. We were just casual then, everything was casual with me. I was twenty three, a Pratt dropout—I had tried practically every course of study available: painting, film, illustration, video, even a brief stint in welding because I always liked to play with fire, and then I came to the conclusion that I could make my life art, I could be a work of art, I could become a part of the New York zeitgeist, just by dressing well, or at least boldly, and putting myself out there in the world every night, meeting the right people, reading the right books, laughing in the wrong places just to throw people off, serving the right drinks in the exact right bar, being there, being present, being a part of it. In torn fishnets on thin, pale legs. (My legs were such slender sausages then. Skinny, but still there was always something to pinch, a little flesh around the knee or up high, inside my thighs.) And I was sharp around the edges, I had a quick response for anyone, and that is appreciated in New York. Particularly in a bar on Fourth Street in the East Village, one that didn't look like much of a bar from the outside, if you didn't know it was there you would pass right by it, just another mystery door on a street, in a city of many mystery doors. Unless someone had taken you there late at night: that guy you met through your drug dealer, you had walked out his door at the same time and decided to get a drink together now that you were both high as kites and discovered you had attended the same law school, just four years apart; or your college buddy who had decided to become an artist, courtesy of a discreet trust fund from his kind, dead grandfather who would be rolling over in his grave if he knew the years he had spent building a successful regional airline that was later bought out by United were being wasted on paint thinner and heroin; or the girl you picked up at Save the Robots, the stunner with the long legs—you never got a firm answer on whether or not she was a model, not that it mattered of course—who told you she knew exactly the place to keep the party going. The new guy in your studio. The slumming real estate agent. The indie filmmaker who would sell out in a minute. The bartender just off duty, a wad of twenties in his pocket and a bone to pick with someone, anyone. There were a lot of men spending money there, and I was the one taking it. Well, me and the girl with the long legs.

So I met some people who were in the same place I was, and then some people who had more money than I did, and a lot of people who claimed to be artists, a lot of this last group talking about who they knew and what they had seen rather than what they were making because they probably were not making anything at all, with just a handful of them actually creating great—or at least interesting—art. All together they were this solid, seemingly impenetrable layer of people who *were eager to meet you*, invite you into their world, which was often comprised of dark basement railroad apartments so narrow two people could not walk side by side in it; and gallery openings for people you're loosely connected to through someone else who knows the guy who had a show here last year and you're there for the free wine anyway; and after-hours parties where people pooled their money to get more beer, more drugs, more more more, keep going until you pass out or find someone to take you home. Whatever comes first.

Art stars, every last one of them.

Until I met Martin. And his entire life, every ounce of it, every breath, every thought, was committed to creating art. Until he met me. He let me in, a small corner, a flap of hot skin, he pulled it up, showed me what was inside like those human body sculptures they had in science class, only inside Martin was color and texture and eyes and lips and nose all in a vast ocean. And he invited me to dive into him, and so I did. It felt cool and lovely in there, so I stayed.

But first: "Cut the coke," he told me. I had been up all night with a young Swedish heiress taking summer courses at Columbia, whatever bartender had been on shift that night, and a DJ, some DJ, there was always a DJ involved. After slipping me bumps throughout the night, the Swede and I had made out in the bathroom right before last call. I didn't mention it to Martin, any of it, but he knew immediately what I had been doing. We made plans to meet for breakfast at the Polish place on Second Avenue, and I started laughing the minute I saw him, laughing at nothing. My hair was in strings around my ears like a brutalized doll. My lips were chapped and I kept licking at the corners. I leaned over him in the booth and kissed him hard. I bit at his lip and he pulled back. I sat across from him and took off my two-dollar sunglasses that made me look (I thought) like Jackie O, slapped them on the table. I kicked up my legs, encased in long black-and-white-striped thigh-high tights, and laid my feet next to him. I rubbed my calf against his thigh. I put my foot between his legs. He slipped off my shoe and rubbed my feet for a second, then retreated.

"Cut it out," he said. He looked serious. He felt serious.

"Seriously I have to," I said. I was playing with him. My toes tapped on his crotch.

"You've got to do it if you want to be with me." He gently moved my feet to the side. "It is . . . unattractive."

Could anything have offended Martin more than the sight of something unattractive? Could anything have scared me then more than being unattractive?

He moved across the booth and sat next to me. He put his hand on my face and traced and spoke. "Bags under your eyes. Adds ten years. You're too white, too skinny. I can see your ribs. They hurt when you press against me. Not sexy. And also, it's not very interesting. To me, anyway. You could probably find someone who likes it, though. Do you want to do that? Do you want to find someone else? Who finds you, this version of you, interesting?"

"Interesting" was said with a slight sneer. Which was unlike him. He was always very gentle with me. His tone terrified me. To be mean was to be serious. Which he hadn't been before.

I doubt he'd thrown too many ultimatums out there in his life, and I'm pretty sure he didn't expect to be taken seriously, and it was also to my great surprise that I did. I quit partying, and then I quit my job, and then I was broke, and before you knew it I was living with him in his big loft in Williamsburg. And here I still am, in his home.

AFTER AN HOUR in the closet with Martin's clothes, it is hard to tell if I am better, or if I am worse, and really what do those words mean anyway when you want to be down? Maybe I'll pull out the big guns later on this evening: a look through Martin's paintings. But for now, I want reality, a substantive record of time and place, so I pick through some of our old photo albums, the plastic page covers crinkling under my fingertips. Here's me and Martin in Vienna, Zurich, Berlin, the requisite tourist shots in front of old and terrifying architecture, and then with friends at group shows, networking, always working, even when we had to look like we weren't; the cheapie vacation to Puerto Rico where we both got sick on tequila, or the water, or both; the formal, and sole, visit to his parents in Seattle, where no one is smiling until suddenly we are all smiling and laughing, Martin's father made some dumb joke, and then we were a family, at least for that one photo.

I stop at that photo. We weren't married yet, but we were living together. I had let my hair grow back to its natural black, and cropped it short, and put a barrette covered with tiny pink rhinestones in my hair. It was superfluous, but it seemed necessary, as if to identify to his parents that, yes, I was a normal girl who did normal things like wear barrettes. I was almost healthy by then, and I had put on a little weight. My cheeks had filled out, and they were pink, flushed maybe. I wore a fitted rose-colored cardigan, and a white collared shirt underneath, and pearls. Pearls! Where did I find those? I doubt I'd worn those before or since. They must have been fake. I must have been nervous.

Who was I then? I was someone who cared. I had parents to impress, a man to keep happy. Before I met him I led a shredded life, my days and nights fractured into slivers of high action and fitful sleep. It was easy to say goodbye to my friends and my life, and to embrace his, because his life was better.

There was one failed attempt at a merger of the two worlds, a disastrous event that sealed my future. Just after I had moved in with Martin—boxes of records and clothes and books and journals and failed art projects shoved in corners, *I'll get to them eventually, honey*—I decided to throw a brunch. I somehow convinced all of my bar friends and art school friends and East Village neighborhood friends that they wanted to come to Williamsburg at noon on a Sunday. I got up early, took the L into the city to buy bagels and lox at David's on First Avenue, eggs, oranges, freshly ground coffee at the A&P at Union Square, went back on the L to Bedford Avenue, bought some sweet sausage at one of the Polish butchers, all of this shoved into a gigantic backpack. I remember I had boots on that laced all the way up to my knees and a short, short baby-doll dress with buttons all the way down the front and a pop of cleavage at the top, and my hair had freshly dyed light-blue tips on the edges to match the blue in my eyes. I wanted to prove to my friends that even though I was living with someone I was still an artist, living my life on the New York edge. No one could domesticate me.

At home I spread the food out on the cheap metal chef's prep table Martin had bought the day before in one of the restaurant-supply stores on the Bowery specifically for the brunch.

"I can't put everything on the kitchen counter, Martin! There's not enough room." I had suddenly panicked at the sight of Martin's dirty paintbrushes, and the dishrack, and the coffee machine, and a stack of cookbooks, and there was all this clutter, his clutter. And so he took off for the city and returned hours later, sweating from the stairwell—our elevator was always broken then, this was before the new landlords took over—and then valiantly assembled it in our living room, packaging and directions and tabletop and rack and legs and screws spread everywhere. And when he was done I let him screw me on top of it.

There was no sex that day, though. I was nervous, I was excited, and I was sober. I wasn't sure if I had ever seen most of these people in the light of day, unless you counted still being up from the night before and watching the sun rise.

"Do you think it's enough food?" I asked Martin, who was lying on the couch.

"They're not coming for the food," he said. "They're coming for the company." He patted his leg. "Come lie down with me."

I paced, rearranged, straightened, and paced some more until one p.m., and then I started to cry.

"No one is going to come," I said. I wrapped my arms around myself.

"They're going to come, baby doll."

"It doesn't matter. Now I know," I said. "Now I know."

But they did come, all of them, starting at two p.m. The Europeans: Mischa and Mirabelle and Franco; and those who had been nicknamed: Twenty-fourth Street John and Philadelphia Bobby and a woman named Tracy who was frequently called "Precious" or "Presshy"; and the NYU grad students: Praja and Foster and Richard; and there may have been a few others, I can't remember now; all of them bounced right through the front door, some of them wearing the same clothes from the night before, some of them freshly showered but still with the telltale saucer eyes or grinding teeth or raw lips. They had all come from a club—I can't remember where, maybe it was Limelight—and they talked as if there would never be another night like it, as if something really important had taken place, as if they hadn't done the exact same thing every weekend for the last six months.

"It was just a beautiful night," said Mirabelle. The glitter she wore on her eyes had drifted down her face and her neck, and some of it dusted the top of her shirt as well.

"Really spectacular," said Mischa, and he wrapped his arms around Mirabelle. He had been in love with Mirabelle at the time, I think, even though he was gay.

"The best night ever," said Tracy. She ran her tongue over her lips. "The way it all came . . ."

"Together. It is perfect when it comes together," said Franco. He was lying down on our couch, tracing circles in the air.

Twenty-fourth Street John and the grad students all went to the bathroom at the same time. They stayed in there for a while.

"You should have come," said Philadelphia Bobby. He walked over to me and put his hands on my shoulders and rubbed them, and then Martin coughed, and Bobby ignored it, or didn't notice, and then I coughed, and he still didn't get it, and then finally, slowly, I removed his hands from my shoulders.

Philadelphia Bobby smiled at me. He was a wide-eyed pharmaceutical rep who traveled all week and went clubbing all weekend. He told me once that he slept, on average, a total of fifteen hours a week.

"Hey, do you think we could . . ." He pointed at the stereo. "You know."

"I don't know," I said.

"Play something. Play a CD. I have a CD."

"Oh yeah, play that one," said Mirabelle. "You know which one." She sat down on the couch next to Franco, lifted his head up, and put it in her lap. She began to stroke his hair.

Philadelphia Bobby began to rummage through a record bag.

"It's from Detroit, you'll love it, Jarvis," he said. "Really hard house." He bumped his fist in the air. "Really, like, thump, thump, thump."

Martin grimaced.

Of course none of them ate, none of them touched a thing. They drank juice, they drank gallons of water, and they put caffeine in their systems just for fun. I saw Franco load a plate with one of everything, just so he could try the textures on his tongue.

An hour later, Martin placed a call to his friends—the older starving artists, the ones who were truly hungry. "We've got all this food here," he said. "It's just going to waste." They were all over in fifteen minutes. Maybe they had been expecting the call. They took plate after plate, the tall ones, the short ones, with their messy hair and their stubble, in their work clothes, jeans, belts with truck-stop belt buckles, in awkward T-shirts that were too big for their skinny frames. "Delicious," they cried. "Thank you so much, Jarvis."

"Martin, where did you find this one? You're a lucky man," one even said.

I barely said goodbye as my old friends left, off to go dancing, one last gasp before their work week began. I was busy making another pot of coffee for the new friends. Flushed cheeks, bright eyes, I laughed at all their jokes and they laughed at all of mine, and then they all sat and talked for hours afterward, and I listened, and I learned.

I tricked myself, of course. I traded one waiting gig for another. But at the end of the day, I was loved. Forever and ever, I would be loved.

SOME OF MARTIN'S PAINTINGS—the ones Alice didn't take during her pillage years ago, specifically the work he did which predates me—are in a storage unit that Davis arranged for and maintains. They have no meaning for me, and also I find many of them inferior, mere sketches in comparison to his later work, which is full-bodied, with a richer voice: thicker, bigger, broader, louder. I care not for the paintings of the Hassids walking across the bridge in pairs, nor the faces of working-men lining up at the bar at the Turkey's Nest, a dive bar over near the park. When he tried to document more than one person, out in the world, the paintings, while still affecting, were too busy, too complicated. There was just too much noise. But then he met me, and I helped him to turn what was an artist's studio in which he slept into a place where two people lived, a proper home. So when he brought people into the quiet, the calm, of our world, and he saw a fresh image clearly, in his creative space, he suddenly found the right voice, the one that sang the highest, purest notes.

So I don't mind that I never see those, and while I'm sad that Alice holds on to so many of his paintings, I know that I've got the best of his work at home, or at least the ones I love the most. Nobody will ever get their hands on these paintings. I drag out my three favorite pieces from his Angels series, the set he did for the Mustard Marathon, an all-day, all-night exhibition and party in an old mustard factory converted into studios for artists and musicians. There were ten floors full of work from all of the artists in the neighborhood. There was dancing on the roof, video installations in the stairwells, art in every corner, you couldn't escape it. And there we were on the fifth floor, a portrait of me, a portrait of Alice, a portrait of Davis, all of us with halos, all of us with wings, all of us with unearthly glows. Davis looks like the cat who ate the canary—I keep waiting for a feather to pop out of that gap between his front teeth. Alice looks strangely soft and lovely. Leave it to Martin to find a way to relax her, to get the best out of her. I have considered giving these paintings to Davis and Alice, but I keep waiting for a special occasion. A birthday. An anniversary. A funeral.

Finally there is the painting of me. When I saw it for the first time I knew exactly how he felt about me. He thought I was beautiful. And I know I'm not ugly, and I know in fact I'm sexy, but it takes someone else to show you the *shades* of you, and in this case it's shades of red. If I were a color, I would be red, that's what he told me with this painting. And I would be pink and tender around the mouth, and darker, rose-colored, the color closer to the base of the petals, in my cheeks. And there is fire in my eyes, the lick of flames bursting out of them, and there are sparks at my temples, combustion, as if I could explode with red at any moment. I am this color, and I am twenty shades of it. I don't know if I knew that before, but I know I'll never forget it now.

And now my depression has wrapped around in a circle, back to the beginning. He saps me, he gives me strength, it starts all over again. I am as new, at least for now.

6.

"I think she's a little too, I don't know, *vagina*, for my tastes."
Alice is describing her new gallery assistant, a blissed-out
twenty-six-year-old with an MFA, shiny soft hair, and long
dramatic skirts that swirl around her ankles. She also has a tattoo on her lower back of the earth. "The motherfucking earth,"
as Alice described it. Alice is brusque and tough and miserable
and sometimes I'm not sure if she has a vagina herself, so I can
see why she might have a problem with the girl with swirly
skirts.

"If you don't like her, you shouldn't have hired her then," I
say. I have a low tolerance for Alice's nonstop catwalk of gallery
assistants. It seems like she's preparing to hire or fire a new
one every few months, and I am starting to find it emotionally
irresponsible. You'd think she'd be worried about getting a bad
reputation, but her gallery is so hot, and she is so good at main-
taining that hotness, that no one cares. Everyone wants to get

their foot in that door. The Alice Dodgson Gallery is the perfect place to start out. I imagine there's a club of her former gallery assistants out there, all bemoaning their time with Alice, and they all probably help one another out along the way. It's almost like she screens the smart kids for the rest of the galleries in New York. If they went through Alice in the first place, there's probably a reason why.

"I need help, Jarvis. I can't run the whole gallery by myself, now can I?" I know that she is making some sort of frustrated face, but it's difficult to tell. It's as if there's a knot at the back of her head that ties together the entire front of it: her tight, straight blond hair and the neat crop of razored bangs, the muscles in her face, the arched cheekbones, her smooth current of skin.

"I've got to go to Zurich this week, and Miami the next week." She thrusts her hands up in the air like a conductor and holds them there. "You have no idea how busy I've been."

Alice has been busy for six years. I know exactly how busy she is. From the minute Martin had his accident and the value of his artwork shot through the fifteen-foot roof of her gallery, formerly of Williamsburg, and currently of Chelsea. Her phone rang only occasionally before that, and now she has two cell phones, one for business, and one for personal calls. As if she had a personal life. As if her personal life didn't revolve entirely around the art world. But I guess she's entitled to her bat phone. I think it makes her feel important. I am hopeful she has some sort of secret romance that I don't know about, but I've never heard a peep. When we meet once a month—tea at a tiny, overpriced café with a koi pond around the corner from her gallery, my one venture into the city sometimes in weeks—we talk about business, we talk about her gallery assistants, and we talk about Martin, but we never, ever talk about her love life. And I think maybe if she just got laid every so often, her gallery assistants would have a much easier time.

"I know that you're busy," I say. "I'm right here listening to you." I point both fingers at my face, at my eyes, at my ears. I wrinkle my forehead. "Right here, Alice." She lowers her hands at last. "I just mean, don't hire someone if you think you're going to hate them in two weeks. If you hate what they wear to the interview, you're going to hate it even more when you see it every day. If she minored in women's studies in college, do *not* hire her. If he spent a summer teaching art to underprivileged children, let the next gallery have him. What I'm suggesting is, don't hire someone nice. Hire a bastard. Hire someone who's going to give you the business. Hire someone as tough as you."

And then we both laugh. As if anyone could be as tough as Alice.

"Moving right along then, we need to give you some money, yes?"

"Yes. I don't know what happened," I say, and then I look away. Thinking about selling paintings always sends me into a different place. It's as if I pull off a bandage only to see that I'm not even close to healing underneath it. I have to think about which ones I care about the least, which ones I want to have staring at me across my living room when I'm old. Which ones will be appreciated best by someone else. Which ones will bring in the most money. Which ones Martin would hate me the least for selling.

"I'm a little embarrassed," I say. "I feel like I never spend a cent, except on Martin."

After commissions and art handling costs of this latest batch, and subtract the taxes while we're at it, too, I should have had the sum of $550,000 deposited into my account. But the sales had moved slowly, and the nursing home wanted two years' rent upfront, and suddenly I found myself in the unusual position of being—temporarily—broke. And then the washer imploded one day, started flooding to the top and a bit over the side—my trusty laundry machine, my urban luxury, betrayed me. I waited for weeks for a check, and went those same weeks without clean laundry. I even wore some of Martin's clothes, a few old T-shirts (Yes, I still had them. Would you have me throw them away? I know Alice would. Or Alice would sell them on eBay. Or archive them. Alice can go suck it), until finally, I had been forced to go to that laundromat.

"It's fine, it's not your fault," says Alice. "The check was late coming to me. But here's an advance, of half the amount." She pulls an envelope from her purse, slides it over to me, swift, across the table. It makes a shimmering sound. I don't bother to open it. Alice has been taking care of me for years. Without her, I'm nothing. I would be broke on the streets, burning his paintings for warmth. She has looked after me—after the both of us, and while I can't say that I like her that much sometimes, I am grateful, and for that, she gets my love.

"And I'll get on those buyers," she says. "Those Australians, they're a bit dodgy sometimes. They think because they're all the way around the world we won't notice when a check is late."

Alice clams up when the waitress brings us our drinks, something hot and minty for Alice, and a cool glass of fruit tea for me.

She takes a delicate sip of her tea, and she pauses to think.

Her face changes for a minute, and I see her as calm, like a full moon reflecting in a still lake, and then she is on again; there is a wind, and she is all ripples.

"So listen, dear, I've got a proposal for you. I've had this idea for a while, but I was waiting for the market to be right, really for quite a few things to fall into place, and I believe they have." She nods to herself. "I think the time is now, Jarvis."

She thrusts her hands across the table and clasps at my wrists, but I jerk back slightly, so she ends up holding my hands, and it is more intimate than either of us would like, but once you set things into motion, it is hard to stop. So there we are, holding hands.

"I want to do a Martin Miller retrospective. Not just a gallery show, but a book, too. Maybe a documentary. And a website and DVD. Everything. The works. All Martin."

I picture posters of Martin's works on the walls of college dorm rooms. Martin Miller postcard books. Martin on the cover of a magazine, in his youth, not as he is now. Martin's face in fireworks above the East River on the Fourth of July.

"He's not dead yet," I say, in a low and tiny voice.

"What?" says Alice.

"I said, he's not dead yet, Alice." We had talked about this before, a few years ago. I had told her then I wanted to wait until he was dead, that it seemed disrespectful to him while he was still around, even if it was in a hovering state. And we didn't really need the money. We were doing just fine auctioning off a series a year. Why market a sick man?

And I remember when it first happened, the day after he fell, there had been a series of articles in art magazines, in the *Times*, even a couple of national magazines, all trying to capture who Martin was, his art, his personality, and they hadn't even come close. It had hurt me, their insistence on turning a man who was all about color into a black-and-white story. The word "sexist" popped up a few times in the articles, and then I stopped reading them. I wanted to tell them: You didn't know him at all. We were equals. I took care of him and he took care of me. He always held my hand in a room full of strangers, and I cradled his head when he ached at night. (Oh, those aches of his.) I was his wife, I was his partner, and he never decided anything without asking me first. There were no pedestals in our house, only easels and tables and bookshelves, and that goddamn ladder. He was my husband, I wanted to tell them, and *you didn't know him at all*.

But when a few journalists contacted me for interviews, I turned them down. I was worried that no matter what I said—and I knew him best, after all—the words would be turned against me, or against him. Artists, I trusted. Writers, not as much. Theirs is a different kind of fabrication, one that is taken as truth, though they have the same urges as any creative person to imagine a better story than the one that exists.

And then there are art dealers.

"I want you to open your mind a bit, darling," she says. "I'm not done yet, so hear me out." She is still holding my hands. She squeezes tight. "MoMA is considering a show in conjunction with the retrospective. A small one, but still. I've told them about these photos of Martin's, the ones he took before he painted."

The photos. The few I've seen are arguably pieces of art in their own right, some in color but most in black-and-white, the subjects standing against the white projection screen Martin had erected in his studio, the light gushing through our high windows toward the opposite wall. (I've since scrapped the screen—I gave it to Davis, told him to just get rid of it, because it made the room feel even emptier. A blank white screen is no fun to have around when there's no chance of changing its face.) Martin felt the direct sun played too many tricks with the subject—suddenly a mysterious shadow would appear under an eye, or what was seemingly a well-defined chin suddenly looked sharp enough to wound—and he didn't want it to influence his paintings. He wanted everything in its purest form for inspiration. "All photographs are accurate, but none of them are the truth," he told me once. "And paintings, well, they're complete lies."

The photos are crisp and detailed, light and arid; they always reminded me of the sky just after a rain, which made sense because Martin was raised in Seattle, though his paintings themselves were always considered very New York, urban and weird and visceral. He shot them with an 8 × 10 attached to a tripod, a cranky old camera that took the crispest of shots. (I think he won the camera in a poker game, or as payback for a loan. It was definitely some sort of payment. I never knew the real story.) He would set up the initial shot, pose the subject, frame them in the lens, and then after that never look at the camera again. He would stand to the side of it and chat up whoever was sitting for him that day, and just when he got them comfortable enough, he would tell them to hold still. Then he would take the one shot, replace the plates of film—this was the most time-consuming part, and sometimes I would help him with it—and start all over again. He would tell them stories about his punk rock days, playing in basements and backyards in Seattle with bands that would go on to be famous—he had a million of them, the "Martin on acid" series alone could take hours—or he would find a way to get them talking about themselves, shoot them sly little questions.

Yeah, you're fighting with your girlfriend, man? You like her more than the last girlfriend? What was her name again? Yeah, I liked her better, too. I don't need to know her, man, I already know she's better than this one. I want to hear about her instead.

The old-girlfriend stories are always more interesting, Martin would tell me. Time brings perspective, and perspective brings much better storytelling.

"MoMA, Jarvis. Not a piece here, a piece there, in a collection. A whole show. We have to do this. Right now. Because there are just enough of his paintings out there that people know who he is, but still enough hidden away that there's a layer of intrigue. For better or worse, there is an interesting story attached to him. And yes, we could make a fortune, and you'll never have to ask me for a check again. But really it's because Martin would have wanted it. He was insanely ambitious, and you know it. He would have killed for this."

I remember a month of open studios, the last summer I had with Martin, every Sunday, industrial fans blowing on art critics and curators and buyers shuffling through our home, sweating bottles of Corona with wedges of lime in their hands. I made deviled eggs and bowls of fresh onion dip, and sliced up radishes and sticks of celery. Once I made margaritas, all afternoon, that sour margarita smell sticky all over my skin. Martin and I smiled so hard our cheeks hurt, and when everyone had left, finally, we would shower together, then sit in silence for hours underneath the fans, the bubble of quiet burst only by Martin wondering out loud how it went. Did that cruel-looking man from the *Times* smile once? Did you see how drunk that Swiss woman got? Did they have a good time? Did I have a good time? Did you? Are we okay?

And then: "Everyone wants video. Multimedia. Avant-garde bullshit. Isn't it enough just to paint a picture of a person anymore?" It was the only time I heard Martin whine, when he thought he wasn't getting enough attention for his work, and that was rare. That's why he loved Alice, I always believed. Because she thrust love on him so regularly, and still does, I think. She visits him sometimes, or so I've heard. They were close friends, and now she's mine by default. I think otherwise I would have fallen under Alice's intolerable-girl category, but if Martin loved me, then she'd love me, too. He was the seal of approval.

"I'll think about it," I say. I know I'm being difficult, but it's stinging me a little bit that she has these photos, and knows them intimately, and I don't. She has possession of a part of him. And he belongs to me.

"Well, think fast, because this offer will expire. We need a year of lead time on everything. There's a lot of legal matters to be hammered out, an entire marketing campaign to be devised—"

"Alice, you never listen to me. I need to think about it." I snap the words out like a belt on a backside. Alice always has to be in control of every situation, and most of the time she's right, and she makes things easier, or at least it's easier to let her, but this was all I had left of Martin, my control of his art, that and our Wednesdays together in bed at the Beverly Home, and I was going to be selfish. "I'll let you know."

We end our tea awkwardly—we had long since released our hands—and when the time came to catch a cab back, we did not kiss each other goodbye. Because sometimes you just don't feel like touching anyone. Because I almost never felt like touching Alice.

ACROSS THE BRIDGE, take the first exit, please, sir, then a right on Broadway, let's take the long way home on the waterfront, let's see Manhattan from the outside looking in. How is Manhattan looking? Still like a gap-toothed child downtown—that hole won't ever be filled properly. And uptown, the island still proudly brims, unassailed, the massive network of concrete and glass and steel, grim, constant, yet changing. New York is like some multiheaded demon: chop off a head, another pops up in its place. And when one person leaves—He couldn't make it here. Back to Detroit. Back to San Diego. Off you go now—another flies in the next day. I have always had the sense, now more than ever, that if I were to leave town it wouldn't make a difference.

The colors from far off are an industrial rainbow: sand-colored concrete, an ominous black shimmer, the occasional color popping through, like the red of the Verizon logo, all set against the sparkling blue spring-sky backdrop. And of course there's the Empire State Building and its ever-changing hues that seem only occasionally to follow a schedule, like red on Valentine's Day, red and green on Christmas, but the rest of the time it's anyone's guess. Martin and I used to sit on the roof at night sometimes and make up silly reasons for the color changes—"He's feeling very blue today, poor thing"—and strain our eyes and look for stars. The Brooklyn sky was always good for a few, unlike Manhattan's.

Kent Avenue is as bumpy and sullen as ever, but I notice it's slowly being smoothed over. Untended and ignored for so long except as a truck route, a warehouse here, a bar there, and the crowning glory, the Domino Sugar plant, a beautiful building that regularly churned out a sour, earthy scent, until its recent closing. But now there are condos to be built on the waterfront, luxury monsters that will tower over everything else in Williamsburg. And people suddenly care about Kent Avenue.

People from the neighborhood have tried to fight the new construction. There have been signs up in my elevator—I can learn more about the politics of my community from reading my elevator walls than I can from reading the newspaper. Once, they lined the waterfront with balloons high up in the air to show how the projected height of the buildings will block the rest of Williamsburg—no more looking in at Manhattan. Now you might as well live in Queens. I know I should have gone to some meetings and held up a protest sign or two. This is my neighborhood, too. Instead I wrote a check to help pay a lawyer to make a small difference.

The cab passes the small riverfront park on Grand Avenue, where Martin and I used to go and watch the sunset from the small beach of rocks. Sometimes he'd make sangria during the afternoon, let the peaches and apples and pears soak in red wine for a few hours, then we'd walk down to the beach and sit. We'd get a little drunk, just a bit, because by then we had stopped drinking a lot. (We'd save binges for things to celebrate, openings, trips to Europe, because he had too much work to do in the morning, and I hated drinking alone.) And while the sun lowered in the sky, achingly slow at first, and then rapidly, as if someone were tugging on the sun with a string, we would talk about the city, make up stories about the people in all the tall buildings, how unhappy they must be so high up in the air. Us against the world, as we sat on the edge of Brooklyn. Then we'd make out like we were in high school, holding hands, sweaty, his palms occasionally brushing my breasts, secretly, sneakily. "I can't wait to get you home, baby," he'd say.

"Take the next right," I tell the driver. I can't stand it anymore.

7.

Another Tuesday, only at last this is one with portent: laundry day. I start making up laundry to do, even though I could easily wait a few weeks. Short skirts, white jeans, a handful of underpants, my favorite tank top, still clinging after all these years, though its blue color is fading. I hoist the laundry bag to my shoulder, lock the door, talk myself out of going, unlock the door, talk myself back into it again, lock it again, and jump in the elevator before I can change my mind.

It's a musty old steel box that is constantly being tagged and repainted, and postered with self-serving documents—sales, and services, and requests. We are all about ourselves in Williamsburg. At the front door of the building I have another crisis of faith, something to do with how much safer it is in my home, away from the world, and also how can I call myself a loving wife if I am out there loving other men, or liking them, anyway, and I do this weird thing where I stand out in front of the building and I turn my head back and forth, all the while keeping my hand on the door, until finally a car pulls up and parks down the street, and a woman exits the driver's side, and I stop moving my head and just look at her instead. She is wearing a long skirt with what looks like a hundred tiny mirrors on it, and a tight tank top, and thick black boots. Her hair unfolds on her shoulders in thick blond dreadlocks. I watch her unlock the trunk and hoist a guitar case out of it. Then she walks toward the entrance of my building. Another neighbor I'll never meet, I think. She nods at the door, the handle of which I am still holding.

"In or out?" she says.

I'm on the fifth floor, I want to yell. You can stop by sometime. I'm not creepy, I swear.

"Out," I say.

I take Berry to the laundromat, one block away from the main drag of Bedford and the masses of beautiful young people and overpriced shopping. Berry is mostly populated with houses, small apartment buildings, an occasional garage or empty parking lot. It's a street on which people live, not work. There's no rapid expansion here, save for the occasional loft-condo building. That I can handle. It's the thought of an impending Subway franchise that terrifies me.

What if the three men—Mal, Scott, and Tony—aren't there? And what if they don't like me like they did last time? It's been so long since I've actually tried to make a friend, I'm worried I don't know how to anymore. The rejection would sting, more than a pinch, more like a punch. I have no men around me anymore, unless you count Davis, who appears sporadically, like some favorite distant cousin passing through town on a business trip. My father is wasting away in Rhode Island, mourning my mother through the bottom of a beer bottle. I haven't talked to my brothers in years; they took flight from our home as soon as they could, with their trembling wings. I can't worry about those men anymore. I have to focus on something new.

And now I walk with bluntness and purpose, long legs in tight jeans. If I am going to do this, then they are going to like me.

THE FIRST YEAR Martin was in a coma I would dream in the mornings that he had never gone to sleep in the first place. I was out for my walk, I came back, cheeks pink from the sun, yellow dress bouncing against my legs, and there's Martin, lying on the floor, only he's sleeping and I tap him with my foot; or he's fallen, that much is true, but he just broke a rib, and he's lying there in pain, but he's laughing—*Oh, Jarvis, I'm a goddamn idiot*—or he's just stretching out, staring up at the sky, contemplating colors, or the sun, or what he's trying to say differently in this painting, something bigger and better than ever before. And then he rises—he *rises*—and sometimes it's drowsily, and sometimes he's in pain, or sometimes he's fully erect and full of so much energy and life and passion and his eyes are full of that thing that I have always loved about him, it was that connectivity, like when two wires spark together, and then he takes me by the hand, whispers, "You look so beautiful right now, at this moment, you could not be any more beautiful, my darling wife," and walks me into our kitchen, bends me over the table, and fucks me. And it is either slow morning sex, or weird but fun jerky sex because he is in pain, or it is the swiftest, hardest sex we have ever had. And no matter what, I always come at the end, because he always made me come at the end.

But after a while I stopped having that dream because the memory of him as alive, as that alive anyway, dimmed in my mind. I miss that dream. Can you miss a dream? I miss it like crazy.

AT THE LAUNDROMAT, my new friends are sprawled out like runners after a marathon, as if standing up would kill them, as if they are spent. What did you do all day? I think. But I recognize how boredom can tire you, and I am often tired when I have been doing nothing but daydreaming.

But they perk right up when I enter.

"We didn't scare you off. Excellent," says Mal. He is seated in the chair. His notebook lies on the floor next to him, an abandoned child. He leans back against his chair, strokes a thick sideburn. I wonder if it would burn my skin, if we rubbed cheek to cheek.

I don't want to tell him I've been looking forward to this all week.

"Good, good," says Scotty. He's half-sprawled on the couch. No carriage, no baby today, I notice. "It's far too easy to disappear in New York. You meet good people, and then never see them again." His beard seems a little unrulier than usual: Santa Claus in the off-season. For the first time I see a small tattoo of a star peeking out from under his shirt sleeve on his wrist, right above the pulse points.

Tony has his cell phone against his ear. He is speaking softly into it in Spanish. He looks me in the eye, but there's no warmth there, just an acknowledgment that I am existing in the same space as he. Yet. I wonder what it is about me that makes him so uncertain of me. Perhaps he's just uncertain of himself. I will make him my friend, though. It will happen.

I drop my bag on the floor and lean against the wall, stick my hands in my pockets, stretch my thumbs toward my belly.

"I wouldn't blow this off," I say. "I get a nice rush from sniffing bleach."

"We're talking about my agent," says Mal. "Sit down. I want to know what you think."

I sit on the couch.

"So I'm on the phone with my agent," he says.

"What's your agent like?"

Mal shoots me a look, like, *Why is this important?* But he says, "I don't know. She's older. She's a pretty sharp lady."

"Older than what?" I say. I'm at the age where I am starting to understand why that word could be offensive.

"Older than me, older than you. Not by that much. Maybe early forties. She's still a very attractive woman. Carries herself well. Great posture. I don't even know why I said 'older.' I just meant she's a grown-up. That's all I meant."

I muse on the fact that Mal is in his early thirties and still doesn't consider himself a grown-up.

"Also she has a sweet loft. With the tall ceilings and the big windows and everything. But in SoHo, not in Brooklyn," Mal says, and there is a desperate crack to his voice. "She lives the high life." We lose him for a moment: he goes off to a dreamy place, far away from Brooklyn, just across the bridge, to a fantastic apartment he thinks will solve all his problems, to a decadent life he thinks he deserves. Real estate corrupts absolutely.

"Anyway, she calls me this week and says she doesn't think I should write a novel. She thinks I should write a memoir. And only part of it should be about me and the band. And the other part should be about my father. Really most of it should be about my father, that's what it's starting to sound like."

"That's great," I say. "So what's the problem?"

"Well, she can't just demand that kind of thing, right?"

I think of Alice, the way she called Martin once, twice, three times a day, and he would slam down the phone each time, there would be a great deal of grumbling, and sometimes I would touch his shoulder and he would move my hand away. But then he always went back to work harder and faster.

"Well," I say carefully, "I think she is trying to help you."

"This is what I said," says Scotty.

"I'm not some trained writing monkey," says Mal. "And I don't want to talk about him. I don't want to be identified with him at all. I haven't talked to him in five years. And he never supported my music dreams. Not once."

I say nothing, because I don't want to be that person who tells him he's wrong, I don't want that role in his life. That's his wife's job.

Mal sits up straight. "I gotta get out of here. This place is driving me nuts. Jarvis, we're going to get a drink. You want in?"

Without hesitation, I nod. To have another moment with them, no matter how small, was thrilling.

Mal glares at Scotty. "Come on, man, don't worry about your mother-in-law. It's your one day in months without the baby. Let's go have some fun."

Scotty folds his arms across his chest, guns on a barrel. "Oh Mal, my friend, you have no understanding of what it's like once you have a baby. Even if they're not there, they're *still there*. And when I go home smelling like beer and cigarettes, she can smell it on me. Deep in her subconscious. And some day, when she's, like, thirty, and she's sitting in a therapist's office, she's going to remember that her daddy used to come home drunk. And then she'll blame me for everything."

I think about my father for a moment. Was there a time when he didn't smell like beer and cigarettes?

"Okay, but what if you don't smoke?" says Mal. "And then you just, like, chew a bunch of gum afterward. Then she won't smell a thing."

"It's kind of more of a psychic thing," says Scotty. I could tell Mal was losing him.

Tony stops speaking into the phone and holds it to his chest. He turns to Scott and says, sharply, "Don't be a pussy," and then returns to his phone.

Don't be a pussy. These are the words that have launched street fights and corporate takeovers and wars. Fraternity pranks. Gang bangs. Racial violence. Manifest destinies, all tied up in the idea that whatever you do, don't be a sensitive, frail flower, don't be less than a man, for Chrissakes don't be a *girl*. And these are the words that will convince a loyal father he really needs to get drunk in the middle of a sunny spring afternoon.

8.

Inside, in the dark, at the Greenpoint Tavern, we are jammed into a booth. Scotty's in his cups, and I'm well on my way to joining him. Tony's too busy working his cell phone over at the bar to get drunk. And Mal, I can't see any difference. His voice hasn't changed at all; it's still that same perfectly modulated, dry tone.

I'm kidding. No I'm not. Oh, you'll never know.

There is a tiny tear in the leather booth and I finger it. It still smells like cigarettes in here, faintly, even though there's no smoking allowed anymore. Next to my head a sign tells me I must be twenty-one years of age to be served. At the bar two men in their sixties, one with pants so low his wiry ass crack is visible, laugh their phlegmy laughs. They are talking about sports. They are talking about the neighborhood. They are talking about politics. They are not talking about women, but I guess men can't talk about women forever.

Scott, on the other hand, his face red like a hard cherry candy, is standing tippy toe on his soap box, arms extended, letting the whole world know: he loves women.

"I just have a lot of love to give. I have always loved women. I remember when I was a kid, five, six, seven, and all the girls at my school used to fight over who got to be my girlfriend for the day. They'd pull each other's hair. Fighting over me. Because I have an *understanding* of women. How to make them feel good. I had older sisters, a wonderful mother. Women are a beautiful thing."

Mal stares at him, opens his mouth to say something, and then closes it. He shakes his head, gets up, and heads to the shiny new Internet jukebox in the back of the bar.

I'm captivated. The spilling of guts makes me happy. Plus, I love men who love women. Because I am a woman who loves men.

"Purity," I say. "I can respect that."

"Well, I'm not totally pure," he says. "I know how to make women feel badly, too. The same things that can make you feel good, that you're charming and sexy and wise and important, it's just as easy to turn that around and make you feel the exact opposite. But most of my life I've been pretty respectful of women. And there are so many bad men out there." His voice is a low grumble. A cowboy trying to save the ranch. "I'm just trying to put a little balance in the world.

"I love to love, is that wrong?" says Scott.

"It is not wrong. It is right," I say. We are connecting, Scott and I. It feels good, but it makes me anxious, too. I turn my head, wishing we weren't alone, wishing someone would join us.

At the corner of the bar Tony glitters under an army of red-white-and-blue Fourth of July decorations, shiny streamers that sparkle in odd contrast with the darkened wood, stained with smoke and beer and sweat. I wave at him, and he gives me a nod, and then I stick out my index finger and curl it toward me, *Come here, young man*, and he puts up his own index finger, *Hold please, miss*, takes a sip from his styrofoam cup, and then leans into the phone. I hear him say, "I'm just trying to keep it real, scungeel."

And Mal is hunched over the jukebox, one hand wedged in his back pocket. He taps a foot. A slow, mournful country song begins to play. A gentle twang of guitar, a bruised heart, the imagined rattle of a train in the distance.

Finally, relief. Tony slides across from me in the booth, next to Scott, who is on the verge of his eightieth epiphany of the day. Behind them the afternoon sun slips through the blinds on the front window, over their heads, and onto my face. Every few seconds another person strolls by the window, and I see them in profile. Outside, the world passes by us, but I don't care, I don't care, I don't care.

"You have a great face, Jarvis," says Tony. He has finally noticed I exist.

I move my head down a bit toward the table, and I raise my eyes toward him, and then I smile my prettiest smile, not too wide, just a hint of teeth. I love men, but I love it more when they love me. It is a flaw, but it is the only way I know how to be.

"Thank you," I say. "And thank you for fitting us into your busy schedule."

"I got a lot of business to take care of," says Tony.

"A man on the go," I say.

Mal appears suddenly at the head of the table. "You guys are not even going to believe this set," he says. "I took care of us, that's all I'm saying." He sits down next to me. I scoot over. Not too close now, I think, but it is hard not to be too close in this booth.

"I have to make a lot of people happy," says Tony.

"I don't have to make anyone happy," I say. "Just me."

Scott bursts his hands forward and grabs mine. "You don't have to be alone, Jarvis. You're going to be okay. We'll help you."

And just like that, my eyes are full of tears. Drinking in the middle of the day, it'll get you every time.

"Would it help to talk? Do you want to talk about him?"

All I do is talk about him, I think. In my head, to myself, all day long. But I begin to speak. Because it is nice to hear the words out loud.

I tell them about the first paintings of his I sold, ten from the McCarren Park series, portraits of local Little League players and their parents. Martin had played loud classical music the day he shot the photos, all of the families traipsing in one by one. I had cooked an Italian spread, big platters of flat, sweet pasta and homemade meatballs, huge loaves of buttery garlic bread with parmesan sprinkled on top, and fresh heirloom tomatoes sprinkled with sea salt and served with basil and mozzarella. Everyone ate and then stood patiently, uniformed children and their parents, one family after the other. It made me stir inside, and later on we had talked again about having children, and again Martin had said no, not now, maybe never, and again I had not listened to a word he said.

Maybe we never would have had children. Maybe he never would have given me what I wanted. Maybe I just didn't listen.

I tell them about the completed paintings: the kids in uniform, scuffed-up pants and cleats, gloves and bats on the floor, and their parents, some still dressed from work, a few suits, more of them in manual-labor or maintenance attire, a few in shorts, and the women in tight jeans and hooded sweatshirts, one of them in a nurse's uniform, another, scowling, in a Mets jacket. It's the most comforting of his work, which is why it made sense for me to turn to it first.

I tell them about how Alice stood there in her sunglasses and six-hundred-dollar shoes in my—our—loft and watched the art handlers wrap the paintings and take them away. How she looked so lovingly at the paintings. The seizing of control made her feel alive. And I felt the same stir inside then. Someone's children, not mine. Martin's children. Taken away.

I tell them about how much it hurt to sell those paintings, how it hurts just as much each time, just when I think it can't possibly hurt anymore than it already has.

When I am done talking, I realize Mal's leg has moved next to mine. He is pressing against me. He is either giving me support or he is hitting on me, I can't tell which, and I don't care.

"I need a smoke," says Tony. "Anyone want a smoke?"

"I quit," says Mal.

"I need a drink," says Scott. He, more than any of them, is devastated by my story.

"I'll smoke with you," I say. I have no one to answer to.

We walk out of the bar into a suddenly overcast day and stand in front of the door. Tony pulls a pack from his shirt pocket, takes a cigarette in his mouth, lights it, and then hands it to me.

He lights another for himself. I lean against the front of the bar and watch him. Somehow he is constantly moving even when he's standing in one spot; his hand moves up to his mouth and he takes a puff, another hand runs through his hair, he takes a step forward, a step back, he shakes his head, he raises his eyebrows; he is a man in motion.

"You know what I think?" he says. "About you."

Tell me, oh wise man.

"I think you need to learn to be a little bit more selfish."

I puff my cigarette slowly. It feels strange, paper to lips, smoke to mouth, through the throat, down to the lungs. Foreign invasion.

"Nobody's going to take care of you but you in this world. And you're in a great situation, believe it or not. You've got all that money. Or the possibility of money anyway. Do you know how many people would kill to be in your position?" He considers what he's said. "Scratch 'kill.' "

He steps toward me.

"You have more potential than any of us, Jarvis. And that includes Scotty, who may win the father of the year award, he's a good guy, sure, but is never going to earn a dime again." He leans in close, his mysterious dark skin glittering with a dewy shine. I'll bet he uses a really nice moisturizer. "Independence, that's what you've got."

"You make money," I say.

"I don't make money," he says. "I make a pittance. The money I make would get me a bed in a closet somewhere. Those guys won't tell you the truth, but I will. We're scared shitless our wives will leave us."

"I'd do anything to get Martin back," I say. "I'd give it all up. I don't even care about the money at all."

Tony shifts again; he's been shifting all day. "Of course, I love my wife. She's my princess."

"Of course you do."

"I'm just saying—lemons, lemonade. *Capisce?*"

I suck in my mouth and think of a sour lemon candy.

"You're very dark," I say. I squint at him. "Almost black."

"Oh, I'm all kinds of colors," he says. He smiles at me, and his lips and eyes meet me at once, refined and masculine at the same time, a sculpture, chipped away by the world. I could chip at him, too, and he would turn into whatever I wanted.

I take another drag off the cigarette. It's starting to feel familiar again, all of this. The comfort we take in our own skin.

And then there is a flash of color in the corner of my eye, a cloud moves and it's the sun, blazing bright yellow down into my skull. I see a hand across the street, waving at me. It's Davis, Martin's best friend, his gigantic frame leaning against the front window of a café across the street, a cell phone pressed against his ear, and then, crazily, his long hair poking out of a ski cap with a bright-blue pom-pom on top. He's squinting to see if it's me, his head cocked to the side, lips pinched together. He doesn't seem to believe it's me. I'm out of context, smoking in front of a bar on Bedford Avenue in the middle of the day. I look away, and pretend that in fact, it's not me.

And I snap back into myself again, the in-between woman, the hoper, the waiter, and I realize I've been misbehaving with these thoughts, these actions, these words; even if I'm not saying them, I'm participating by not arguing. I shouldn't even be here, I realize.

"I shouldn't even be here," I say to Tony. "I don't know what I'm doing here. I've got to go." I drop the cigarette and hustle myself inside to the booth, where Mal and Scotty are arm wrestling.

"Can you hand me my bags?" I say. I squeeze my hand at Mal. Mal and Scotty drop their arms and look at me. Scotty is red-faced, and Mal looks exactly the same, always the same. "The laundry bag, my purse. Can you give them to me please?" I realize there is a hysterical ripple to my voice but I can't seem to control it.

Tony comes up behind me and puts an arm around my shoulder, whispers that he's sorry in my ear, and I feel like a gentle wind just blew through me.

"Why don't you just sit down and have another beer?" says Mal. He pats the seat next to me. "No one's in a hurry today."

"I have to be home by six," says Scotty.

Mal looks at Scotty and gives a slight tilt of his head, a raise of his eyebrows. *Shut up, dude.*

"That's when my wife gets home from work," says Scotty.

Mal rolls his eyes. "Fine. Except for Scotty."

"But you, you've got all the time in the world," says Tony. He steers me into the booth, next to Mal, who promptly returns his knee next to mine, as if I had never been gone.

"Maybe I could stay later than six," says Scotty.

"We'll all stay here until Jarvis feels like leaving," says Mal.

"We're here for you, Jarvis," says Tony.

Here they are, here I am, here we are, together.

9.

At home, a phone message from Davis.

"Sugar pie, you doing all right? Now you call me back, okay? Just let me know how you're doing."

Erase, erase, erase.

I NEVER WOULD have met Martin if it weren't for Davis. Specifically because Davis likes to talk to the ladies, any lady, including me. He's a dirty, dirty bird, or at least he was, I'm not sure if he is anymore. There's a legendary story about the height of his dirtiness that got passed around the artists of Williamsburg for a while, until no one knows if it's true anymore, or how much of it was true in the first place. Martin told it to me one afternoon, not too long after I met him.

We were walking back on Manhattan Avenue through Greenpoint from Davis's place. Davis had thrown a pig roast with a few of his neighbors in the backyard that adjoined their row houses. They had spent hours the night before spicing and stuffing and binding the pig and had then cooked it in a hole in the ground overnight, until the next afternoon the pig was finally ready, the meat so delicious and tender it fell from the bone with the slightest tap. All of the men had grown rowdy and drunk with the fantasy of the kill (although of course the pig had been purchased already slaughtered from a farm upstate), and then the ritualistic preparation, which had taken hours, and when we left they were singing and smoking weed. Strangers were flirting with me. Davis was flirting with me. I was laughing, but Martin didn't find it funny. Finally someone opened a large bottle of whiskey, and Martin said, "That's our cue to leave."

So we walked, arm in arm, through the throngs of Saturday shoppers, past all of the Polish businesses—the bakeries and groceries and bars and travel agencies and butchers—until finally Martin stopped me in front of a donut shop and said, "Davis is a great artist and a good friend, but sometimes he's a bad man."

"Does Davis do dirty things with the donuts?" I said.

Martin smirked. "No, with the donut girls," he said.

IT HAD BEEN a few years since it happened, and probably none of the girls involved still worked there anymore. No one lasted very long at the donut shop, it being some sort of underground donut railroad for recent émigrés. They're there six months, max, and then they move on, get married or sponsored some-how, move to New Jersey, find work at one of the clubs.

Anything to get them out of the donut shop. "It's like their training ground for seduction," Davis had told Martin. "Their early introduction to the deviance of New York."

Davis has always had a thing for Eastern European women, so he was the target customer for this donut shop. His first wife was Latvian, an aspiring art historian named Vivika. They met first in Geneva, where she was an assistant at a prominent gallery featuring some of Davis's work in a group show. He promptly imported her to the U.S. like a bottle of vintage wine or an expensive truffle, found her a job at one of the few good galleries left uptown, where someone of her appearance and background would be prized more than downtown, where she would seem just like everyone else—foreign and beautiful; and then after six months he married her at City Hall in order to ensure her continuing welcome in our fair country. Martin said the entire wedding party was drunk on Polish vodka, shots of which had been consumed as they walked across the Brooklyn Bridge on a sunny Friday afternoon, awash in crowds of tourists from all over the world. I've seen Martin's photos from the day, and once, late at night at a loft party, someone showed a Super 8 film: a half-dozen longhaired artists—except for Martin, he was always too punk rock for long hair—in tuxedos, swigging from a liter-sized paper bag, cut a crooked line across the bridge, as did one woman, a short one, in a white lace minidress, straight blond hair cut at different angles and layers, the tiniest wisp of a nose, baby-pink lipstick, huge plastic hoop earrings, also baby-pink, fair skin coated with makeup (she reportedly had terrible skin as a teen, plus pores of a woman twice her age— probably from all the drinking—but it was her only physical flaw and the scars ultimately only added to her appeal), and these huge blue eyes with long dark-brown lashes, like one of those collector's dolls you might see on a cable shopping show or in the homes of middle-aged women who never had children; or worse, had children who turned out to be nothing but trouble. She was crying, wailing practically. Her mascara ran like sewer rain down her cheeks.

The film showed a bulky Davis—he's six-three and has natural brawn—putting a thick arm around her, whispering in her ear, and as they walked, they swerved. What was he saying to her? Was he trying to convince her to go through with it? Was he telling her he loves her like no other?

And then he turned to the tourists taking pictures of the Statue of the Liberty, winking off in the distance. It's possible to read his lips in this moment. "I love this woman," he yelled. The tourists looked at him blankly. They clearly did not recognize a New York moment.

Davis tried again. "I. Love. Her." He was wearing a cowboy hat. He took it off, waved it in the air. He was bald by then, but still kept his hair long on the sides, almost down to his shoulders, and he was wearing a powder-blue rented tuxedo. ("Why didn't they just go to Vegas where they would have been properly appreciated?" I had asked Martin at the time.)

At last he received a smattering of applause, two hippies on bikes passing heard his cry for attention and saluted him.

She left him six months later for an art handler from South Carolina who played drums in a punk rock band. He lived two doors down from Davis and Vivika. They met at their local pub on the nights Davis was stuck at the studio. She took a few thousand dollars from their joint account and they moved to Baltimore, where she had an aunt. Last Martin heard she was pregnant, and her boyfriend was on tour with Fugazi. But that was years ago, of course.

WITHOUT DISCUSSION, Martin and I walked inside the donut shop—how could we not go in?—and took a long look around. It was an overheated no-name joint: fluorescent lights with one bulb flickering, a Polish flag on the wall, held up by thumbtacks, day-old crullers for sale (a dozen for a dollar), a shakily written sign denouncing the use of personal checks. I imagined the coffee was terrible until the third sugar, and then it was just fine.

"Do you want a donut?" said Martin.

I was full from the pig roast, but it smelled great in there; hot blasts of sugar and butter dripping and melting together.

"I'll take an old-fashioned," I said.

"Is there any other kind?" said Martin, and he approved of me in that moment, I could tell by the way he looked at me, as if I were brilliant, and then he brushed my bare shoulder with his lips. We were in those early stages of judgment then, when every choice we made, every opinion expressed, was getting us closer to the moment of love. We were moving fast, and we both liked it, Martin because he was tired of dating, and me because I always wanted quick solutions, convenient exits and entrances to the stages of my life.

A thin, young blond girl, her eyes glazed and tired, was manning the counter as we approached. Martin ordered and she lazily shuffled to the stack of donuts, and wrapped two in individual sheets of wax paper.

"You want bag?" she said. The pink gloss on her lips had glitter in it.

"No bag," said Martin. "We'll just eat and walk." He lingered for a moment longer, as if he were waiting for the counter girl to reveal a secret password, and then handed me my donut.

Outside, Martin was thoughtful as he nibbled on his donut. "I was hoping to see the guy," said Martin.

"What guy?" I said.

OLD-FASHIONEDS WERE the specialty of the shop, or they were when Davis used to hang out there. There were always fresh ones coming out of the oven hourly all day long, the sheets of which were managed by a quiet older Polish man who usually had whiskey on his breath in the late afternoons, a fine row of hair sprouting up from his chef's shirt. Two tattoos on his arm. One bearing only numbers. He only talked when he was angry with one of the girls who worked there, and then he talked quickly, spitting out Polish in bursts. He could make any girl cower in less than a minute; as soon as he opened his mouth, she would lower her head, maybe pull a fine set of bangs down over her eyes, or pick at a hangnail until her finger was bloody. Davis had seen it happen a million times, but he never said a thing.

"I BET HE didn't like that," I said.

"Oh no," said Martin, extending the "o" sound for a few seconds, squeezing his lips into the shape of a tunnel. "You know how Davis is. He thinks he's the perfect southern gentleman."

"But he's not," I said. By then I had seen Davis in action a few times, the way he could never sit by himself at a party, there always had to be a girl he was captivating, who by the end of the night he would pull into his lap. Most girls would shriek and giggle, but some girls would pull away.

"He is, and he isn't," said Martin, and his tone was wounded on his friend's behalf. Martin still loved Davis more than me then.

DAVIS HAD BEEN single for a while, a tricky act for a man like him, who was born to love, as he so often says. He started hanging out in the donut shop in the morning, getting coffee with three sugars, staying until the early afternoon, when he went to work. (He was the right-hand man for T. Wilhelm, arguably the world's most important video installation artist, in an enterprise that rivaled Warhol's factory in its time. It left Davis in a curious position of power. He had his finger on Wilhelm's pulse, which connected him to the art world in a unique and important way. But his finger was also stuck on the pulse, rendering him mostly immobile, unable to do his own work, most of which involved the videotaping of demolitions and the display of surrounding artifacts as sculptures, sometimes authentic, sometimes manufactured. "Detritus" was the name of his most famous series. To this day Davis hasn't resolved which direction he wants to go. Some say he's just waiting for Wilhelm, who's well into his seventies, to die.) And sometimes he would come in late at night, after a dinner with Wilhelm and out-of-town guests in Koreatown. Davis had this very full, very rich life surrounded by people who counted on him or listened to him, but at the end of the day he preferred spending time with pretty blond girls barely out of their teens who spoke broken English.

Eventually Davis got the girls to warm up to him. Even with his wild crown of hair and the goofy space between his front teeth, Davis is still sexy. Maybe it's his height. Maybe it's his drawl. He's a generous man, too, and he started leaving the girls larger tips each time, tips that far surpassed what he spent: a five here, a ten there. And then he began to hire them, one to do housecleaning this week, another to do his book-keeping, neither task being particularly taxing as Davis was rarely home and merely required someone to total his expense receipts for him on a monthly basis, no different from ringing up two Bavarian Cremes on a cash register. The girls would come and go frequently, whispering to themselves in Polish; they would make their money and leave Davis again and again, which was fine by him. He just liked to see them out from behind the counter, to place them in different scenarios, like Barbie dolls in every room of their dream house. Everything was free-flowing and warm and familiar. He knew he could go to the donut shop and be received as a sort of sponsor, he had his place there, he wasn't doing anything wrong. Of course there was a layer of wrongness to it. But he didn't ask them to wear French maid uniforms or dress up like a naughty accountant. He allowed them to be who they were, and he paid them to do it.

And then at the end of one rough night—Wilhelm had thrown a temper tantrum about the hue of a series of bulbs. *Amber, I said*—Davis went to his refuge and ordered three donuts and coffee with whipped cream on top. The waitress across the counter, a nineteen-year-old by the name of Kryztyna, smiled at Davis. It was the end of spring, probably a pleasant day—blue and clear, the kind of day when New Yorkers began to have faith they could be happy again—but Davis had missed most of it, stuck in the studio.

"Now how are you doing today, sweetheart?"

"Good. It was beautiful day."

"Yes it was."

Davis smiled at her, her long blond hair, a little dirty, falling all around her shoulders, and her young, pale skin, and her long nose that reached out far beyond her face, her high cheeks, her warm lips. She was wearing a tight knit shirt with stripes across the belly. The shirt was a size too small—deliberately or hand-me-down?—and he could see her belly button.

("You know those belly shirts? You know what I'm talking about?" Davis had said to Martin. "Oh, those belly shirts get you everytime.") She had her fingers hiked into the back pockets of her jeans, like Courteney Cox in that Bruce Springsteen video, the one where he pulls her up on stage to dance with him. Davis liked Courteney Cox, with her huge eyes and deep scratchy voice, always a little impatient. He liked women who demanded attention.

"I go to beach soon," she said. "Coney Island." Her eyes, lined with powder pink eye shadow, widened with excitement. "Swim." She pinched her nose with her thumb and index finger, and shimmied as if she was jumping into a clear beautiful pool. Davis pictured her in a bikini, her blond hair flying up in the air as she crashed into the water. Oh, she was delightful. He took a swig of coffee.

"You need a bathing suit for the beach," said Davis heartily. And then, quieter, "You got a bathing suit?"

"No. Well. Yes, I have my sister's bathing suit. She left it when she move to Chicago. No ocean there, she say."

"That's not acceptable," said Davis. "You need your own bathing suit for the beach. This your first summer here?"

She nodded.

"Girl like you should have a new bathing suit. You want a new bathing suit?" Davis was excited, he was nodding his head. He was inspired.

"Yes!" She started laughing.

"Would you like me to buy you one?"

"Yes, but . . ." She looked down.

"Oh honey, ask anyone around here. I'm safe as a kitten."

And that's how Davis started buying the donut girls bathing suits. The first girl he took shopping told another girl at the donut shop, and then she mentioned it to Davis, and then suddenly Davis was shopping every weekend. One after the other, department store after department store: Macy's, Bloomie's, Barneys if they were really special, the tallest ones, the blondest ones, the ones in the best condition. Bathing suits for big girls, too. Davis was okay with the big girls. Yeah, he was okay with them. He would sit in a chair near the dressing room, and the girls would parade out, one by one, in the barest of bikinis. Davis would sit and watch and smile and laugh. Keep his cowboy hat on his lap. Thank his lucky stars. Hate himself.

Once Davis even borrowed Wilhelm's truck and took a girl to a mall in New Jersey. Later on she gave him a handjob in the backseat ("She insisted," he told Martin), but as much as Davis enjoyed it, that's not what he wanted from these girls. He wanted to see them model the suits for him, and he wanted them to wear them to the beach, and he wanted them to serve him coffee and donuts with a smile.

. . .

MARTIN AND I were at McCarren Park by now. We had finished our donuts and were licking our fingertips.

"I just thought he was a flirt," I said. "I didn't realize he was so . . . What is that? Is that perverted?"

"My man was going through rough times, I think," said Martin. "We've all talked to him since."

"But they were so young," I said. "You don't think he was taking advantage of them?"

"I'm not sure if you're in the best position to judge someone," said Martin quietly.

I stopped licking my fingers and stared at him.

"Neither am I," he said. "We're not so innocent. That's all I'm trying to say."

Then we looked each other in the eye, and I knew he was ready to forget my past, but I also knew that we would never discuss his past. Everything that happened before we had met was irrelevant. We could be good now. Good together.

DAVIS KNEW HE WAS BAD, but he couldn't figure out how to stop himself. He was slowly ruining his relationship with the donut shop. He used to pay the girls to work for him, and now he was giving them money for nothing. Money just to look good. Now when he walked in the door, the donut girl on duty would slip to the back bathroom and hurriedly reapply her makeup. Now when he walked in, the smile he got was larger than usual, more excited, perhaps less sincere. He couldn't tell. Everyone was always smiling at him all the time. Except for the donut maker, the stiff Polish man in the rear. With him it was a stare-down from the minute Davis opened the door, bell jangling, until he shut it behind him. He would stop working, lean on the counter that separated the kitchen from the front service area, and stare. He had Davis's number, and Davis knew it.

He was running out of donut girls, too. He had attired all but one, a quiet girl, older, not quite as pretty as the rest—arms lumpier, shirts covered with powder, hair in a ponytail when it might look nicer down, but what did Davis know anyway? She'd been working there for as long as Davis remembered, and she seemed to take her duties more seriously than the rest of them: reminding him that if he bought just one more he'd get a free coffee, wrapping the donuts in wax paper expertly, folding the paper bags that held the to-go orders just so, a clean, crisp line at the top of the white paper, firmly between her thumb and index finger.

On a night when he was feeling good—Wilhelm was in London opening a show at the Tate and wouldn't be back for a week; Davis was running the show in New York, and that seemed right, that seemed like the way the world should always work, everything was just as it should be—he finally nailed her down in conversation. The old man was out back taking a smoke break. Davis had noticed him as he rounded the corner, kicking at imaginary stones with his feet.

Davis opened the door—bells jingling, a wave of sugar and heat blowing in his face—and sat at the counter. The joint was empty. The TV in the corner showed the local newscast, sound off, fuzzy reception. Rain tomorrow morning, blue skies later in the day. She walked over, in her shrug of a sweatshirt, a hole in the sleeve, and stood in front of him patiently. He ordered a coffee. She pulled out a ceramic taupe mug from underneath the counter, walked to the coffee station, filled it, gently placed it in front of him.

"Nice night," said Davis.

"It's okay," she said.

He looked her in the eyes. Prettier than he had thought. The blue was hazy, but the pupils were fierce. She had her hands on the counter.

"What's your name?"

"Paulina."

"I'm Davis."

"I know. I know who you are."

"What else do you know?"

"I know you take girls shopping."

"Would you like to go shopping?"

She looked down at the ground, held her head down for ten seconds, fifteen, thirty. She nodded. She didn't look up.

"I could take you shopping."

He heard the creak of the back door.

"We could do it tomorrow," he whispered. "In the morning."

The oven door opened and then slammed.

"Would you like that?" said Davis.

The old man stuck his head over the counter. He began speaking in Polish, loudly and slowly, and the girl stood at alert instantly. She took a step back, turned from Davis, and walked to the kitchen. He heard the back door open, and then quietly shut. The old man disappeared for a moment, then appeared in front of Davis. He was carrying a large rolling pin. He clenched it in one fist, and patted the base of it in his other palm.

"That's my niece," he said. "You like my niece?"

Davis sipped his coffee. He felt his bladder fill. He felt wet inside.

"She seems like a lovely young woman."

"You think so?"

Davis put his coffee cup down.

"You want to marry her?"

"No."

"Why don't you want to marry my niece?" He patted the rolling pin.

"I don't know her."

"But you want to watch her dress and undress. You want her to dance around in front of you."

"No," said Davis.

"With no clothes. My niece in no clothes!" The old man sounded wounded.

"No, no," said Davis soothingly. "She'd be wearing a bathing suit." As soon as he said it, he knew he had fucked up, but it was done.

The man slammed the rolling pin on the counter in front of Davis. The coffee cup shook.

"No bathing suit. No more bathing suit."

And Davis wanted to say: "Well the summer's almost over anyway." And that he had thought about what he would do in the fall already—short plaid skirts and knee socks—and he knew the girls would want to go shopping again.

Instead he said, "It's a free country, man."

And the old man said, "Yes, I know. I live here, too." He rolled the pin back and forth on the counter, both hands on the end. "Get out of my shop."

Davis pulled his wallet out, and extracted two single dollar bills, which he placed next to the coffee cup.

"Get out now," said the old man.

"I just wanted to make sure I left a tip," said Davis. And then he left the donut shop forever.

Which is why Davis stopped eating donuts. Which is why Davis moved away from Greenpoint to Williamsburg, one block away from Martin, his best friend: *Blood, hombre, for life*, they would joke at the end of the night when they were drunk. Which is why when I met Davis and Martin for the first time at the bar on Fourth Street, me in my short skirt and pink hair serving them scotches on the rocks, and Davis asked me if I needed a bathing suit, Martin told him to shut the fuck up already with the bathing suits.

Martin, my hero.

I PICK UP the phone. I call Davis. He can be over in a heartbeat, he says. Just let me take care of a few things around the office.

No, tomorrow, I say. I've had enough of men for one day.

10.

I have no food in my house, at least not any Davis would want to eat, just a head of lettuce, some strawberries, and some pale, watery tofu. I can't have any of Martin's friends going hungry. It would be a disgrace. So I head out the door to Greenpoint. There's meat there. Davis, hungry, lusty Davis, is unapologetic about his love of meat.

Down in the elevator, a whistle on my lips, a flier for a loft sale taped to the wall. CDs, books, a scanner, a VCR, a futon, a couch. All day Saturday. They're moving out of state. Everything must go. Out the front door, and I see the woman with the guitar approaching again, the one who saw me holding the door too long for my own good yesterday. This time I walk confidently through it, and then hold it open for her. We smile at each other, like good neighbors should, and I notice she has a space between her front teeth, and that she is younger than I am, just by a few years, but her skin is distinctly smoother than mine, and that there are turquoise beads weaved into a few of her blond dreadlocks. "Good morning," I say, and I surprise myself. I sound so cheerful. It is almost as if I am approaching normal. Before I know it, I'll be making idle chitchat. How about this weather? How about those Yankees? Have you heard, my husband's in a coma?

Maybe I'll stick with "Good morning" instead.

I reach in my bag for my sunglasses, then relent. I've been out in the world so much this week, I'm getting used to the sun now. I am getting used to the world now. I round the corner, and walk on Berry toward the park. There is some graffiti along the way, slapped against a block-length warehouse: a green octopus—or maybe it's an alien—and a hot dog that looks suspiciously phallic oppose each other, and there are swaggering tags around them, different artists, one with a 1970s influence, like auto detailing on a Camaro, another looks hip-hop, but old school, Run-DMC era. I stop and give the wall my full attention. The hot-dog bun is sprinkled with a few dots, like sesame seeds. The octopus makes me a little nauseous. At the far end of the block, written in lowercase cursive, is a simple "i love you."

Off to the park, past the pale, shirtless hipsters getting their first brush of sun, and I hope they're using sunscreen; and the dog people, they all gather together like parents on prom night, staring proudly at their children, one dog sniffing another's ass—*Aren't they cute?*—and then I see the Little League team on the diamond in the warm-up stages, kicking up dust, as their parents on the bleachers pull out their coolers and chips and scorecards, warming up their vocal cords for a fine afternoon of screaming, and I get a pull in my chest, and I miss those paintings I sold, and I remember those people in my home, and how warm and close they all were together. We were together.

Martin is all around me, but I still have to get to the butcher. I see the farmers' market up ahead on the corner of the park. A paltry showing of goods—one vendor has two small tents of vegetables, there's an orchard represented by a table covered with a dozen or so crates of apples, and the trunk of a small dairy truck is open, dispensing quarts of milk that are promised to be from fairly treated cows.

At the vegetable stand a worker chops off the stems of a bunch of radishes for an elderly woman rocking a shopping cart and nodding. "Perfect," she says, and some spit flies out of her mouth. One Little Leaguer chases another, and as they run past me the chaser yells to the chasee, "I'm going to knock you on your ass." A young woman, pale in a polka-dot blouse, short black hair tied in a knot at the base of her head, walks her bike, shifts a plastic bag full of carrots, dusty with dirt, into a milk crate strapped to the back of it. Another woman—a stunner, blond hair tumbling down her shoulders, a gauzy white shirt belted by enormous silver hoops around an even gauzier skirt, cowboy boots poking out underneath, the tips of which are immaculate—redirects a baby stroller firmly, as if she were shifting gears in a race car. She points out a cluster of tomatoes to a stocky, bearded man dressed in dark-blue jeans, new and crisp, a faded oxford, one elbow gently shredded, hanging down almost over his rear. *Effortlessly casual*, the fashion magazine would say. I could fit into that picture, too. I am wearing expensive jeans (even if they are six years old), I am wearing a wistful T-shirt—a flower and birds are drawn in a style reminiscent of some southern outsider artist, childlike, an inspired doodle—and I am wearing no makeup except for a pale lip gloss and overpriced mascara, and I am limber, I am in motion, and yet I am so far off from being them. I will never, ever, be them. I will never have that purity that comes with a marriage, at least not a first marriage, when you're still proud of yourselves for doing it right, beating the odds, when you haven't yet felt loss and remorse or like you've fucked up something really big, and at least part of it is your fault. I will never again wear that glow of innocence, even if I were to find someone to love. But to find someone I would have to look, and I cannot imagine looking.

"Not those. *Those*. Nope. Still not there. Darling, *please*." She jerks her finger.

Must she do *everything* herself? I think. Oh, the pain of domestic discord shining bright under the light of a spring day. It pinches me in the gut. There's an uneasiness that accompanies witnessing other people's frailties, but also it makes me jealous. To have one more fight with Martin, just to hear his voice when he was angry, the low growl that grew suddenly sharp when he was making a point, I would take that moment.

"Honey," he says. Lost. "I don't know what you want. Tell me. I don't know what I'm doing here." I swear I hear him say, "Jesus," but of course he is just standing there with his hands out, paused, waiting for direction.

"The ones on the bigger stems. And there's four of them. On the bigger stems. Those."

He shakes his head. "They all look the same. They're all on stems. They're *tomatoes*."

I almost laugh, and then he turns and I see a golden beard glinting with bits of gray in the sun, and I feel a jolt of something zoom up my torso—Adrenaline? Blood? Love?—and back down again: it's Scott, my new friend from the laundromat. I feel like turning around and going home. Who did I think I was this week, prancing around all over town as if I had a normal life? Pretending I could function like everyone else, like I can talk and move and maintain myself in public when really I know I should be hiding out at home, boxed in but safe, comfortable, under the white comforter.

He sees me, raises his hand, waves once, a short confirmation that I do exist.

"Well," he says. "There you are." As if he knew I was there all along and had been expecting me to walk up and witness this minor marital traffic accident at the vegetable stand. He rubs his hand to his chin. He smiles at me. He takes a step toward me. "How are you?"

"I'm good." I feel all right. This is going to be all right.

Scott walks over to me. His wife executes a deft turn with the stroller and wedges herself and their child between us. He doesn't even look at her, but he knows she's there.

"This is Jarvis. Jarvis, this is my wife, Elizabeth."

I look at her straight on and notice she has a small dent in the tip of her nose, but beyond that she is as beautiful as I initially thought. She extends a hand. It is gentle, and small, and highly moisturized. French tips. A forty-dollar handshake, easy.

"Jarvis is thinking of joining our book discussion group," says Scott. He winks at me, so quick I almost don't notice it.

"I thought it was boys only," says Elizabeth. The baby starts to chatter to herself, and Elizabeth moves the stroller back and forth.

"No, now we're being more inclusive," says Scott. "It seemed like the right thing to do."

"Maybe you can get them to start reading books besides ones that have been made into movies," she says. "I don't know how many times one person can read *Fight Club*." She purses her lips into a smirk. Her eyes are wide and blue and shine like cut glass in the sunlight.

"As many times as it takes, I suppose," I say.

Here I am, making polite conversation with a couple at the farmers' market. I am here. I am doing this. I am out in the world, making nice with new people. I am not performing, they are not performing, we are *interacting*. This is what people do. I want to sink into it, to enjoy it. It might even be a little bit thrilling.

"That's what I think," says Scott. "So many lessons to be learned." He pats me on the arm. "No, she's just kidding. We read all kinds of books, not just *Fight Club*. I think next week we're going to do *A River Runs Through It*."

"Which was a movie," says Elizabeth. She wags her finger.

Oh, her and that finger. She's *fun*.

"Don't let her sway you, Jarvis. She hasn't read a book in the last two years besides baby books." He adds, "She just doesn't have the time with work." His tone and eyes and stance during this statement are all so comfortable that it feels almost practiced.

"Plus pumping and dumping," says Elizabeth.

"I understand." I don't, really. But since I'm pretending I'm normal, why not pretend I understand?

"Breast milk," she adds. "I've got way too much of it. I'm just an overachiever, I guess. And we're trying to get her off it entirely at exactly the six-month mark."

I realize: now we're having a baby conversation. Books to babies in twenty seconds flat.

"I'm sure Jarvis doesn't want to hear about that."

"Sorry," She laughs, sharp, direct, but maybe a hint of embarrassment. I can't tell. She's a tough one. A woman so pretty, you'd think she wouldn't need to be insecure. But there you are. "New-mother syndrome. I seem to have lost all other interests. Maybe I should join your book club, too."

"If you want to, honey, of course you can," says Scott. And there is that ultra-comfortable tone again. I knew it! He's a big, fat liar.

"Right, like I have any spare time."

"We can make the time," he says soothingly.

"Oh, I don't know, it's your thing anyway . . ."

I am suddenly not there, though of course I am required to witness at the same time. Finally I raise my hand. "I'm going to go," I say stiffly. "Shopping." I point in the direction of Manhattan Avenue.

"God, we just do that *all* the time," says Elizabeth. "Our own little world."

"We'll see you next Tuesday then?" says Scott.

"Oh, I'll be there," I say.

I walk toward the park, turn back for a moment, and see Elizabeth fondling the tomatoes while Scott rocks the stroller.

I cross the street, dodge a Hassid barreling through a light in a dented SUV. My phone vibrates in my pocket. There's a message from Alice. "I hope you've decided to move forward with my proposal. I've got the paperwork ready. Do call me."

11.

Davis ate everything I gave him with great gusto: the cheese pierogi, deep fried and nestled under a dollop of sweet onions and sour cream, the kielbasa, sliced lengthwise, slathered with mustard and laid gently, albeit briefly, to rest on a bed of rye bread, scoops of sauerkraut, and two bowls of tomato soup, plus pint after pint of lager. He chewed and gurgled, a low hum under his breath, and viciously wiped at his skin with napkins, tossing them into a growing pile to the side of his plate. I poured, I ladled, I sliced, I spread it all out before him and he took and took until finally he rubbed his belly and said, "I couldn't take another bite." And then he belched.

Now he is pacing the apartment, talking about his job, talking about the art world, and I find this part the most comforting, the listening, the learning. Davis has the power to make anyone feel like they're a part of something important just by knowing him. I watch him pace, I feel a little dizzy, I lean against the kitchen table. He is talking about Miami, about how the galleries down there might as well be hotel lobbies. "And that makes the gallery owners fucking doormen," he barks. He squeezes his massive hands into giant fists and stands with his legs spread, calls up to the skies. "Doormen, do you hear me?"

"I hear you," I say quietly, but I know he isn't talking to me. *He's not up there*, I want to tell him. *He's over in Queens. Visiting hours are over, but you could go tomorrow.*

Davis rarely visits Martin. I don't care, I know Martin doesn't care, but Davis, he feels badly. But he can't deal with it, seeing the unplugged version of Martin. Pain, it's not for everyone.

Davis turns, makes an exaggerated pout.

"Here I am, talking about me, when I'm supposed to be checking up on you." He crosses the room to the black couch and sits, spreads his legs. "You come sit here." He smacks his legs with his palms. "Right here. Come on." He sounds so fresh and happy. Should I? This man, this artist, this lover, he likes it when women sit in his lap. Cling to him like he's King Kong. Or Daddy. I know that he respects women—as friends, as artists—but I still think he prefers they just sit in his lap, rather than face them head-on. Anyway, it's almost like sitting in Martin's lap.

I go, I sit, I put my arms around his neck. It feels nice. It's a lap, after all.

"You tell me what's going on in your life," he says.

Do I tell him about my new friends? Alice's plans for world domination? Before I can answer, Davis says, "I hear Alice wants to do a retrospective."

"Yeah, and the book thing. And of course the MoMA show." Davis smells like kielbasa. "I'm not sure what to do. I'm still deciding."

"Well, here's the thing, Jarvis. I'm not sure if the timing is right for a retrospective. Martin's name is out there, but no one knows who he is in Kansas, you know what I mean?"

I nod.

"But I think you should do the MoMA show. You'd be a fool not to. Martin would have killed for something like that."

"I know that," I say. "I just feel a little uncomfortable signing over every last piece of Martin to someone else."

"To Alice," says Davis.

"Maybe," I acknowledge. "Maybe to Alice."

"Let me do it," bursts Davis. "I mean, screw Alice. You can go around her, you can have me curate the show. You've got what they want, not her."

I consider what he says for a moment. Davis and Alice have always been competitive when it comes to Martin, and I'm pretty sure they're not speaking anymore, though no one has ever said as much. I asked Davis to catalogue all of Martin's work after the accident, not Alice, and she was furious. She made so much noise about how long Davis was taking, and the accuracy of the information.

"I believe he's engaged some foreign girl to type up the information," Alice said at the time. "It's rife with errors."

"Alice, *you're* foreign," I said.

"No dear, I'm *British*."

There were millions of dollars involved then, I understood. And now there could be even more money, not to mention credibility. It might make more sense for Alice to handle everything—she has always looked after me in the past, and it's probably good to have everything centralized through one source. But maybe Martin would want me to share the wealth? This could mean a lot to someone like Davis.

Davis bounced me on his knee.

"I have to think about it, Davis. I need time."

"Well, you know, sugar, here's the thing. I wouldn't necessarily trust Alice to be . . ." He pauses, mid-bounce, and I was briefly lofted high, so I could see directly into his eyes. "I don't know how responsible she would be to you, or to your feelings."

"What's that supposed to mean?" I say.

"Don't get all bunched up," he says, but he's too fast and too smooth and I think of Scott earlier in the day, and now I do feel exactly as he said: bunched up, a quickly forming mass of questions intertwining in my stomach, unruly and unanswered. *Responsible to my feelings.* Fiscal responsibility I understood, when it came to Alice. She and I had been dealing with lawyers and accountants and checks and bank statements for years, and I have never worried for a moment. I trusted her to take care of Martin and me. But emotional responsibility— that was new territory.

Davis continues talking, and his twang has become more pronounced, and it is charming, though I am in no mood to be charmed. He isn't going to tell me a thing, I know that much.

"You could sign over the photos to me," he says. "I can go through them all for you. There's probably a lot of crap in there, fuckups, missteps. I think I would know what Martin would want, you know, *out there*, in the world." He adds quickly, "Plus I've got proper storage equipment, everything you need to archive. Do it up right, like I always do, sister." He gives my thigh a good squeeze. I shift in his lap. I want off. How do I get off this ride?

"I think I'm going to wait a little while before I decide."

"Are you sure? Because I could get started next week. I have a few personal projects I'm working on, but I would happily put them on the back burner for this opportunity. And, of course, to help you out." He puts his hand on the back of my head and pats me gently. "You know you're my favorite girl in the whole world, don't you?" I look deep into his eyes, all the way through, through the glint of gold around the pupil; and it is hard, because that gold is lovely and shiny; I look deep down inside of him and I see: it is not necessarily a lie in there, but he is hiding something.

I put my hands behind me on the couch and slide off Davis's lap. I smooth my skirt, I clasp my hands in my lap.

"No," I say.

"It'll just take no time at all. Jarvis. Come on." There it is; there is that tiny desperate whine. I knew it would come.

"I'm tired," I say. Game over, I think. There is no Martin left in the evening.

"Positive?" I think he might be sweating. Maybe it's from all that kielbasa.

I get up. I step over his extended leg.

"I will let you know as soon as I decide," I say.

Were your friends this irritating when you were here, Martin? Or are we all just lost without you?

I WAKE UP at midnight, and then again a few hours later. Covers off, covers on. I am naked, now I am clothed. A black slip, with lace at the top. I pace. I wish I had something to distract me: a cigarette, a drink, or, jarringly, a bump of coke. I feel depressed, as always, but also there is the tickle of elation, as if I am on the verge of something great, or at least good.

I can't stop thinking about those goddamn photos. Everyone wants to put their hot little paw prints on them, piss on them, mark their territory. "Psssss," I say. Piss away. Piss off.

And then it clicks in my head, a little shift of brain membrane from the back to the front, mixed with adrenaline, a memory rush, an overdose of external voices, external egos. What do they want to see so badly? What do they want for themselves? Or maybe, what is it *they don't want me to see*?

12.

The Alice Dodgson Gallery sits, placidly, on Twenty-fourth Street in Chelsea, down the block from the majestic Gagosian, and Mary Boone's gallery, and a host of smaller galleries. It's a thin sliver of a gallery, with high ceilings, slotted with a small second-floor loft. The windowed ceiling lets in an astonishing amount of light, which gives the room a stunning glow: the hardwood floors seem shinier, the colors in the artwork appear more vibrant, and the visitors to the gallery themselves are suddenly a little more attractive. This has always been Alice's gift: to make everything—and everyone—look their best, even if they don't deserve it. "You can take shit and coat it with chocolate," said Davis once at one of Alice's openings. "But it still tastes like shit." But Davis is a competitor, and I am just a fan of art, and I almost always think the artists Alice represents taste just fine to me.

Right now the gallery is showing two artists. In the front, there's the work of an outsider artist named Frankie Taylor from Oklahoma, a man who has long suffered from bipolar disorder, a fact that has only enhanced his cult status. His work portrays superheroes living next to bits of scripture, coffee-shop girls he had once loved (and stalked, reportedly), and occasionally talking mice and rabbits, cartoon bubbles spouting angry thoughts, all alternately drawn in crayon, colored pencil, and marker. His work makes me feel less lonely, and also glad I'm not him. Last year, after a *New Yorker* article spotlighted his physical frailties (obesity, various speech impediments, prescription-medication-induced flatulence), Frankie tried to kill himself. Then he declared he would never show his work again to the world. Somehow Alice convinced him otherwise. I'll never know how she did it; I only know that she is very good at her job.

And in the back of the gallery there's a video installation (Martin would kill Alice if he knew; he was never a fan of video, except for Davis's work, but that's just because Davis blows stuff up in the process) by a Moroccan woman that relates a narrative of a prostitute visiting clients and a steam bath and then finally falling in a heap on the steps of a mosque. This is one of Alice's pet projects, bringing the work of women from the Middle East to New York. I would say it was because she's media savvy and knows she'll get attention for it, but she's been passionate about it since the day I met her—I know she journeys to Casablanca twice a year, and has traveled extensively in the Middle East—and I can only conclude that—in this one way at least—Alice is righteous.

I stand and cool myself in the darkened room, watch the woman fall and moan on repeat. I'm gathering up my guts and will all around me. I feel like I'm about to commit a crime, even though I know I'm entitled to possession of my husband's work. Still, there's no way Alice would let me walk out of here with these photos. She'd tell me that I'd be disturbing her process. "How can I keep getting you those big checks if you keep mucking everything up?" she'd say. Or she'd ask for my respect. That's what she'd do. "Darling, this is what I do. Give me that much respect. Let me finish what I've started. You can't argue with that."

Alice, the impenetrable.

So here I am, sneaking around the back way by forging through the front: I am going to ask her favorite new assistant for a little help.

I have come prepared, of course. I walk to the front of the gallery and stand before the woman seated at the front desk. I can feel the sunlight rushing all over me. I give her a smile, and she, with straight brown shimmery hair so long as to make it almost inappropriate for anyone other than an eight-year-old, and the long, tan arm, stretched longer perhaps by yoga, encased in a cool, gauzy shirt, and the tapered nose with the tiny uplift at the end, and the tan, clean face bereft of makeup save for a pleasant sweep of lip gloss across her lips, she of the vastly healthy glow and spirit, smiles back at me with a sturdy row of bright white teeth.

"Is Alice here?" I say.

"Alice is out of the country," she says. Confirmed, I think.

"I'm supposed to be picking something up from her." And then before I launch into a further lie, I say, "I'm sorry—is that shirt made of hemp?"

"It is," she says, and there's a little bit of excitement in her voice. And I can tell she is the kind of person who appreciates thread count. Maybe it's because her skin is so soft. "And I noticed your bag—that's hemp too, right?"

"Yes I got it in this little shop in Williamsburg," I say.

"The one on Grand Street?"

I nod.

"I *love* that place," she says.

"Me too," I say. "It's lovely."

Oh yes, I think. You will be mine. This is going to be easier than I thought. I've got an organic apple in my bag as well, ripe for consumption, red and shiny, ready to be displayed and eaten with great enthusiasm. We earth mothers have to stick together. If I can just keep Alice's voice out of her head.

"I could talk about hemp all day," I say, laughing. "*All* day. Believe me." I slip into a casual tone, a little lazy. My sentences become questions, so that she can answer in the affirmative. "But I'm kind of in a hurry? And I'm hoping you can help?"

The phone rings, and she glides one gentle index finger up in the air, asking me to wait. She maintains eye contact with me as she picks up the phone and continues to smile. I flip through a binder on the desk, which lists the prices of the work of the artists displayed, their biographies, some of their press.

And then I hear her say, "Yes, Alice." She is not looking at me anymore, her tone changes from the musical to the dull, her back stiffens against her chair and I can see the light outline of ribs through her shirt. I'm scared I've lost her, that I'll never get her to break any rules.

She hangs up the phone, and there is the hint of an eye roll, I can tell she wants to do it, but she is restraining herself.

Come back to me, I think.

"Alice can be so difficult," I say, and I infuse my voice with honey-coated sympathy.

"I love this gallery, and it's a wonderful opportunity," she says. It's rehearsed. Goddammit, she's gone. She's one of Alice's trained minions once again.

"Of course it is," I say. I suck on the inside of my lower lip. I'll just plunge forward. I'll tell the truth. I'll beg for mercy. I'll ask for help.

"So you had a pickup?" she says. "Alice didn't mention anything to me."

"I'm Jarvis Miller, Martin Miller's wife." I extend my hand.

She stares at me for a moment, a blank look washes through her eyes, and I can't tell which direction she's going in—Does she care? Does she think he's overrated? Did his work offend her? She could be one of those women who thought he represented everything wrong with men in art. I've heard it before, I'm prepared to hear it again.

She reaches out her hand to mine, and then I notice the flush of color at the base of her neck, creeping up toward her chin.

"I've been waiting to meet you forever," she says. "I wrote my thesis on your husband."

"You're the one?" I say.

"Yes. I'm the one."

MELISSA IS TALKING excitedly about Martin as we walk down the hall toward Alice's office, and I hear the words "ironic" and "reconstruction" and "male gaze" and I'm sure there's an entire sentence there, and someday I would like to have a discussion with her about all of this, but for now, I just want to get the photos and get out of here.

We stop at the end of the hall, and Melissa rifles through a set of keys, stopping to examine a few.

"I can never remember which one is hers," she says. "We're not really supposed to be in her office unless she's here."

"I really appreciate you breaking the rules," I say, and for the first time it occurs to me that Melissa might get in trouble for helping me, but I can't worry about that now. I'm almost there.

"Oh, I'm sure Alice wouldn't mind," she says. "I know this show is really important to her. It's all she thinks about. Any level of insight you can offer into Martin's work will be wonderful."

Together we walk into the office. It is tiny and compact and it reeks of cigarettes, nasty little ones, the butts of which are still sitting in an ashtray on Alice's glass desk. There are also yellow stickie notes all over the desk, except in the middle, in a laptop-shaped space. There is a stack of banker's boxes in the far corner of the office. Melissa kneels on the floor and removes one of the tops of the boxes, and peers inside, replaces it, and then begins to make her way through all of the boxes.

"I'm not sure why she keeps them in here," she says. "We usually keep everything in the back storeroom." She turns toward me. "She really does prize this collection."

"Yes, well, they aren't hers to keep," I say sharply, and then I remember I'm supposed to be long-suffering and loyal, and not jealous and bitchy. "I just mean it's great that the whole world will get to appreciate his work."

Melissa nods her head, somber and sincere. "It's so true," she says. She peeks through another box and pulls it out away from the rest. "This is part of it." She looks in two more, and then stands and drags them toward me. "I've badly wanted to look in them myself," she says. "I haven't seen them yet. No one has but Alice."

I am tempted to share them with her, but my need to fully possess Martin has me in its thrall. I feel like a little kid being asked to share her candy with a new kid in the neighborhood. Maybe someday we'll be friends, but for now, this is all mine.

"Are you sure you can carry all of that when you get home?" she says. "It's too late to get a delivery man today, but I could get it sent to you tomorrow."

"I got it covered," I say, my voice deep and gritty. And then I remember to smile.

THERE WAS A long cab ride over the bridge, my left hand tapping the edge of the box in my lap, my right arm spread across the other two boxes, clutching them as if they might fly out the cab door, and then a sweaty trip hauling the boxes from the elevator into my apartment, through the kitchen to the base of the black leather couch in the living room, which is where I now sit, boxes in front of me. I crack the lid of one, and the scrape of cardboard makes a satisfying noise.

Inside the box are binders filled with photos, and I flip through them quickly, barely stopping to admire the quality of them. I've seen all of the subjects before, only as paintings, of course. There's nothing new here, no information. The second box contains a mess of negatives; some have been organized

and marked in protective plastic sleeves, and there are nota-
tions on each sleeve in Alice's handwriting: years, subject
matter, some are starred. I hold one up toward the window,
and it's more of the same, more Williamsburg. This could take
hours. I pull out a stack, drop it in my lap, then pause for a second. Maybe it would be easier to hand this over to someone
else. Maybe this is why Alice wanted to take care of it herself.

Then I remember: there is nothing pure about her when it
comes to Martin. And I am seized with a feeling of greediness
for a moment. I am not so pure either.

I drop the negatives back in the box and lift the top off the
third box. Inside there are three thick manila envelopes, one
with Alice's name, one with Davis's name, and one with mine.
Each is labeled in Martin's handwriting, firmly, as if he knew
exactly who we were.

I remember my mother, and I allow myself to miss her,
something I don't do very often, because there's no point to it,
she's never coming back to me. But still I wish she were alive. I
pray very hard and squeeze a wish out of me. I wish that she
were sitting next to me, right now, her arm around me, and that
she would tell me what to do, whether I should look in those
envelopes, or whether I should put them back in the box, hide
them away forever, from Alice, from Davis, from myself.

Is it better not to know what's in them? Is it better to
live your life not knowing everything? Sometimes it has to be
better, right?

But Alice knows everything. And I suspect Davis does, too, so
eager was he to get his hands on these photos. No one of us
should be any more powerful with knowledge about Martin than
the other. I cannot be the one left behind, waiting, faithful,

ignorant, forever. I open the envelope that says "Davis" on it, and empty the contents onto my lap. These photos were taken with a different camera. Looks like a rush job. Definitely not art. They fall all around me, around my thighs, on the couch, on the floor, but even at a glance, I know the truth.

My bones, my spine, my veins, my muscles, my blood, my cells collapse within my skin. There is a small pause, and then I am suddenly fucking freezing, and I feel them begin to re-form. It starts with the cells, one by one, I can feel the individual chill, and then all at once they are collectively freezing, and then they are frozen, and chills shoot through my body, and I am hard now, a hard, frozen woman, frozen with hate and anger, and oh my God, Martin! You son of a bitch. I could just *kill you*.

PART TWO

13.

After weeks of hard-thumping, bone-shaking techno music, it's suddenly, surprisingly *reggae day* at the laundromat, and the four of us are slumped quietly in response: me on the couch, as I pair socks; Tony lying next to me, curled up, his head—skin tan and moist, almost glistening—resting near my lap, and his fingers occasionally anxiously thrumming; Scott across from us, looking sharp with a freshly trimmed beard, lazily tickling Nina, who is stretched out on his lap; and Mal in the corner, always in the corner, hair wildly sprouting from his head like a thousand bolts of angry energy with his matching set of infuriated sideburns, notebook clenched in his fist, glaring out at the tableau, clearly offended by the change, and yet powerless to explain why.

"I don't know that I liked the techno," says Scott. "I'm not sure if I ever have. And I may even prefer reggae to techno in certain areas in my life. But it's what I expect from this place.

I'm all thrown off." Nina reaches out two tiny fists and grabs his meaty hand, but he persists in his delicate torture.

"Don't worry. 'Bout a thing," sings Bob Marley.

"I'm ambivalent," says Mal. "Actively." He nods his head firmly. He has made a decision. "Who is to say techno is any less or more appropriate than reggae for the washing of clothes?"

I turn to the washers. They seem to have fallen in time with the sluggish rhythm, just as easily as they were in time with the techno. Is it possible that they are moving more slowly?

"Did Bob Marley have the power to slow time?" I ask.

"It's just laundry," says Mal. "And we are just customers. I don't know if we have any rights."

"We're human beings, we have the right not to listen to crap," says Tony, who suddenly shoots straight up on the couch. He's too high-strung to handle anything less than full speed ahead. "Hey, Mr. DJ. Yeah, you. Get over here." He waves at Pando, the pretty young Asian manager bouncing slowly over by the register. It had taken me a few weeks of seeing him around to realize he was in charge, he was so young, his face so free of guile and worry. But then I began to notice that he knew how to turn things on and off, how to massage machines, get them to work with the flick of a finger; he could make decisions, like what entrance a deliveryman should use, or whether one of the old neighborhood ladies who worked there could go home early to baby-sit a grandchild. He was likely dipping into the registers, he had far too many quarters in his pocket not to be copping some sort of financial feel. And then, of course, there was his side business: Mal had determined Pando was dealing pot to every hipster slacker in the 11211 zip code, based on the trail of young men who flowed into the laundromat, through to the back room, and then out again.

"What is it, world music day?" says Tony, and he points to the speakers.

"I'm trying to mix it up," says Pando. "Why? You hate it?"

"We're not saying we hate it," says Scott.

"We're wondering why," says Mal. "After months of techno, why reggae?"

"Hey, do you know if it's possible that the machines are running slower today?" I say.

"No, we're saying we fucking hate it," says Tony.

Pando crosses his one hand, then another, loosely across his chest, and grasps his elbows with opposing palms.

"What else you got back there? You got some other CDs?"

"Come on, you picky bitch, let's go," says Pando, and off they walk together.

We all exchange looks, roll eyes, shift back into place, into order: What are you gonna do? Oh, that Tony. What a character. I check out his ass and the skin on his arms and the outline of his back through his T-shirt as he walks away. Nina cries, then turns it into a gurgle as Scott bounces her on his legs. Mal raises his eyebrows at me, puts his thumb and index finger to his lips, and takes an imaginary puff. We sit, we wait. Outside the laundromat, someone races by on a skateboard, a dirty goatee dragging down his chin. Then, after a few minutes, the unstoppable insistence of beats kicks in overhead. I turn and look at the washing machines. Are they going faster now? And then a few minutes later, Tony returns, eyes glazed like a fresh donut in the morning, smiling and happy. "Everything's taken care of," he says.

We all sit quietly, absorb the music.

"Now I kind of miss the reggae," says Scott. "Don't you?"

. . .

I FEEL LIKE I have been having an affair with Tony and Mal and Scott for six weeks, the last four of which I've not seen Martin. Not in a sexual sense, of course. I don't think these men are looking for that. No, they want to flirt, to smile, to feel like they're being understood. They want to feel an unusual new warmth inside them, the birth, the click, of new love. They want to be made to feel special. And so do I.

None of them ever thought this would be his life, this quaint, calm, boring existence they all lead, folding their wives' panties every Tuesday afternoon and dining out on their expense accounts every Friday night. Mal and some of his friends from college had put out a few albums on a small indie label before they were snapped up and subsequently abused and abandoned by a major label. There was even a quirky video, played late at night on MTV. Scott was some sort of tech guru before the dot-com bust. Tony had studied theater for years and had an M.F.A. from NYU. He had even taught a few classes, though now he was seemingly so mired in his real estate deals that whatever intellectual or artistic intentions he had once held had vanished.

They try to fill their lives with activities. I see them trying. But eventually it all comes back to this. Sitting around, tending to undergarments and egos.

And so I am a mistress in the sense that I get their best, most carefree moments, the time when they are single, at ease, free of responsibility. I get them when they're loose, and funny, and silly. I get to hear their secrets. I get them during their days, which are sponsored by their three rich wives (or rather, by the original-programming division of a successful cable network, a stalwart interactive advertising company that has somehow managed to survive the crashes and burns of its industry, and a multinational record company that specializes in the future of urban contemporary music). It is when they feel light, and airy. Everything is casual. Everything is easy.

And I don't have to be anything but me, be Jarvis, the child-like, fragile half-widow who has quietly slid into their lives, smelling different, less perfumed perhaps, and looking different, fresher perhaps, than their wives. I am soft. I am vulnerable. I am slightly nuts. I am special. I have not spent the last six years under fluorescent lights, bound by office walls, even if I have been bound by other walls. I haven't been going to eight a.m. meetings for six years, taking lunches, problem-solving, fighting for raises and promotions. And I certainly haven't been fighting them for six years.

I have been, strangely enough, embalmed.

WE DRIFT OUT of the laundromat together, and I groan as we leave the air-conditioning behind. It's officially summer. Spring seemed to last only for a minute, as it has for the last few years, and the New York heat is in full effect. Blue skies, bright sun, pretty on the surface, but the humidity holds everyone hostage, and you have to fight to walk against it. There is no busy click-clack New York foot traffic in Williamsburg; we are all in slow motion.

I've got my laundry bag slung over my shoulder, and Mal takes it from me, shuffling in his flip-flops. We both live on the north side, so we've been walking home together. Tony takes a call—he has to show an overpriced condo today on the south side to a hip-hop star his wife knows. "A million five for a penthouse with a view of the projects," he shrugs. Scott stops, bids us goodbye. It's naptime for Nina. He and Mal knock fists, he and I gently kiss on the cheek. Tony walks off, throws a finger our way—*one minute*—and so Mal and I stand and wait.

"I love them both equally," he says. He hoists the laundry bag a little higher.

"What?" The word "love" makes my heart jump, for some reason.

"Techno and reggae. It was like *Sophie's Choice* in there for me."

Mal is rarely sincere, I've noticed. I think he spent so many years on the road with his band, having back-of-the-van conversations, or making late-night bar chatter, that he can barely remember how to shoot straight.

"You don't have to carry that," I say. I reach out for my laundry bag.

"Let me treat you like the lady you are," he says.

I snap my fingers at him. He hands it to me, but then doesn't release it right away.

"What are you doing on Friday?" he says.

"Nothing. I am never doing anything ever," I say. Why pretend that Tuesdays aren't the highlight of my week? They should know the truth.

"Fantastic events await you," he says. "If you choose to accept this mission." He releases the bag.

"English, please," I say.

"There are a couple of parties," he says. "And my wife's on location all weekend."

Was he saying what I thought he was saying? Was he asking me out on a date? I mean, I had thought there was a connection between us, something dark and weird and sexual, but I never thought he would actually act on it. I imagine the bruise of his lips on my neck. And then I quickly throw that image away, I ball it up and throw it in the air and suddenly there is a baseball bat in my hand and I am taking aim and I've knocked it all the way into left field, it's high, it's wide, it's going, it's gone, it's out of the park. And we're good again. He's just my friend. My married friend.

"So I can, you know, play." He winks at me, and it's back again, and I'm useless against it.

"I just think you should go out and meet some new people," he says. "We all do." All right. I see he's just being friendly. I am an idiot. My neck burns red and I look down, away. What happened to me? I used to be way cooler than this.

I feel an arm around my shoulder, a cell phone dangling from the hand at the end of it. "We want you to get out in the world, baby," says Tony. "Get a little action."

"And you should wear something pretty," says Mal. "Show off those pins of yours. Guys love a nice set of legs." What guys?

A deep car horn honks twice, and I hear my name being called.

"Did you call a car?" says Tony. We all turn to the street, where a luxury sedan, one door with a slight dent, idles. As I walk up to the car, I hear, "Want a ride?" mixed with an overripe flute backed by a guitar. *Aqualung.* Jethro Tull.

It's Missy.

"Get in, stranger," she says.

14.

I've never sat in the front seat before, amidst Missy's detritus:
a pair of pink-tinted disco sunglasses with rhinestones on the
frame, an empty Orangina bottle, a lipsticked straw protruding
from it. A crumpled Doritos bag lies at my feet, next to a map of
Manhattan. The car smells strongly of a chemical-based fruit
scent, likely emanating from the pear-shaped air freshener
dangling from her rearview mirror.

"How's your grandmother?" I say, as Missy pulls out,
directing the car west. The air-conditioning is blasting, and
I shiver.

"She keeps hanging in there. We are all like, not, waiting
for her to go, but, you know, expecting it. And she keeps
surprising us."

"How does she feel?"

"She says she feels mellow." Missy pinches her lips together. "I think Freddy's been getting her high on top of her

pain medications. I swore I smelled weed the other day. I don't know, is that terrible?"

"If it makes her feel better, Freddy probably has the right idea," I say.

She turns the car right on Berry Street, and then pulls over, parks, but leaves the engine running. "So you haven't called me lately," she says.

"Yes," I say.

"It's been weeks," she says.

Yes, more than a month since I've seen Martin.

"Did I do something wrong? Are you using a different driver now?"

"No, no—"

"Because I thought we were friends. I don't know, maybe it's crazy to think that. Wouldn't be the first time I was wrong about someone." Missy pushes her hands up in the air—*I give up*—and then runs her hands back through her hair, tightens her ponytail. "And I just think if there was something wrong with my driving, you would tell me."

"Missy, please, would you please cut it out? You are a wonderful driver, and yes, you are my friend, too. It's not you. It's Martin. I'm mad at Martin."

And so we sit there, in her car, the dispatch blaring requests for pickups, street names abbreviated, intersections merged, *South Eleven Division*, *Metropolitan Driggs*, and I tell her what I found in two of the manila envelopes, the one marked "Davis" and the other marked "Alice," because while Martin was very good at hiding things from me, I now know he was not perfect.

I tell her about a series of photographs of naked blond women, Polish girls I am assuming, young, maybe teenagers, maybe early twenties, it's hard to tell at that age. Most of them have long, blond hair, bangs, slightly feathered on the side, and beautiful bodies, skinny legs and curved hips, pretty little pot bellies and tiny mounds of breasts perched high up on their chests. Occasionally they are wearing bathing suits, bikinis, plain dark colors mainly, one polka-dotted. Only a few are smiling; most are looking dead center into the camera, very seriously, as if this were the most important picture ever taken. Straight and serious, but not dull, not dead. Just intently. There is a lot of life left in their eyes.

I tell her Davis makes a guest appearance in a bunch of them. In most, he is just talking to the models, adjusting something, maybe a strap, or pushing hair back behind shoulders. In one photo he is shirtless, his tall torso still young and firm, a massive intersection of muscles and flesh. And in one photo he stands, arm around a girl, smiling, and I didn't know where to look, at the nipples of the woman standing next to him, rose-colored in real life, I would imagine, but in this photo gray and bullet-shaped, jutting straight out toward the camera, or at that gap between his front teeth, dark and cavernous, the center of his delirious face. Smile nice for the camera, Davis. Say cheese.

And then there are a good dozen photos, all of different women, different bodies, their pubic hair is a different color or it is trimmed differently or it is entirely absent, and they are all taken at night, in different parts of Martin's studio, on the ratty futon, on the floor, against the wall, the camera hovering over them, and all you can see is a little of their belly and all of their crotch, and a finger, sometimes two, slid inside of them. In three photos, the thumb is on the outside, pressed against their flesh, mid-massage. In one photo, fingers are spread against the leg, and the fingers are slick and shiny and wet. These are the most pornographic, but they are not the worst.

Because then I tell her about the other set of photos I found, several series taken over a span of time, maybe a few years, with Alice in different outfits, different haircuts too, a bad perm, pre-bangs, her brunette phase, one in what looks to be a wig; and she's seated against the white screen, smiling, relaxed, her eyes calm in all of them, not a line on that face, almost childlike (as I had flipped through them I was reminded that Alice used to be nicer, that we all used to get along so well, all of us stars and planets and moons that rotated around Martin's sun), and she seems quite lovely. And then at the end of each batch of photos where Alice is seated and clothed, there were a handful of photos where she is lying down, naked, in the bed I shared with Martin. They had clearly been taken post-coitally, after they had *fucked*, in my bed. Snapshots of her ass, plump yet small, side shots of her thighs, the shape of them, the arc almost a silhouette; and another of a thatch of faint pubic hair reminiscent of willow trees, a mild streak of light flesh, almost imperceptible, peeking out.

The one that killed me—it really fucking killed me—was of Alice with her head cocked, her lips are molded into a kiss, and her eyes are pinched slightly, and there's a saucy glint to them; her hair—this was post-bangs but pre-blond—is pushed back behind her ears, and there is a light hitting her face, revealing a soft down curling on the edge of her face. God, she looked gorgeous.

"Love letters," I say to Missy.

And there were photos of me, too, in the envelope bearing my name. But I didn't bother looking through them because I was so pissed off. I didn't want to confuse the issue. I knew seeing those photos would be like Martin arguing: "Do you see? I loved you, too. I loved you best. Alice, it was only a few times. And it was before I met you. Maybe a few times after. Only once while we were married. Twice. You weren't around. You left me alone, in the house, when I needed you to be there, when I needed you to look at my work and tell me what you thought, tell me that it was great, that it was the best thing in the world. I needed your reflection."

I couldn't be there all the time, every minute of every day. I had to leave the house. I had to breathe every so often. But he got me good for six years, didn't he?

Missy turns away from me, presses the automatic window button, lowers it, raises it. She shakes her head slowly, considering everything I've just told her. "Men are such dogs," she says.

North Seven, North Seven, says the radio. The words run together and it sounds like *Norse Heaven*, and I think of angry gods in the sky with hammers that turn into lightning bolts.

"I feel like I want a divorce." I start laughing, and I know I sound psychotic. Missy is the first person I've told, and I can't decide if it feels good or not to utter it out loud. "If he were alive—I mean, awake—I would leave him." I think about it again, for the thousandth time. "If I knew he was fucking Alice, I mean *Alice* of all people, for Christ's sake, I would leave him the next day. Just pack my bags and go."

I slump down in my seat, rest my head in my laundry bag. I inhale. Ah, the purity of the fresh load of laundry. I wish I could leave my head here forever. Hide in the laundry. But I know everything is changing, my habits, my rituals, my unwavering faith in Martin, all of that has changed since I found out the truth. I'm not free of him totally, not yet anyway, and maybe I never will be, but the way I lived through him, breathed through him, breathed *for* him, that has been altered forever. I am done with taking care of you, Martin Miller.

I jerk my head up and say, "So, you know, here I am. I'm not seeing him. I'm not going to watch over him, nurse him, whatever. Anymore. He's on his own."

"I know you're mad, but I don't think you can leave him there all alone."

"Why not? He left me," I say. No, I shout it.

Missy grabs my arm, steadies me even though I am sitting.

"I don't trust myself," I whisper. I am on another planet for a moment, or in another town, or on another street at least, and I am not me. I am the girl with the guitar in my apartment building. I am Missy's grandmother. I am a cat making its way through the streets of Manhattan.

"I don't know what my next move is," I say. "But I know things are going to keep changing." That much I know is true.

15.

More posters on the elevator, a fresh batch Scotch-taped: I learn there are pollutants in the air, all over Williamsburg, courtesy of power plants on the waterfront. *Citizens, Unite!* There is a time, a date, a place to make our voices heard. Otherwise, it's over, and we're poisoned, we might as well buy the funeral plots right now. I try to make myself care. I squeeze it out of me.

Also, someone is offering guitar lessons in the building, a woman named Alison. Any weeknight but Mondays. Price negotiable.

Guitar lessons would be nice. Maybe I need to learn something new. Maybe I need to go back to school. Even though I feel like I know everything there is to know now.

My floor, I step out, I see Davis sitting outside my front door, and I step back in.

"I saw you," I hear him yell.

I press a button, the door opens again, and I find myself standing there, one foot out, one foot in, looking at him. He has an armful of flowers wrapped in paper, purple and white petals mixed together. Also he is wearing a dumb red-white-and-blue-striped sweatband around his head and his long tendrils of hair around his shoulders in a ponytail and a black and white T-shirt with some Japanese lettering on it and I'm certain it translates into something dirty. He is trying to make me realize I miss him. It is not going to work. When he stands the paper wrapped around the flowers crunches, and because he is Davis and he is always moving, the bouquet continues to crunch. I experience a small seizure of annoyance, but how do you tell a grown man to sit still?

He offers them to me as I approach, and I take them only because it has been a long time since anyone has given me flowers, not because I am in any mood for forgiveness. I open the door and he follows me inside. I drop the laundry bag behind me. I hope he trips on it.

"I can only stay for a minute," says Davis.

"Oh, you got that right," I say. I look at my watch. "Starting now."

I walk to the kitchen, find a vase under a shelf. The flowers are pretty and smell nice.

"Baby girl shutting us—me—out isn't doing anyone any good." The way he talks, so lazy and easy, it could almost be convincing.

"I feel pretty good," I say.

Of course this isn't totally true. I still feel sad in the mornings, alone in my bed, except on Tuesdays, and sometimes on Wednesdays, when I wake up and realize I don't have to go to the nursing home. I guess that's two more days a week of feeling good than usual. Ever since I decided Martin and I were separated, I have cut out not only Davis but Alice, too. I have stopped returning their phone calls. I send back Alice's messengers with contracts unsigned. I haven't returned any phone calls from the nursing home either, not from their social workers, not from Martin's doctors. I am trying to cut out that portion of my life right now. So I can *let the healing begin*.

"If I pressured you too much, I'm sorry," says Davis. "I will gracefully rescind all control to Alice. Or you can hire a third party. There are a lot of options, Jarvis. Only don't fuck this up for him. This one's important." Now he is using his authoritative artist tone, the one that Martin had also. He's not playing. Forget about everything else, whatever might have happened. I'm sure he's used it before on women. *I'm sorry I was late but I had to have drinks with this critic from the* Times. Or: *this dealer from Zurich*. Or: *You remember Olivier? Sure you do. He was in town from L.A. Don't snap at me. It was business, baby*. Davis and Martin, these men that merge their work and personal lives, the whole world is just one big art project to them. It's a brilliant whirlwind, but there are no boundaries, no rules, just the pursuit of success.

God, I wish he would shut the fuck up. I think I shall shut him the fuck up.

"I have the photos," I say.

"What photos?"

"The photos of you and the Polish girls. How old were they anyway, Davis? Sixteen? Seventeen? Did they even speak English? Did you tell them they were going to be famous? Or did you just pay them and send them on their way?" I am spitting. A whirling dervish of words.

He is surprised, but he is not surprised. He knows who he is, he knows what he's done. Still, he has been caught, and there is even photographic evidence. There are no denials, no shades of gray. For once, Davis is silent.

"That's why you wanted the photos, right? So you could make sure no one else saw them. Or maybe you don't care. Maybe you just want to jerk off to them. Filthy. You're filthy. Do you know that?"

Davis looks through me, as if I were a windowpane, and on the other side of me is blue, blue sky. He is trying to check out, move space and time, move me out of his mind. He is technically listening to me right now, but he can't hear a thing I'm saying. I am speaking French. I am speaking Spanish. I am speaking backwards. I am speaking too softly. I sound like the roar of a truck. Whatever he needs to do to the sound of my voice to make it unintelligible, it's working. There is a glaze over his eyes, a thick lacquer, as if he has been baked in an oven. Davis is cooked.

"Tell me what you knew," I spit at him. I know that it's not his fault, but he's going to pay for it anyway. "Tell me about those other women. Tell me what he did late at night in the studio. I know you know something."

"I know that he loved you more than anyone else in the world," said Davis. "He loved you best." That's just what Martin would say, I think.

"And what about Alice? Did you know about Alice?"

"I don't know what you're talking about," he says, flat and airless, and now he is so far gone I can't tell if he's telling the truth.

"I have worn my heart on my sleeve for six years while everyone around me has been keeping secrets. Every time you looked at me, every time Alice looked at me, you were thinking about what you were hiding. I thought you were taking care of me. I thought you loved me. But now I see, now I know."

"Yeah, you've really been suffering," he mutters. He glances around the loft, and starts to say something, then stops himself. Too late.

"What did you say? What the fuck did you say?" Then I am throwing flowers and vases and now it's broken glass and more flowers and my hands are wet and there may be a cut, but I am backing him out the door, a little bit farther, until it is open, and he is gone.

And this is exactly why I can't go see Martin right now. Because he can't talk his way out of it, and he can't back away. It wouldn't be a fair fight, and I haven't decided yet if I want to win this one.

16.

Mal and I dangle our feet over the edge of a warehouse rooftop as the sun sets over Manhattan. We are at a party on the south side hosted by a coworker of Mal's wife, an art director on interstitial ads. ("I have no idea what that means," I tell Mal later. "And fortunately for you, you don't have to," he says.) I have a plate of barbecued kielbasa in my lap, a chunk of salty potato salad impaled on a fork, and a red plastic cap full of strong sangria resting on the concrete next to me. A large group of Germans stand nearby, laughing, deep gunshots of laughter. One of them pops off a beer bottle cap with the handle end of his fork. Behind us stands the rest of the party, golden and glowing from the setting sun. Mal is into his fourth beer, but he could just as easily be on his first. He takes off his glasses and cleans them on the end of his shirt. I notice for the first time that he has a scar near his eyebrow, a thin, white stitch with a little bit of red around the edges. He is wearing a vintage button-down shirt and his hair is a little messy on top and I am feeling warm, and I'm not sure if it's the summer heat, or Mal, or both.

"There's nothing like a sunset over an island of office buildings to remind you of the beauty of nature," he says.

Mal has just finished telling me the entire history of his band, how they were all such good friends when they started out, living next door to each other in broken-down row houses in Baltimore, two of them in art school, Mal a Johns Hopkins dropout turned bike messenger, how much he loved playing in tiny rock clubs for drunk college kids, and then touring the country with his two best friends, living off whatever they could sell in CDs and homemade T-shirts, how they were so close until they moved to New York after a major label threw a little money at them, how their label screwed them over by holding their album—"If we could have leaked that shit on the Internet, we would have, Jarvis. People were just starting to do that then. But they had us by the balls"—then cutting their promotional budget when they finally released it, and in the end, the excitement and joy turned to disappointment and they weren't old enough or savvy enough to work through it so they all ended up hating each other. The drummer went to law school and now works eighty hours a week in Chicago; the singer/guitarist, arguably the dumbest but the hottest of the bunch, went on to release three solo albums while working part-time as a host in a hot Cajun restaurant in NoHo, the last release achieving some sort of mainstream credibility when one of his songs was played for thirty seconds on a teen drama on Fox; and of course Mal, bassist and lyricist, released one disappointing solo album, and now was writing his book—"How far along are you?" "Oh, pretty far." "How long have you been writing it?" "For a while. You know. A while"—the book that was going to shatter the music industry into a million pieces; and when Mal explained this last part, he turned his right hand into the shape of a gun, cocked it with his left hand, took aim, and then shot an imaginary bullet right at the Manhattan skyline.

"There were some issues with drugs, too," he says. He leaks this out gently and carefully, testing me to see what I think. He looks me in the eyes, directly, perhaps at my pupils, searching, to see if I'm like him. And he finds what he's looking for right in the center: I am, in fact, just like him.

I cut off another bite of kielbasa with my plastic knife and fork.

"Didn't everyone have those?" I say.

Mal smiles. Yeah, go ahead. You're safe with me.

"Hey, do you want another drink? I can't believe how thirsty I am." He hoists himself up.

I hand him my cup. "Fill 'er up."

The sky above Manhattan is orange, and the buildings look dark, drained of their daytime color. A wall, an outline, of edges and points.

NOW IT IS DARK, now we are up the street at another party, slowly making our way north, toward something. I can feel a gravitational pull, but to what I don't know. We stop at a building, a newly renovated squat four floors up, and the paint is still fresh and shiny, and we watch the rocker kids walking in and out. "Seven bucks, it ain't worth it," one sneers at us, and I tell Mal, "It's on me," and he laughs and squeezes my arm.

Inside it is hot, and the crowd is diffident and sluggish, but the band is great, a little off-key but I think it's deliberate, and there is a rush of energy, and I love the way they bounce around, and the bass line makes my stomach swell. Mal brings me a cold can of PBR, and I run it along my forehead and cheeks and the condensation drips a bit. I pop the tab, drink it fast, half of it is gone by the time the band ends their song.

A young man, straight dark hair cut like a third-grader's, wearing the same glasses as Mal, walks up and shakes his hand, leans in, yells something in his ear. I hear the word "love" and I hear the word "project" and the young man raises his eyebrows. Mal smiles, says nothing, shakes his head, then leans in to him, pats the guy on his back, says something short and quick, get rid of him, Mal, that's right. We don't need to answer any questions tonight.

OVER ON THE Grand Street waterfront, a couple of Hassids standing nearby, smoking cigarettes, nervous—they shouldn't be out cavorting, it's Friday night—we grasp our cans of beer in paper sacks and sit awkwardly on the rocks that line the East River. I am trying to sit gracefully in the skirt I was instructed to wear for the benefit of other men, though of course I realize now it was only to make Mal happy. Mal, however, is not that happy.

"And you know, the album got good reviews," says Mal. "Some might say great reviews. But by the time it came out we were already broken up. I know it's pathetic to want you to know—but people really liked the album. When we were together, it was *good*." He drinks the rest of the beer, crunches the can in his hand. "I tried to ride it out as long as I could. But at a certain point, you have to give it up. Or start over anyway."

"You could always go back to it," I say. "At least you have something to go back to."

"No, Lily and I have decided it's best that I move on. And she's been so supportive. I know I complain, but really, she only asked that I make a decision and stick with it. She doesn't care if I never make a cent as long as I'm doing something." It of course sounds like a lie coming out of his mouth. Or I want it to sound like a lie. Or maybe it's just that he's slurring his words.

"But what do *you* want to do?" I say.

"I don't know," he moans. "I don't know."

What I know is, it's not right for me to be poking any holes in the fragile skin of their relationship, but I cannot resist, and I don't think he wants me to resist. Tonight, at least, he is mine.

WHERE ARE WE NOW? Some bar, somewhere, it's a new bar in an old space. They sell hot dogs, and chili from a crock pot, and three-dollar bottles of Budweiser. "Every Rose Has Its Thorn" is playing on the jukebox, and it's unclear if it's an ironic selection. The bar seems familiar, but now I am drunk, and every person I look at is starting to resemble someone I used to know, and I am worried that if they see me, they will know I am being unfaithful in some way.

But don't you understand? He did it first.

"Do you remember this place?" asks Mal. "What it used to be?" I have stopped counting how many drinks he's had, but I notice he's switched to whiskey. "This used to be that coke den. Did you ever come here?"

Of course I remember. They sold terrible coke—"Diet Coke" we used to call it, because it was probably fifty percent baby laxatives, and it gave you a few minutes of the runs right after the first line—but there was never any wait, just walk through the door and—"Remember? There was that back room, and you went behind the curtain," says Mal.

"And that little old Spanish man was there," I say. I am suddenly so happy. It's nice to remember who I was before Martin, as lost as I was. I have a hard time doing that sometimes. "God, I was just fucked-up all the time then," I say. "God." I shake my head, so fondly, and I try to make eye contact with Mal, but I feel like my eyeballs are full to the brim with alcohol, and now my head, and my neck, so I look down instead at his hand, and then I take it in mine, and I put it on my knee, and we sit like that, quietly, guiltily, tiny threads of heat making their way up my body from where we are joined, starting little fires along the way.

"So, you know, I have a number. For a guy. I had it from this bachelor party last spring, and it's still in my phone. I could call him. I don't know if it's even working anymore—"

Liar. You use it all the time.

"That would be bad," I say. "A bad idea."

"Terrible," says Mal.

"We're too old," I say.

"Hey, I'm not that old," he says.

We are quiet. We laugh. We are quiet again.

WE STAND OUTSIDE a bar on North Fifth Street, off of Bedford, smoking cigarettes from a pack Mal has bought from a corner deli. If we're going to fall off the wagon, let's make a magnificent leap into the air, arms spread wide open, before we hit the ground. Mal is waiting for the phone to ring, a second callback. The first told us to come to this bar and wait, the second will tell us that the dealer has arrived.

A woman next to us—a dead ringer for Jennifer Beals, the *Flashdance* years, with her creamy skin and curly hair spilling over her shoulders, a cut-off T-shirt dipping to one side, and even a set of leg warmers curling around her tiny calves—bums a cigarette off Mal. He leans forward and lights her cigarette.

"You guys are sexy," she says. "A hot, hot couple." She pulls a digital camera out of her bag. "I want you to kiss for me."

"No, that's okay," I say shyly.

"Why not? We're hot." Mal is enjoying himself.

"We're not together," I say. I choose not to tell her we're married to other people, though it is on the tip of my tongue. Mostly because I am enjoying myself, too. It is nice to feel young and single and like I could be on a date, or even just playing the field.

"One kiss," she says.

Mal's phone rings, he puts it to his ear, puts a finger in his other ear, and walks up the block, toward Bedford. The door to the bar opens and I hear a Joy Division song playing. Love will tear us apart.

"We're really not that hot," I tell her.

MAL'S APARTMENT IS lined with bookshelves filled with vinyl records, a testament to a different kind of testosterone.

"Two thousand and twelve," he says proudly, as he cuts up one long line of coke, then another, on top of a CD case. I join him at the kitchen table. There is a vase of flowers in the center of the table. Gerber daisies, bright yellow. "I've been collecting since I was a kid. My first album was *Off the Wall*." He rolls up a twenty-dollar bill and hands it to me, pushes the CD case across the table.

"That's not very rock-and-roll," I say. I lean forward, take in half a line. It's still the same feeling, and it takes me back to my life in New York before I met Martin: the click in the back of the throat, a rev of engine, a flood down toward my chest, and then there is a shift. I pinch my nostrils together gently and sniff harder. I feel very measured and in control. Mal, on the other hand, is staring at the CD cover, waiting for his turn. I push it back toward him. "It's been a while for me," I say. "It doesn't take much."

He snorts his line enthusiastically, rubs the end of his nose when he's done. "You don't like MJ?"

"I like him fine. I just thought it would be like, Bad Brains, or something like that."

"Let's listen to MJ," he says. "Let's listen to every album he's ever done, in order, from start to finish, because you know what? I have all of them."

"I bet you do."

"Let's just do one more line real quick, and then I am going to school you, my lady." He cuts four smaller lines, does two, pushes the CD case toward me, gets up, bounces, really, and heads to a shelf.

"Is it all in alphabetical order?" I say. I take on the other half of my original line. My eyes brighten, everything comes into a sharper focus.

"By genre, and then alpha," he says. He slides out an album. I see white socks glowing against a brick wall in the distance, a flip, and then there's young Michael, dark-skinned, big-haired, proudly wearing a tuxedo.

"Come on," says Mal. "We're going to have ourselves a little dance party." He winks at me, and I catch it all the way across the room, and send it right back at him.

WE ARE DANCING, we are jumping, we are singing. Sometimes we look each other in the eye, but we are too high to be serious. Mal grabs me and dips me, and leans in close.

My heart, it pounds.

No, no, no, I shake my head. He pulls me upright.

"Bathroom," I say. My mouth is clogged. I point in one direction, and he points in another, and I follow his hand. Away from the kitchen, around a secret, dark corner, past the bedroom—I peek inside for a moment: they have a huge bed with a half-dozen pillows, the comforter pulled aside, a cat curled up on top of it, a vintage lamp on a nightstand, three books stacked next to it; my mind is shooting off like fireworks, I am gathering it all in at once and then spitting it out again—and then I bump into the wall, feel for a door handle, and then I'm in, at last, I can lock the door and be by myself for a minute. I am unaccustomed to spending this much time with someone else, and the night doesn't seem to be ending anytime soon, and whatever I do, I can't look in the mirror, don't look in the mirror.

I look in the mirror.

I could look worse. The lips are still red, and the way that I am holding them, with just a few front teeth glistening through, I look inviting, so I will hold my mouth like that for the rest of the night. My hair is sticking out a little on top, a soft haze of hair, and I turn on the sink and pat it down with water, comb my hair into a slick scoop with my fingers. Two tiny crumbs of white in one nostril, not bad. My eyes, there's no fixing them. They're bloodshot from the drugs and the cigarettes and the alcohol, and it's late, not only am I not used to being around someone else, I'm not used to being up this late, and I *am not faring well*.

One more splash of water on the face, and a pinch of the cheeks for good luck.

He's waiting outside the bathroom for me.

"I wanted to make sure you didn't get lost," he says.

"I'm not lost." It feels like someone else is talking right now, my voice is lower, my tone wavers; I am simultaneously confident and pathetic.

There's a hand on my stomach now, and I look down, and I'm surprised to see it's his, although I don't know who else it could belong to. I lean up against the wall. The hallway is almost a perfect pitch-black, but the light from the living room peeks around the corner, a brief flicker of yellow, adding a tint to the proceedings.

And what are the proceedings? His hands are on my legs now, pushing up the skirt a bit, crisp, cotton, light, short, with a subtext of a starry night. "You look so good in that skirt," he says. "I'm so glad you wore it." He pushes it up some more, and then he kisses me, one flat kiss on the lips, one suck of the lower lip, and then he's in, tongue on my tongue, and I can taste a confluence of chemicals, the cocaine, the nicotine, the stir of the whiskey. If I lit a match right now our mouths might explode.

The skirt, higher, and now he's cupping the warm pockets of flesh between my ass and my thighs, tiny bulbs of hips, and I know soon he will move forward, he has no interest in the back of me, he is all about the front.

"Did you want me right away?" he's saying between breaths. "I wanted you." And now he's kissing me all over, breasts through the shirt, on the stomach, arms, and I hear grunting, base, guttural noises, and I realize it's me, I'm the one. It's me.

EVEN. NOW, we are even, Martin.

Funny, I don't feel even.

THE THING ABOUT fucking on coke is, afterward, there's no rolling over and going to bed. I'm usually not going to come in the first place—this time I did, but he didn't, and his dick still stands upright—and now I'm stuck with him, I've got to talk or leave, those are my choices. And there is this mixture of intimacy and aggression that makes things truly dangerous. Grand, inappropriate gestures await.

"What do you think?" he says.

We are in their bed. It is bad to be in their bed. He is wrapped around me, one arm on top, one arm underneath, and he is twitching slightly. He is, as I suspected, beautiful naked, the strong legs, the muscles pulsing underneath his torso and arms, as if there were a trigger somewhere waiting to be pulled.

But he is heavy, too heavy for me, and I can feel every part of him all over me. I think about that expression I heard one of my brothers use once, something to do with how animals chew their limbs off to get out of a trap. I wonder how my arm would taste.

"About what?"

"About us. I could move in with you," he says.

"I don't think that would be a good idea," I say.

"And then I could write," he says.

"You can write now. You *are* writing now."

"Actually I'm not writing now," he says. He shifts over on his side, strokes my cheek, my hair, kisses me gently beneath my ear. It is tender, but I do not like it.

"You said you were almost done with your book," I say.

"Can you keep a secret?" he says, and I start to laugh, and then he laughs, too, and I hope that he'll stop there, but he doesn't. "I haven't written in months," he says. "I've never really written anything."

"Then how do you have an agent?"

"It's complicated. It doesn't hurt that my father is who he is. Plus Lily introduced us, and that helped. And . . . I think my agent likes the way I look. I think she looks at me and sees the book jacket photo."

I thought about the myth of Martin Miller, the fallen artist. All those people all over the world waiting to get their hands on paintings they've never seen painted by a man they've never met.

"I just said I was going to do it to get Lily off my back. She wanted me to make some sort of decision, wanted to be able to report something to her friends, her parents. It is very important to her that I be doing something. She doesn't care what, just something."

"So what do you do all day instead?"

"I play my records," he says. He pulls away, stares at the ceiling, one arm left underneath me.

"Over and over again," I whisper, and then louder, "I bet they sound good."

"They sound fucking great," he says.

I WATCH MAL do the rest of the coke, just because it's there. Some people can put it away for a rainy day, but not Mal.

Mal tells me to think about what he said, about him moving in with me. About what he wants, about his needs, I think. He doesn't know how lucky he is now. *Shove a feeding tube in your arm, and then we'll talk.*

And now I'm thinking, I'm almost ready to pay a visit to Martin.

I wait till the sun comes up before I leave, just to make sure there will be some life on the streets, so I won't be totally alone out there.

17.

I dream of firecrackers exploding across the Williamsburg Bridge, me watching from a distance, high up, maybe from the roof of my building. Bright yellow sparks of light popping in an orderly fashion, one by one, like dominoes cascading down a line. Pop, pop, pop, and then Brooklyn explodes into Manhattan. Incendiary devices.

I DON'T KNOW what day it is when I wake. It was always like that with me and coke, back before I met Martin. The great time-stealer. I'd lose days, entire weekends, time that I can never get back, but it never bothered me. I have always been so willing to give up my life to something—or someone—else. The only time worth being awake is when there's someone to wake up next to.

My cell phone buzzes and I jerk. A noise in this house be-sides the quiet patter of my feet? Or the low occasional hum of traffic in the street below? It's been a funeral parlor in here for six years, and now it's one big party, what with me cursing and throwing vases, and now, an actual phone call.

"How does a nice Irish girl like you get such a dirty mouth?"

At first I think it's Davis, but then I realize: it's Mal.

"Practice," I say, but of course I was out of practice, it had just spilled out of me from parts unknown. I had almost felt as if I were speaking in tongues at one point when we were having sex. Making love. Fucking. Whatever.

"I'm getting hard just thinking about it," he says.

Oh, I do not know what to do with this attention at all. I feel a little panicked. At least I think it's panic.

"Can you hold on a second?" I say.

I put the phone down and pull off the covers. I get out of bed—I'm naked. I don't even remember taking off my clothes—and drag myself to the bathroom. Water on the face, a splash of mouthwash, fingers in the hair. I notice my nipples are hard. I swipe a finger between my legs. Nope, definitely not panic.

Back to bed, back under the covers, I pick up the phone.

"I'm here," I say. "I apologize for the delay, but I needed to confirm whether or not I was still alive."

"Are you?"

"Yes." I say, and the s slides along for a few seconds, hissing out of me, though I don't feel deflated; I feel full.

"What are you wearing?" he says.

"Oh, you can do better than that," I say.

"Okay, I'll tell you what I'm wearing. I'm wearing my glasses and a T-shirt and jeans and my fly is down and I have my dick out in my hand and it's so hard."

I reach my free hand across to my breast, rest a fingertip on my nipple. I rub around the tip of it. Whatever was stirring inside of me before is now at full speed. I squeeze my thighs together and it feels nice, hard and full and hot.

"That was a lot of information," I say.

"Now you," he says.

"Well," I say. "I'm naked."

He groans. I know I could have said anything and he would have groaned but I still enjoy the sound; the fact that I made him make a noise.

"I want to see that," he says. "I want to see your breasts again."

"My tits," I say.

"Tits are good too," he says.

I know that it is wrong, he is married, I am married, but I have already been wrong once this week. Is it possible to get wronger? But I say it anyway: "Do you want to come over?"

"If I come over I'm never going to leave," he says. "Are you prepared for that?"

I picture Mal showing up at my front doorstep, duffel bag in hand. All of a sudden there would be someone else here, all the time. Whatever life I have created for myself, my solace, my loneliness, would be gone forever.

No, I am not prepared for that. Not yet anyway.

"I need to think about it," I say.

"You do that," says Mal. I can't tell what he's feeling.

Later I try to masturbate—I think this is finally my time, now that I have a new visual, Mal's face hanging over mine, as he stretches me wide open—but Martin still looms, watching in a corner, eyes open, staring into the abyss between my legs.

18.

Out front, outside my building, I hover waiting for Missy, in the sticky heat, drips of sweat lazily but consistently spiraling down my body. The girl with the guitar sits on the sidewalk, in a loose cotton dress that runs all the way to her ankles. She is strumming her guitar, singing a Dylan song, something about a leopard-skin pillbox hat. I think of Jackie O, the ultimate widow. Sexy, yet pristine. Well-mannered. Graceful. JFK was a philanderer too, but you never saw her doing lines with someone else's husband. Although she did marry Aristotle Onassis, perhaps a curious offense in and of itself.

I drop a dollar in the woman's guitar case. She sings another verse, then thanks me, and strums her guitar gently.

"Are you Alison?"

She nods.

"Guitar-lesson girl."

"That's me. You interested?"

Was I? "Well—I don't have a guitar."

"I can loan you one for a while, if you live here in the building."

"Is it fun?"

She squints up at me, the sun behind me briefly blinding her. I step in front of it, provide her with shade. Her eyes wander briefly to my breasts. What a brazen young lady, I think. But then she looks me in the eye and gives me a blank smile. Maybe I'm not her type.

"I think it's fun," she says. "I better think it's fun. And it gives you something to concentrate on. Lose yourself in. You're not going to think about anything else but where your fingers are going next. I guarantee it."

Missy pulls up in the sedan, honks the horn once. She waves, I wave, I see a little hand waving from the passenger side, too.

"I'll think about it," I say. I won't do it, but I enjoy imagining it, picturing me and Alison sitting together in her living room, purple tapestries hanging next to a Janis Joplin poster, an industrial fan blowing in the corner that she turns off so we can hear each other better. When the lesson is over, we'll split a bottle of wine and I'll tell her my sad, sad story. Maybe she'll make a pass at me, a curious hand on an upper thigh, testing the waters; and then I'll gently move it away. I can go see her shows in the East Village, she can throw a smile in my direction from the stage, and people will wonder how we know each other. Later on when she becomes famous I can tell people I used to see her sitting on sidewalks, dreaming of a better life for herself. "I knew her when she was just another cute lesbian in Williamsburg," I'll say.

"I can do it anytime," she says to me, but my back is already turned, and I'm headed toward my next destination: Martin, asleep in his nursing home.

MISSY BROUGHT HER DAUGHTER, Mira, in the car with her today because shit was going crazy at her house, as she put it, stretching the *a* in "crazy" out for a few precarious seconds, making me think she was going a little bit crazy herself. I lean my head up through the two front seats and greet her, and she turns, her shiny dark hair, thin and feathery and long, her face like her mother's, open and accepting, wide, flat features that could go either way, make her look unremarkable or make her beautiful, you won't know until she opens her mouth.

"I'm five years old," she says. "And I have been for forty-six days." Beautiful. Definitely beautiful.

"Mira likes to count," explains Missy. "Tell her some other numbers, go on."

"There are twenty-four kids in my class at school. I have three teachers, except on Thursdays, when I have four, Miss Costas teaches music then. There are forty stairs to our apartment. It is twenty-eight blocks from our house to your house." She stares at me for a second, scans my face. "You have eight gray hairs. Right here." She points at the tip of her forehead, where her hair sloped gently into a widow's peak.

"Mira, that's enough," says Missy. She pulls out, heads east, toward the BQE.

"So there's some unrest," I say. I slide into the guarded language of adults, like crossing a stream on a path of jagged rocks, searching for the flat one, the long one, the safe one.

"She's not feeling well at all," she says. "And neither is Freddy."

"My cousin Freddy is crying all the time," says Mira. "And then Mommy told him he cried like a girl."

"I did not," says Missy. "I said he was being a baby. He's been crying for like, three days, Jarvis."

"He locked himself in the bathroom," says Mira. "With all the beer from the 'frigerator."

"You're welcome to stay at my house," I say.

"I think it's going to get taken care of today," says Missy in a voice so careful and controlled it's as if she's tapping out a telegraph with it, one that says, "Believe me." I see a pair of sandaled feet stick in the air and then land on the dashboard. "Feet down, Mira." She fiddles with the radio dial. "Look out the window and tell me what you spy."

"I spy, I spy," squeals Mira. She begins to rattle off colors and letters cheerfully. I spy something blue. I spy something that begins with the letter *g*. I spy something red.

"A stop sign," I say.

Missy asks how I am. I try to think of any part of my life I feel comfortable sharing with her at this point. Drugs. Infidelity. Hangovers.

"I'm fine." I lie now just like everyone else.

"Now you spy," says Mira.

I look out the window. I see a bakery, a laundromat, a deliveryman riding by on a bicycle, his wire basket filled with a large folded brown bag, stapled neatly shut with a receipt. I spy a homeless man, lonely in an alley, examining his hands. Streetlights, license plates, billboards, the blue sky, a few low-hanging storm clouds, an apartment complex, an innocent bug

trapped on the windowpane, green, foreign, lost. I spy quietly
all the way to Queens and don't even realize it until the car pulls
up in front of the Beverly Home, and Missy turns back grimly
to me and says, "We're here."

"Stay here," I tell her. This won't take long at all.

INSIDE, everything is the same, same colors, same smells, different Linda at the front desk, but a Linda nonetheless.
But I feel like I've been away for a very long time. Who knows
what could have happened in my absence? Someone new
could have moved in, someone could have died. Medication
could have stopped working. I cruise past the front desk
without even saying hello, afraid I'll be judged for my time
away.

I'm walking my Manhattan walk through the halls, keeping
my eyes straight ahead, one glance the wrong way and I'll be
trapped in some quaint conversation, and that's the wrong path.
There is something about the air in this place. It pumps so
slowly, like fluid through an IV. It's narcotic. I've accepted this
different reality for so long, but I've got to punch through it now,
get to the other side. Now I know better. Don't be charmed,
don't be swayed, don't get caught up in this eternal swirl of *trying
to stay alive.*

I see Philo as I pass through the cafeteria, head down flat on
the table, one arm in the air. A nurse's aide stands next to him,
checking his pulse. Ignore Philo. He's fine. He doesn't need
your help. The smell of fresh donuts, cinnamon and sugar
mixed together, warm and steamy, spurts from the kitchen. A
month ago I would have stopped to buy one. I would have

walked over to Philo and given him a donut. But now I'm racing, I'm on a roll, I can't stop now.

A young woman, her hair tied back with a bow, walks by with a bouquet of roses. Yellow, cheerful, pristine, as if they were manufactured. She has an exceptionally serene look on her face, as if she has accepted fate, or some sort of religion, into her heart. One of those people who has all the answers.

I have no answers, I just know I have something to say to my husband, or rather, that I should say something to my husband. I don't know if he'll understand a word I say, but I will be heard.

The photographs lining the halls leading up to Martin's room—the ones by Sylvie Porter, those curious black-and-white shots of the city in the sixties, maybe it's the seventies—are practically glowing, but maybe it is me, maybe I am the one who is seeing things, making things glow. The cat races through the photographs, leaving a little trail. I notice the edges of the photographs are yellowed with age today, crinkling around the edges beneath the frames, as if someone had set a flame to them.

I stop for a moment, press my hand against a frame. The photos are definitely wounded. I wonder if anyone else has noticed this. I wonder if anyone else would care. The cat captured in this photograph looks toward the camera, a halo of sun around him, two black dots for eyes, a hazy stare. He is sitting on a street corner, alongside the feet of a half-dozen hippies and one man in a dark tailored suit, their feet in motion, and I swear it's like he's waiting for the light to turn.

I catch a wisp of my reflection in the glass, a spare black bang. I am almost inside the picture. I shiver. I fight it, I win. I head on, to Martin's room.

Outside I stand and wait, hand on door, then handle, thinking about what I could say, what I should say. Why didn't I write a little speech? Isn't that what wronged women do? Or they make a list of points. I was never one for winning an argument with Martin, though. I just wanted him to love me all the time. And now I guess he didn't. How could he have been loving me at the same time he was loving Alice?

But this can't be about questions, because he can't answer me. I think some people would be happy with this situation, they could yell and scream and the other person can't say a thing. But part of me wants him to make me feel better, too. If he could say something back, an admission of guilt, an understanding that he has wounded me, just to hear him utter, "I'm sorry," it might take some of the pain away.

But there will be no questions, Martin. So you just listen to me. Listen now.

I push the door open and stand in the space between the hall and his room, the air from his room slightly warmer, stuffier, than the air in the hall, so I feel different on the front of my body than the back. Isn't that how storms are made?

I don't step in, I am magnetized into place by something. There is this invisible threshold, and I am held, I am being kept.

"Martin," I say. The top of his bed is angled slightly, and his eyes are wide open, and on his stomach rests the same yellow cat I saw the last time I visited. The cat opens its eyes, yawns, turns to me, and lets out a tremendous hiss, and I know that if I take a step farther, with one swift, merciless swipe of paw, this cat will scratch my eyes out.

19.

"So how long has the cat been there?" I ask.

Martin's nurse, Vaz, and I are sitting in the solarium, door closed, quiet, our conversation punctuated intermittently by the polite chirps of a caged parakeet in the corner. This is perhaps the most peaceful room in the whole building; the walls are of the faintest blue, so faint they are almost white, and there are green, lush plants everywhere, spilling out of their pots, and of course there is sun pouring through the vast corner windows, blindingly so. Vaz has her hair back in braids, and her wide, dark head holds up a sincere but serious set of lips, and she reminds me of a professional athlete, the determination and focus, but also the physical bulk collected together in one solid network of muscles.

"The cat moved in just after your last visit," she says, a slight lilt to her booming voice, a faint hint of an island somewhere, the West Indies, perhaps. "So, maybe a month? Is that how long it's been then?"

I nod. I've been busted.

"He's been slipping in and out since your husband moved in. He finds a favorite and sticks with them. That's his way. Martin's his new favorite, that's all."

"Who was his favorite before?"

"Leonard Porter."

"Sylvie Porter's husband?"

Vaz looks at me, crosses her arms, invites me to say something further, and I feel a tiny catch in my throat, a milder version of the magnetic pull that held me back from going into Martin's room earlier.

"Well, look. He hissed at me. He looked like he wanted to kill me. I know he's just a cat, but I can't imagine this is safe, or healthy. What if he turns on Martin?" I try to sound imperious, but it's exhausting. It goes against the flow of the nursing home, like I'm walking into the wind on a gusty day.

"And I spend a lot of money to keep Martin here. I expect to be able to see my husband when I want to," I say.

"Of course, Mrs. Miller. I understand." She is managing me now with her tone. "The cat just likes to keep people company."

I relax myself, and as my eyes loosen, they suddenly fill with tears from nowhere. That's the last thing I ever wanted, what I've been fighting all this time, for him to feel lonely. For me to feel lonely, too.

"Because I was gone."

"That is correct, Mrs. Miller." Her fingers are intertwined in front of her, calm in her lap.

"What do you think I should do?"

"Well, some of the nurses don't like it when the cat comes around. I don't think it's wrong, though. I think it's . . . natural. And I believe in nature taking its course. It's selfish to do anything else."

I feel a sting of color around my ears and neck. I've been reprimanded.

"If you're asking me, I'm just telling you, that's all," she says. "That's what I think."

The bird in the corner chirps daintily, a voice comes over the loudspeaker, asking for assistance, there is the thunder of footsteps outside the door, and then I feel the whole building move, as if it has let out a long breath, an exhale of time, an exhale of emotion, and I know that things have slowly shifted forward.

20.

In the car, in the backseat, on the way home, there is a void, an absence, and I'm missing something, and then I see: no one is talking. Missy has her hands on the wheel, and she has turned the radio off, and I can hear Mira shifting in the front seat and I hear her take a deep breath like she's about to speak, but then she says nothing.

I say, "Did something happen—"

"Yes," Missy says, and then I know. It's amazing how death washes over you, just like that.

Someone was there, and now she is gone, and everything changes at once. It's terrifying.

Missy drives faster than I've ever seen before, playing with traffic like it's a video game, and I realize she's been taking her time driving me all these years. All those fares she gave up to spend time with me.

Mira plays with the automatic window, up and down, and Missy doesn't stop her. I hope Mira won't remember this afternoon, years from now. But that won't be true, of course.

SO THERE WAS a lusty and lovely Irish family from Providence, Rhode Island: a mom, Bette, and a dad, Daniel, and two sons, Ian and Lawrence, and at the very bottom of it all, a little girl, Jarvis. All the children looked just like their mother, Bette, with black hair and light-blue eyes, and strong, long legs, like those of a regal animal, and pale, pale skin. Also they all had a healthy laugh. The father, Daniel, was part Scottish, too, so he looked different from the rest of the family, ruddier, with red hair (and was often said to resemble the tennis player Boris Becker by strangers on the street, who would occasionally point), but still he had remarkable blue eyes, though of course different from his wife's. This was a favorite game they all played: Who looks like who? How are we all related? They took a constant delight in their appearance, and though they were poor—both parents were artists of a sort, Bette was a potter and worked at RISD part-time, and Daniel switched specialties from year to year, painting one year, photography the next, and then he started writing, but mostly he worked as a bartender— they were the best-dressed family in town.

Most of their clothes were bought in thrift stores, and then Bette would rework them all. The boys would get T-shirts with screen-printed designs of their favorite Saturday-morning characters, or whatever sports they liked at that moment—a soccer ball, a football—and blue jeans previously torn in one knee were suddenly outfitted with the coolest patches, peace signs, guitars, designs that made them look like tiny rock stars. They pulled off their fashion-plate look, they were interesting little boys, artists already from an early age. Lean and dreamy. They wore the clothes as if they were handmade and special, not hand-me-downs from the bottom of a Salvation Army bin. They wore them *correctly*.

And, for the little girl, Bette made belts of ribbon, and skirts that flared out in surprising ways, and shirts with shiny spangles, and jeans with faux leopard-skin fringe, and handmade bows for her hair, pink and purple bows that looked like flowers, and hand-knit sweaters, warm and lovely and honey-colored, and dresses made of swirling velvet, perfect for a little girl to wear when she felt like dancing around in circles, which she almost always felt like doing when her mother was around.

When they walked down a street together, en masse, the McMahons, Daniel with his boisterous smile and wind-stung skin and wild red hair that would stick straight up when he ran a hand through it, and Bette with her red lips, all of her gorgeous angles, and her row of identical black-haired ducklings, sometimes one on Daniel's shoulder, the littlest one, the girl, they were knockouts, you could not help but stop and take a look at the proud, beaming, noisy family.

That is how I freeze-frame it in my mind. Walking down the street, to church maybe (we went only occasionally, out of habit for my parents—the "If it was good enough for me, it's good enough for them" sort of mentality on my father's part probably sounding just like his own father's in the process), or walking together on Federal Hill, before going to one of the cheap Italian restaurants there, on a side street, eating family style, bowls and bowls of pasta spread out before us.

Here come the McMahons. That's where I usually stop it now. An unfinished story. That's all I have room for.

But then, with Martin, I could fill in the rest. With stories like those we tend to perfect the telling of them in order to protect ourselves.

METROPOLITAN EXIT, and Missy finally speaks.

"Is anyone hungry for ice cream?"

"Ice cream!" says Mira.

"I like ice cream," I say. "I could take Mira for ice cream. For a while."

"You could?" says Missy, and I know that I have just checked something off her list for her, one less thing to do on a day when she has a million horrible things to do.

"I could," I say.

"I like chocolate," says Mira.

AND FOR A TIME Bette made all these clothes in the garage, in a workspace Daniel had set up for her, a sewing machine atop a wooden table with one leg uneven so when she sewed it rocked back and forth slightly, making a ritualistic click on the ground, containers for all her materials, the buttons, the scissors, the needles, the thread, the patches, the fabric; she never threw anything away if she could see how it could be used in the future; if she could see the right place to put it in her mind, even if that place didn't exist yet, she wouldn't throw it away. She sold some of the shirts to neighborhood moms for their sons, and then a Little League team asked her to spruce up their uniforms with baseball-bat screen-prints, and then a local children's store asked her to start making her belts for them, and they couldn't keep them on the shelves, that's what she told her family proudly at dinner. A woman who owned a few stores in New York City came into the children's store once and asked for Bette's card, and then she called, and Jarvis and her brothers sat at the kitchen table quietly and listened as Bette walked in and out of the kitchen, the long spiral phone cord stretching and then winding up again, as she pretended to be calm, but all the kids knew how excited she was. This is exactly what I wanted without even knowing that I wanted it, she told her children.

Life gives what you need, she said.

And she stayed up all night coming up with new ideas, working away in the garage, and the next day she was tired, too tired to make jokes at breakfast, though she smiled sweetly as ever, though drowsily. And the next day she was tired, too, even though she hadn't stayed up late. After that she was tired every day; but looking back, she had probably been tired before that, they just hadn't noticed. Everyone was so thoroughly nestled into their lives, they didn't notice the downshift.

"Don't sew anymore," said Jarvis. "Play with me instead."

"I have to make ten more belts, and then we'll do cartwheels on the lawn," said Bette.

But there she was, hunched over the machine. In the mornings she was crankier and crankier. She had done it all before, the children wondered. Why couldn't she do it now?

Eventually she stopped sewing entirely, sent off an order to New York and she was done. She was still sleeping a lot. The children tiptoed through the house when they came home after school. Their father worked happy-hour shifts, and wrote in the mornings. He was missing everything, he knew it, but he couldn't keep up. They never took walks anymore, the family. Sometimes Jarvis would take naps with her mother, just to get close to her, just to feel some warmth, just to smell her natural, sleepy scent. She loved the smell of her mother's neck, sweat and vanilla. She loved her mother. She just wished she would wake up already and play with her.

THERE'S A FROZEN-YOGURT place near the L train (not ice cream, but close enough), and Missy drops us there with a promise to call soon. She tries to shove money in my hand and I have to walk away from the car window to keep her from throwing it at me.

I take Mira by the hand and we walk inside.

"Can you believe there's a frozen-yogurt place on Bedford?" I say to Mira. "This neighborhood has *really* changed."

"I want sprinkles, too," she says, ignoring me, as she rightfully should. What does she care if the neighborhood has changed?

THERE WERE FOUR LUMPS, at first, all in the armpits. Three in the right, one in the left. Then they started attacking the breasts, these landmines of the flesh. It was like she was a deer hit by cancer buckshot: a spray of bullets from the inside, a handful of months, loosely grasped, and then she was gone. She died so quickly, it was almost as if she had never lived.

And then after that it's the usual: Daniel started drinking, the three kids ran wild. Jarvis was protected a bit because she was the youngest, and she was the girl, and she resembled most the woman who wasn't there anymore. They would look at her sometimes and get a chill. Ian and Lawrence would come into her room late at night, stoned on whatever they could get their hands on, and say don't fuck up like us. "You gotta promise not to fuck it all up Jarvis." Then Daniel would come home drunk after work, after a *happy hour*, no less (the earlier the better for Daniel), miserable, nothing written, nothing sold, a handful of bills in his pocket, and sit miserably in the living room, till finally when Jarvis passed by him, he would yell, "Don't fuck it all up like me."

Everyone needed her to not fuck it all up.

MIRA AND I are stoop-sitting, one of the greatest pleasures of life, even in this heat. I've got red-velvet yogurt with chocolate sprinkles, and Mira has chocolate with rainbow sprinkles. I convinced her it would be more fun to eat from a cup, easier to count the swirls, the sprinkles, the spoonfuls. I am not prepared to clean up any messes today.

A chubby little girl rides by on her bike, a tiny rim of belly popping out from under her T-shirt, and she waves. Mira waves back and screeches, "Hi Alicia I like your bicycle."

Alicia slows down and curves back toward us, stopping on the street in front of the stoop, awkwardly balancing herself on her feet. She is wearing a Hello Kitty T-shirt, and her hair is in braids. "Do you want to ride it?"

"I'm eating frozen yogurt with my friend," Mira says.

"Hi," I say.

Alicia looks me up and down, my long peasant skirt, my brightly dyed tank top stained with sweat under my arms.

"She's too old to be your friend."

"She is too my friend." Mira frowns.

"I am," I say.

"*Whatever*," says Alicia. She makes a little W with her fingers. "Can I have some yogurt?"

"No," says Mira.

I want to say scram but I know you have to let these things work themselves out on their own.

"Come on," says Alicia. "You ride my bike and I'll hold your yogurt."

Don't do it, I think. She's a con artist.

"I need to sit here and talk to Jarvis. She's sad." She pats my hand. "Maybe tomorrow I'll ride your bike."

"Okay come find me," says Alicia. She pulls her stubby little legs up and motors down the street.

I hear Mira whispering under her breath, counting something.

"Don't get hit by a car," I yell, and she looks back at me and scowls. "I'm not that old, am I?"

"She doesn't have any friends because she's fat," says Mira matter-of-factly, and spoons another bite of yogurt into her mouth.

"No, she doesn't have any friends because she's annoying," I say.

"I try to be nice to her," says Mira. She puts both hands around her cup and centers it on top of her tiny knee. "You never know," she says.

"You never know what?"

"I don't know what. You just never know."

IT IS A strange thing to realize how quickly it can all fall apart once one person is gone. That the relationship and strength of their family was predicated on one person. They didn't have enough time with her, maybe, to learn how she kept them all together. Or maybe they weren't that strong to begin with. Maybe they were held together by aesthetics only.

They tried to come back together a few times. Daniel was in AA for most of '96, Ian was touring as the sound guy with a metal band from the eighties that played fairgrounds, so he had a regular paycheck, and Lawrence had moved to western Mass, from town to town, but he was working, an unremarkable file clerk in an unremarkable office, a job his parole officer had helped him get.

Jarvis called everyone consistently, tirelessly, just to keep people talking. Let's get together for Christmas, she said. Hopefully. And they all said yes, let's do it, we need to see you, little girl, you hanging in there in New York, you making us proud, don't fuck it up now, that's the last of the money, you need to make it happen, we'll love you anyway, but if you don't mind, could you please make it happen?

Her brothers canceled a week before. There would be no grand reunion. Ian was going to the Bahamas with the band to play some resort, and Lawrence was going to stay at home and drink by himself quietly. He just wanted to be left alone.

"You could come be with me," said her father, but then Jarvis realized she didn't want to spend Christmas with her father, with his fading memory and angry outbursts at inanimate objects and the way he stank, especially later in the evening. Sometimes he slipped and called her "Bette." He wasn't proud and strong anymore. He was withered, and he was miserable. She didn't want to be alone with him.

"LET'S SWITCH," says Mira, and we exchange cups. We eat slowly. I think we both recognize we've got nowhere to go for a while.

"Count for me," I say.

"Okay, let me see . . ." She starts talking under her breath again.

Across the street there is a flash of black glasses, a wry smile, a button-down polyester shirt with a wide collar, a strong arm around a beautiful woman: Mal, with his wife. I catch that Bettie Page haircut, vintage dress, high Mary Janes, a sway of the ass, a swagger. Okay, we get it. You two wish you lived in the 1950s, a much simpler time. Or at least you want us to think that.

"Two fire hydrants, six trees." She uses my arm for support, stands for a moment, looks both ways, then sits. "Eighteen stoops. On both sides of the street."

Let's see if we're admitting we know each other. I look at him, he looks at me, he looks away.

All rightie. I guess we don't know each other today.

I guess yesterday's phone call meant nothing. Or maybe it was a test, and I failed it. But if I hadn't failed it yesterday, I would have failed it in the future. I can't be the next woman to keep him. I already know his tricks, his lies. I know he must love his records more than he loves anyone other than himself.

His wife's skirt swishes, just below her knees, as she walks. I realize I haven't blinked in a while when my eyes start to sting with tears.

IS SHE CRUEL for abandoning her father? Because the man she knew as her father is no longer there. If he could have just died with her, they all used to think that. But of course now she realizes he did. There is an exterior, there is a shell, a skin, but inside, he's gone.

"IT'S SAD, ISN'T it?" says Mira. We are almost finished with our yogurt, our spoons scrape the bottom, plastic against plastic. "About my great-grandma."

"It's always sad when someone doesn't feel well," I say. "But I think it is *particularly* sad that your great-grandmother is sick."

"I think she died," she says.

"I hope not."

"Mommy didn't say she did but she was on the phone and then she got quiet and she told me to be quiet too."

I feel nervous talking to her about it. I'm in no position to provide wisdom on matters of life and death. I'm clearly no expert.

"I'm more sad for my mommy than for me."

"You're a nice person," I say. I wipe my forehead with my hand. "It's too hot."

"She'll miss her the most. She knew her longer." She holds her hand up and unfurls each finger. "I only knew her five years."

"You can still love her as much your mom does, though," I say.

"Maybe."

"No, you can. You absolutely can," and I have no idea why I'm being so fierce all of a sudden, but I am. Mira looks a little scared, and I apologize, and then she forgives me, which is just what I needed, forgiveness, for someone to say that to me, and there we sit, side by side on the stoop, sweating, Mira counting the leaves on the trees, the pigeons, the cars, the children, the men, the women, fingers, toes, breaths in, breaths out, until Missy calls to tell me her grandmother is dead, and it's time for Mira to come home.

21.

At home, front door slammed, purse cast aside, air conditioner on, shirt off, skirt off, and then, in my bra and panties, I haul out the last banker box for another look. Under the Davis photos, under the Alice photos, is the envelope with my name on it. Block letters, thick black Sharpie. Firm. As if he knew exactly who I was.

I get in bed, on top of the safe, white covers, prepare myself for the emotional disaster zone that surely awaits. I open the envelope, spill the photos onto the bed in front of me. At least one hundred of them, Polaroids, black-and-whites, full color prints, a few contact sheets; photos taken when I wasn't looking, and photos where I'm looking directly into the camera, the look of love in my eyes. So many different hairstyles for me over the years, just like in Alice's photos, different lengths and colors. I was very fond of pink. I am much skinnier and younger in some; high, drawn cheekbones, the end of the drug years I'm guessing, right when we first met. Most are taken in our home, when I'm sleeping. So intimate. He somehow managed to make me look like a child in some of them, with the right light, the right angle.

There are a few from our travels together. I recognize a hotel room in Geneva where we once stayed for a week, small with dark wood panels. A painting of a vase of red roses hung above the bed. There are six pictures of me sleeping, each from a different morning, the sun drifting in through the curtains, lighting me unevenly, but perfectly of course, and one of me sitting on the toilet, laughing, drunk, legs clamped together, waving hello.

Me at one of his openings, a blur of people in the background, no one I can recognize. I am wearing a white ruffled shirt and a lot of eyeliner and false eyelashes and dark eye makeup. I am smoldering with love for him. You are going to get some later, that's what I'm telling him in that picture, with that look, with those eyes.

Me, full length, napping on the couch in the afternoon. Black-and-white. My mouth's slightly open, and there's a teacup resting on the middle of the table next to the couch, so it looks like I'm attached to it. A teacup lady. Alice in Wonderland.

There I am on Grand Avenue, the city looming behind me. I'm not smiling in that one. I'm letting him take it, but I don't want to be there. Enough already.

Coney Island, with a hot dog, extra mustard. Chinatown, wearing pink heart-shaped sunglasses I had just bought for a dollar from a street vendor, holding a bubble tea, the straw between my lips. A beer garden, the one in Queens, a half-eaten sausage in front of me. I couldn't eat another bite.

High heels and nothing else, a smiling rose of a woman. I take a breath.

Me on the mountain, Mount St. Helens, maybe ten years ago. During the trip we took to see his parents. They were fascinated with the aftermath of the eruption in 1980—"the blow," as Calvin called it—and they visited once a year, the same trail, to track the changes. We took the long drive to the mountain from Seattle, passing fir trees planted by logging companies, an occasional sign announcing their year of planting, but many of the trees were still tiny and thin, thatches of green crisscrossing the ridges, aspirations of life. To the east all I could see was gray land, formations of ash and rock, in rounded hills—"hummocks," said Meryl—and of course, Mount St. Helens.

"A minor mountain, considering everything else," said Calvin. "It wasn't the tallest, it wasn't the oldest. But now it's got a place in history."

We took a trail, a dusty loop. Martin and his father walking ahead of Meryl and me, chatting and pointing. They had the same arms, the same shoulders.

"Martin and his father were always so happy hiking together," said Meryl. "And during the blow, they were glued to the television set." Meryl seemed lighter than usual, a happy pink glow to her cheeks, watching her husband and son engaged in each other. "Practically the whole state felt it, I tell you. Ash everywhere. The air quality changed. And of course, those poor people who died. We all prayed for them. You can't help but feel that here." She touched her heart. "But God has his reasons. For everything."

Meryl's God talk always made me feel uncomfortable. I changed the subject.

"So why don't they plant trees everywhere?"

"The plan is to let it grow naturally," she said. "But of course it will never be the same."

And indeed there were small patches of wildflowers, yellow and purple and pink, and small streams winding their way through the trail, and bringing with them moss to build on the stones, and tiny stumps of trees, green poking through the barren ground, like springtime, but springtime for beginners.

"There's no bugs yet," said Meryl. "When the bugs come, then we'll be in business."

We stopped in front of two dried-out tree trunks, taller than us, one curved over at the top, as if it had been sculpted by a powerful wind. The land opened up to reveal a valley, a flat valley of pumice, and then again behind it, that powerful, dangerous mountain. My husband, my beautiful husband, turned to me and said, "Just stand right there, Jarvis," and he motioned for me to move next to the tree. Meryl and Calvin stood behind him, nodding and smiling at both of us, as Martin arranged me just as he wanted. And then he took a picture of me, with the pumice plains splaying out behind, a vast desert waiting to explode with life.

I FEEL SOMETHING heavy in my chest drop to my gut, like a thick icicle falling from a roof in winter, landing on the front porch, and there is a shudder—I shudder—and then the shards begin to melt. I am not angry anymore. I am still hurt, and I am still fragile, but I am not angry.

And now I'm empty inside, there's room for something new, and I feel it build up instantly, fill me, as if it had just been waiting all along for everything to clear away. A trickle, and then a rush, up from the gut, to the chest, the breasts, the neck, the lips, then flooding my head, and there it is: a decision.

It is out of love, not anger. Love for myself, love for him. And out of necessity. If I am ever going to be a whole person again, I am going to have to stop being the half-widow.

I pick up the phone and dial Seattle. I owe them this much, at least. To let them know what I'm about to do.

PART THREE

22.

Freddy is sitting on the fire-escape stairs leading up to the floor above Missy's apartment, and I am leaning on the railing next to the window that opens into Missy's kitchen. His eyes are still swollen from tears, but he is calm now, three puffs from a thick joint did the trick. His suit jacket is off, strewn somewhere inside amongst an array of family members and hot dishes, large aluminum trays of tamales and fried plantains and rice, one stockpot of chicken and rice soup, and another full of some sort of fish soup, and bowls of mango and papaya and coconut. Everyone is talking and eating and occasionally crying and then laughing, it seems, at nothing at all. Laughing to fill up space in the room. Before I went outside with Freddy, I had been leaning on a wall in a corner by myself, feeling a little freaked out. What am I doing here anyway? I don't even know this woman. I don't know how funerals work. I guess I need to learn, that's what I'm thinking. I had started plotting Martin's wake—who I would invite, what I would wear, where we would have it, what I would serve, what music I would play. How much Xanax I would need. In six years, I've never once pictured how it would all end, how I would end that phase of my life, of his life, and move onto the next one. A gush of air and energy flushes through me. There could be an end to it all.

And then Missy sees me standing in a corner by myself; she jerks her head up and around and over an older woman with thick dark dyed hair and penciled-in eyebrows that make her look cruel; and she pinches Freddy's arm, whispers in his ear, and then he sails across the room, kisses my cheeks, takes off his jacket and leads me outside. There I watch him roll the joint efficiently, a pinch from a plastic bag, a swift turn of paper, a lick, a twist, and he's done. It all happened so fast, and now everything is slow because of the one hit I took, cautiously, knowing full well that if I took in too much I would head down a long, uncomfortable path.

I haven't smoked pot regularly since high school, when I began falling into the same pattern every time I smoked: my head swirled too much, closed in on me, and I quickly found myself thinking in circles. I was always doomed by the end, doomed to miss my mother, to hate my father, to wish my brothers were near me to protect me, or, alternately, so I could protect them.

This same path is one of comfort for Freddy. I can see he suddenly feels easier in his skin after the first few hits, as if he's been thinking of it all day, like a businessman at the office waiting to come home and put on his slippers and pick up the remote control, sit back, and relax. I would think his habit was sort of dangerous but it's only pot, and also, I simply couldn't tolerate any more of his tears tonight.

Freddy moves the joint in my direction, unlit end facing me, and motions his head toward it. I shake my head. "One is enough for me," I say.

Freddy laughs. "One ain't enough of anything," he says, but he withdraws his hand. His light-blue eyes beam, the dark pupils in the center engorged. "So Maritza's been telling me about you," he says. "You and your . . . situation. With your husband and everything. And I extend my sympathies to you."

"Thank you," I say.

"And out of respect for your husband"—Freddy pumps his fist against his chest—"and the difficulties you must be going through, and also because I have respect for my grandmother, God rest her soul"—Freddy crosses himself, the joint leaving a trace of smoke behind, for a moment in the shape of a cross—"and for life and death and heaven and God and Jesus"—he motions at me with the joint, and again I shake my head, he takes a puff, then continues—"and because of all of that, I am *not* going to tell you what a fine-looking woman you are tonight, and how if you were mine I would take care of you in every way imaginable. Baby, I could make you so—"

A hand shoots out of the window and lands on Freddy's knee, hard enough to make him howl.

"Freddy, I'm going to fucking kill you." Missy pops her head out toward Freddy and says something in Spanish, and then she slaps his leg again. She hoists herself up and through the window, stopping to pull off one black high heel, and then another, which she tosses back inside the apartment, one clunk, then two.

"I told you to be nice to her," she says. "Not hit on her." She stalks him on the stairwell.

He pokes his head around her. "I promise you sweetheart I would be *so* nice to you, like you wouldn't believe."

"Cut it out," she says.

Freddy breaks out laughing.

And then she says, "At your own grandmother's funeral. You got no respect, Freddy."

Freddy stops laughing, puts his head down, stares at his hands, which are giant, I notice. Monster fists.

"Move over," says Missy. She is more tender with her swat this time. Freddy squeezes his legs to the side, and she sits below them, so that her torso is astride Freddy's feet. She wedges her feet between the narrow metal slats of the base of the fire escape, then wraps an arm around Freddy's ankle. Light pools in her hair. Were we anywhere else, I would think it moonlight, but I know it must be a reflection from the streetlight. Her lipstick is still perfect. Her gold hoop earrings dangle. A hefty cross lies at her throat on a thick gold chain.

"Say you're sorry," she says.

"I'm sorry," he says.

"I know you are," I say. "It's okay."

"I'm exhausted," says Missy.

"You're doing great," I say. I reach out a hand toward her and she takes it and then we hold hands for a moment, and I am surprised at how soft her skin feels, so young, like a child's. It is softer than mine. She is softer than I am.

"I'm exhausted, too," says Freddy, and he reaches a hand toward me. Missy hisses at him and he quickly retreats, mumbles, insulted, "Damn," and stretches out the *a* for a few seconds, so she knows he's been chastened enough for one day.

"What about you?" says Missy. "And him?"

"Him" is Martin, "him" is the husband, "him" is the man huddled up in bed in Queens. How could a practically lifeless lump of flesh have so many identities? And I forgot the fourth of course: son.

"I'm going to do it," I say. "It's time."

"You're going to pull the plug?" Missy seems excited by this for some reason. I guess it's big news. I feel more resigned to it than anything else.

"Yes. Well, they take him off the ventilator. I don't know if there's any actual plug-pulling." I picture a cartoon version of myself tripping on the plug end of a cord attached to the back of Martin, and then the long, cold beep of a flatline. "And then he stops breathing. I guess," I add. The finer points of his death are more disturbing when uttered out loud. I lower my head, I shrug my shoulders, I pray for a strong wind to whip around me and carry me away, Dorothy, Kansas, etc., but it looks like I'm staying put on this fire escape.

"Man, that's some rough shit," says Freddy. He cocks his head on the railing of the fire escape and locks his eyes on mine. He looks sorry, and I believe him, but I know if I stare too long his sympathetic stare will turn to one of flirtation.

"When are you going to do it?" asks Missy.

"Two weeks," I say. Two weeks till freedom. Two weeks till doom. Two weeks until I see the light of day.

I AM WAITING two weeks because Martin's parents asked me to hold off until they could come to New York. Well, first they asked me not to do it at all.

"It's time," I said. "We've been holding on too long. It's selfish of us." I said all these words slowly into the phone, which I had jammed up to the side of my face as some sort of support. A breeze of moist air, murky and sexy, brushed through the window off the East River. That seemed to comfort me, too, the life force behind it, making its way through the neighborhood.

"We urge you to reconsider," said Calvin. "We know you're not religious, but surely you must have faith in life."

"I don't think he's really alive anymore," I said. "The bones and the flesh and the blood are all still there, and his heart is beating, but his mind is gone, Calvin. And it's never coming back. He is never going to wake up."

"Is it the money?" said Meryl. She had been whimpering through most of the conversation, and I had been successfully ignoring her, but now she was trying a new tack. "Because we can take over the bills. You keep everything else for yourself, dear. The paintings, whatever money is left over, it's yours. Just let us keep our son."

Meryl had never particularly enjoyed Martin's work. She had made it to exactly one opening of his since I had met him: the NYU series, paintings of young, breathy coeds with shiny doll eyes and bright eyelashes and, the problem area for some, all with oversized breasts (they didn't look that way in reality, Martin just painted them that way), their limbs set in poses reminiscent of old *Playboy* centerfolds as they engage in NYU freshmanlike activities—studying at the library, gabbing at the student union, sitting and contemplating life in Washington Square Park. Martin had written a seemingly sincere artist's statement about how his work was feminist, which sent a young critic, Darcy Goldberg, into a frenzied, though articulate, headspin in the *New York Times*. In her review she had not-so-jokingly called for a protest, a preposterous idea if only because it was just a show in Brooklyn, of all places, in Alice's tiny, unknown gallery, and yet some NYU students (not the ones Martin had painted, they were thrilled to see these glamorous versions of themselves preserved for eternity) had heeded the call; and so they paraded in front of the gallery, holding posters imprinted with cutouts of Martin's head atop a naked male body with various dastardly things done to the genitalia, extra-large testicles, extra-small penises, vegetables stuck in orifices, that sort of thing. They stuck their middle fingers up at Martin as we passed them to enter the gallery, and it was actually so brilliant and funny that we invited them inside after all the guests had arrived, and they brought in their posters, and I think a few of them sold for a couple hundred bucks each, the protesters wildly, drunkenly auctioning them off in the front corner of the gallery, while Alice insisted she get at least twenty percent, and there were cameras flashing, and later, at home, in bed, under the covers, smelling of cigarettes and sweat and wine, Martin said, "Baby, it was a *happening*," so in the end I suspected he knew exactly what he was doing in the first place.

But he had neglected to consider what his parents might think, which I suppose is how an artist should act; I had heard someone say it before, probably Davis, "You must paint as if your parents are dead." Little did Martin know his work might actually make his parents keel over in front of him. I remember Meryl in the back of the gallery, as far away from the protesters as she could get, eyes glossed over, her skin burning with embarrassment, a delicate hand clapped to a cheek. Her posture—her "very American posture," as Alice cruelly pointed out later, a bottle of wine into the evening—betraying her feelings, which seemed to be that she wished she could shrink up into a ball and disappear.

And Calvin tried to admire the artistry, the craftsmanship, but I know all those tits really threw him for a loop. Still he pounded a hand on Martin's shoulder, even posed for a few pictures, and smiled wide. Calvin showed each and every one of his teeth to the gathered crowd of artists and musicians and writers and beautiful young NYU freshmen, and later, he allowed himself to puff on a cigar out front with Martin and Davis, the exhaust of the B-61 mixing with their smoke at a nearby bus stop. I watched them through the front window of the gallery. I could see how the three of them were the same all of a sudden, three powerful men unafraid of the world because they were physically strong, and also because they were convinced entirely that what they were doing was the exact right thing. (I tried to picture my own father standing next to them, and I couldn't; he was so broken-down by then, a man convinced his life was all one big mistake. This was a club he was not qualified to join.) It had started to rain softly—it was mid-October and the pregnant humidity of the late summer had given way to unpredictable bursts of rainy weather—and the men took in their last puffs. Meryl came up next to me and stood sort of close, closer than usual anyway, with her arms crossed, a cup of water pinched between two fingers.

"Men," I said, because I felt like I should say something.

"Aren't they wonderful creatures?" said Meryl. On the one hand, she sounded dreamy: she was a proud mother and wife, and she had spent most of her life tending to one or both of them, and it must have been nice for her to see them together, especially for a celebration, even a strange celebration. It was a fine moment for her. On the other hand, she sounded a little obsessed—her voice was all wavery and emotional—and it kind of freaked me out.

"Sort of," I said. "Sometimes I don't understand them. But I just try to make Martin happy."

"That's right, dear." She beamed at me, then put an arm around me. "That's what we're put on this earth to do. Take care of our men."

"They should take care of us too, Meryl." I was trying really hard to maintain an even tone. I had been drinking, and I'd stolen a few cigarettes from Alice, I remember, so I was a little bit more wired than usual. And this was my chance to bond with Meryl, Meryl in her neat white collar and quilted vest and pleasant taupe heels. I wished for a moment I could go ask one of the NYU students if they were holding. I'd even smoke weed. The lines to the bathroom had been kind of long all night. Someone had to have something.

"It should be equal. All relationships should be equal," I said. Of course it was preposterous to lecture a woman who had been happily married for forty years on how relationships work, I realize that now. Whatever they were doing, it was working for them. But then I thought I knew everything about love.

Meryl squeezed my waist, friendly, and we looked each other in the eye, and I don't know what I was putting out, but she didn't like it. She released me. The men walked inside, Calvin to her, Martin to me, and Davis standing in the doorway.

"Dear, Martin has explained everything to me, and I completely understand his work now," said Calvin. I think maybe he was a little drunk, too. "He's being ironic."

We all started laughing. Oh, how we laughed. We laughed until it stung.

"WHEN FREDDY was little he was really little," says Missy. "Really short and kind of chubby. He didn't have his growth spurt till like maybe, junior year of high school? We used to call him Gordito. Remember that, Freddy?"

Freddy says nothing, looks out over the fire escape, toward lands unknown. He rubs his hand over his smooth shaved head, small points of stubble poking at the surface. "Why you gotta tell the same stories over and over again?"

"Oh, don't be a fool. It's a nice story." She looks up at him, says something quietly in Spanish, I don't catch it. Freddy lets out a sigh. She pats his knee and continues.

"So all the other kids picked on him. Because they could. You know how kids are."

At the window, Mira's head pops into view. "Are you talking about me? I'm a kid. How are kids are?"

"Kids are perfect," says Missy. "Come here, baby girl. Come sit with your mama."

"No, come sit with me," says Freddy.

I gently help Mira through the window. She is so light. Her skin soft and new. Her hair smells like nothing, just clean.

"No, I want to sit with Jarvis," she says, and then she pulls me from where I'm standing down to the floor of the fire escape and curls herself into my lap. Her dress, a dark-purple velvet, brushes against my legs, and it feels nice. Missy leans back against Freddy's legs and smiles at us, a proud smile, proud of her little girl's capacity for instant love. I never want to leave this fire escape. Inside, at this exact moment, I am completely full. I have not felt this way in years. Six years, at least.

"I'm telling a story about when your cousin Freddy and I were kids."

"Is it when you saved him from the mean kids?"

"It is," says Missy.

Mira claps her hands. "That's a good story."

"Okay, so I was always having to save Freddy's behind," says Missy. "But I couldn't be there all the time. We walked to school together, and back home again, and I would sit with him at lunch, but there were still times he fell off my radar. Like at recess I kind of wanted to play with my girlfriends. And Freddy had his own friends. That little Mikey Vasquez, he was a good kid, he looked out for him, too. He walked him home sometimes."

"He lives outside of Hoboken now," says Freddy. "He called me last Christmas. He's got a kid, a house, everything. He's a dentist."

"A dentist! Good for him, good for him," says Missy. She nods to herself, musing. "You could learn a little something from him." As soon as she says the words, she claps her hand over her mouth. She waits for Freddy to respond.

"You're not my mother, you're my cousin," says Freddy.

"You're right, I'm sorry," she says. "You'll learn someday, Jarvis. Once you're a mother, everyone starts to feel like your kid."

Her words shock me a little bit. That someone could consider me somehow ready or even capable of motherhood. Missy can see some sort of future I can't even begin to imagine.

"Anyway, so one winter, there's a huge blizzard," she continues. "It happens right before Christmas break, and we all got to stay home for a few days. But then they opened the school back up, because you know, for most of the kids, their parents worked all day, and they couldn't afford day care. So some kids went back to school, but the kids who had a parent at home, they just stayed there. Their parents figured, why not start Christmas break early. There was still snow on the ground, piles of it everywhere. So Mikey Vasquez, his mom didn't have to work, his dad owned like three dry-cleaning businesses.

"But we had to go, me and Freddy. It was crazy at school, kind of. Like half the classrooms were empty, and it was the last day before vacation, so no one wanted to pay attention anyway, and we'd all been playing in the snow for days, so we were just like more hyper than usual. And I just wanted to hang out with my little girlfriends after school, and one of my friends, Tara, her house was across the street from the school, and her mom said we could all come over afterward for hot chocolate. And her mom was not messing around with that hot chocolate, there was whipped cream and sprinkles all over everything. And if you finished half the hot chocolate and all the whipped cream and sprinkles was gone already, she put more on top for you. Everybody wanted to be Tara's friend."

"I want to be Tara's friend," says Mira.

Freddy squeezes his lips together, squints his eyes. He bends his hand at the wrist and makes a back-and-forth motion with it. "Tara wasn't all that," he says. "In my opinion."

"That's because she never invited you over for hot choco-late," snaps Missy. "So I went over there after school, I had my hot chocolate, I played with my girlfriends, and then I realize—I've totally forgotten about Freddy. So I grab my coat—I remember getting dressed so fast I almost broke the zipper—and my book bag, and I run outside, back toward the school, cross that beat-down basketball court, which was frozen over, so I was kind of slipping *everywhere*." She starts to laugh, a big boisterous howl, and Mira laughs, too—I can feel her body quiv-ering on my lap—even though she doesn't know why. Just be-cause her mother is laughing. "You should have seen me, Mira, I fell on my behind so many times. Your mama was such a klutz."

She wipes tears away from her eyes.

"Anyway I start hollering 'Freddy' everywhere, and I can't hear nothing back. The streets were real quiet too, no cars, everyone's staying home, because there's snow everywhere, and you *know* they always clean up our neighborhood last. So I'm like"—she cups her hands to her mouth—" 'Gordito,' and I swear it was like I was in a cave, it must have been echoing off the ice or something, and I'm yelling it everywhere, running around the school, the streets. Nothing. Then I finally hear this little voice." She turns her voice high and squeaky. " 'Maritza, help me.' Oh, it was so sad. So I'm running down the street, I think it was maybe South First or something."

"Right off Bedford," says Freddy. "By Manny's place."

"Right. So there's little Freddy, hiding behind a dumpster. I'm like, *what* are you doing? And Freddy's eyes are all bugged out, like he's seen a ghost or something, and I grab his shoul-ders and like, shake him a little bit? Finally he goes, 'They're coming for me. You have to help me. Please Maritza. Please

please please.' And he takes his fat little hand and squeezes mine. Oh! He was so scared." She lets a little giggle spill out the corner of her mouth.

"Was it monsters?" says Mira. She is rapt.

"No it was sixth-graders!" says Missy.

We all start to laugh, except for Mira, who shakes her head. "Sixth-graders are scary," she says. Utter solemnity.

Missy ignores her, cups her hands again—"*Gordito!*"

Freddy responds: "Maritza, help me." They laugh harder.

She continues: "Then I had to get this sorry thing home. They'd been nailing him with snowballs for at least an hour, and he'd been running scared all over the neighborhood. So I come up with this plan."

"She could have been in the army," says Freddy. "We could send this girl into Iraq and she'd have everything settled in a week."

"We made this stockpile of snowballs—must have been fifty of them—and then I send Freddy for a walk around the block. Not too fast, not too slow. 'As soon as the first snowball hits you, you run to me,' I told him. Sure enough, a minute later, here comes Freddy, pumping those stubby legs and arms as fast as he can, two sixth-graders running after him, a couple of snowballs in their hands. He runs up behind the dumpster, and then I say, 'Now, when I say go, you run all the way home and don't stop.' When the kids come closer, I just start to pummel them with snowballs, and I yell, '*Go, Gordito, go!*' He takes off, and those kids, they never knew what hit them." Missy looks at her daughter. "Not that I am telling you it is okay to throw snowballs at anyone. This was an extreme situation, Mira."

Freddy puts his hand on Missy's head, strokes it. "But your mama's my hero," he says.

Whatever jealousy I feel for their connection and history with each other, their life, their energy, is subdued by my admiration for them. They are alive, even while dealing with death. I need these lessons.

CALVIN HUNG UP on me first. Then a moment later I heard a click from Meryl's end. I waited; I knew it wasn't over. I scribbled in a notebook. I drew cords. I drew wires and plugs. I drew cobwebs. I drew a complicated series of interlocked diamonds and triangles and I tried hard to see things from a different perspective, but I could only see this new way of thinking. Once you make the leap, there's no climbing back up that mountain. They called me back.

"I think this involves a larger discussion," said Calvin. He was quiet, tentative maybe.

"I understand how you feel. It's a hard thing to accept," I said gently. There was no response. I could almost feel the collective ache of their hearts, a tremble, and then a moan, through the telephone. I faded for a second, a flicker of regret, and then I remembered: I had made a decision. Someone had to make a decision already. I continued: "But I am not open to discussion on this. I have been thinking about this for six years."

"We think he's still there," said Meryl. "Dear, you have to have faith."

"I have faith that this decision is what's best," I said. "We need to let him go."

There was a rustle of noise, and I could tell the phones were being covered. A minute later, Calvin spoke. "I can see that we're not going to be able to change your mind. I ask only that you give us time to prepare. Emotionally. Spiritually. And that you allow us to be at his bedside when he . . . passes."

"Of course, of course." I felt excited, even though I knew it was perhaps an inappropriate response. I could not help but let myself feel it, though. I was happy to feel something new. Here is a new emotion. Feel it. I hadn't expected it to go this easily. I was one step closer to moving on in my life. Martin, too. It was all fitting together so neatly.

"And Jarvis?" said Calvin. "I recommend you prepare yourself, too. You might want to have a little conversation with a priest. He could surprise you."

"I appreciate the advice, Calvin, but I think I need to handle this in my own way," I said.

"It's your soul," he said. I imagined him shrugging those broad shoulders. And then he added, "God loves you anyway," and hung up the phone.

I hung up the phone. I wrapped my arms around myself, and stood still. I tried to hold my soul. It was a shadow, a silhouette, a ghost of me. It rushed through my fingertips. My soul was liquid, but it was there.

I think I'm saving myself all on my own.

23.

Could it possibly be laundry day again? I am still flush with the notion of family, the red, rosy hues of Missy's life tinting my cheeks. And now it's time for me to go see my family, or what's passing for a family these days.

As I walk to the laundromat, I am trying to ignore this pulsing mass of independence surrounding me, though I am vaguely aware that it is all there, that it is always there: the kids, the almost-adults, who own these streets in their carefully chosen messy ensembles, and the ever-changing array of posters promoting art shows and moving sales and drunken parties, and the street art that redefines every surface not already owned—ephemera, all of it.

I pass an empty lot on North Seventh where a construction worker sits at the controls of a relaxed crane. He twists and turns the knobs, and the crane begins to unfold. I wonder how high it can go.

There is nothing permanent about my neighborhood anymore. It used to be different from Manhattan. I loved Manhattan for its transitory nature, but I was glad when I moved to the other side, across the river, far enough away from it. I was happy to be involved in something solid with Martin. I was happy to have a home. And now when I see how Manhattan has infiltrated the streets—my streets—I wonder if I will have to move again.

I can start over again here. I can build my own family. I am doing it already. Before I met Martin, every few years I found a new, spontaneously created family. An explosion in the universe, as if a star had formed, unbidden. Now I remember who I am, and what I'm capable of. A clean break, and then I can start anew. Explode the star into tiny bits and see what remains.

AT THE LAUNDROMAT, Scott sits on the couch with Nina, reading to her from a book covered with bright-green fake fur and yellow paper cutouts in the shape of triangles. Nina is wearing a pink sundress with tiny purple flowers, and she is barefoot. There is an empty laundry bag next to Scott, and one at his feet. I slap myself down across from him, the backs of my thighs, free in my short cotton schoolgirl's skirt, making a smacking noise on the chair. I hunch forward, legs arched, and clasp my hands together.

"So where is everyone?" I say. "What's going on? What's the good news?"

"Tony's in back. *Again*." He clucks his tongue. "And Mal's not here."

"Why not?"

"I don't know," said Scott quietly. "Well, he left a message but it didn't make that much sense. There was one part about going out of town and another part about using a laundry service and a third part about how he really needs to work on his book. But the sentences were . . . they weren't connected. It's hard to explain."

Fine, I think. I don't need him to be part of my family.

He claps the book shut, looks around, and leans forward. He lowers his voice further. "I think his marriage might be in trouble."

"Oh," I say. I almost say about fifty things at once but then I realize I should keep my mouth shut, change the subject, do some dance moves, a cartwheel, anything, to move this conversation along.

He raises his eyebrows and nods, a slightly scandalized expression on his face, and then pulls back. He begins to bounce his leg, and Nina squeals. She grabs at his face.

"You're such an old lady with all your gossip," I say to Scott.

"But gossip is fun. Why should women have all the fun?" says Scott.

He's wearing a plain blue T-shirt with a smudge of white paint on the sleeve and a small tear right above the waist; a square of hair and stomach, the round corner of it, flashes me. I want to press my hand against that corner and hold it there. That's not very familial.

He dips Nina forward off his knee, swoops her around like a tiny plane and she whirls her hands in the air, and then he holds her above his head, and she kicks her little legs and laughs.

"Good thing you had a girl," I say. "Someone to hang out with and gossip all day."

"Oh, I would have been fine with a boy. Whatever we had, I would have been ecstatic. But I do love my little girl." He lowers her onto his lap, puts his hand on her belly. "It really was like I was waiting my entire life to meet this person, and to give her everything she needs, and to pour my love and energy into her." He begins to bounce his legs again, slower than before. "I didn't know exactly, but I was just waiting for her to get here. For that moment to arrive. Like that Beatles song."

"Blackbird," I say.

"I play her that in the mornings sometimes. I sing it to her." His hand is on her head. I notice she has more hair than last week, and it's red, and it's shining in the light of the laundromat. "There is never going to be a moment in her life that she doesn't feel loved," he says. "Not as long as I'm alive." And then he looks me in the eye, and I believe in his total and complete purity, no matter that I know he lies sometimes, and then I feel it, I feel his love for me. Not that he's in love with me, he just makes me feel like I am worth loving.

Over his shoulder I see Tony, arms crossed, listening. He's got a funny look on his face. I wonder which version of Tony we're going to get today. A doubting Tony. Finally he throws his hands on Scott's shoulders.

"Can you believe this guy? Huh? Scotty freaking Poppins. Where's your umbrella, buddy?" He jumps over the couch, slides in next to Scotty. "Nice skirt," he says to me, and glances casually at my legs. Whenever men compliment your skirt, they're almost always talking about your legs.

Tony's tight polo shirt is unbuttoned. The shirt is light blue. He's a little sweaty, the front of his shirt is moist. He's wearing tight white denim pants. He's tanner than usual. He and Paula have a timeshare in the Hamptons, and they were probably there last weekend. Drinking and swimming and tanning. Maybe fucking, too.

Come to think of it, I'm not feeling familial toward either of these men. But they're all I've got to work with right now. They're all I have left.

My cell phone—Why do I carry it with me? Because you're supposed to have a phone. That's what normal people do—rings through my purse, raindrops of beeps, high and then low. I ignore it. I hate phones. Phones are for bad news, bad jokes. Misinterpretations. You can't see the whole person, you don't know what they're wearing that day, if they're in their favorite color, if they're sitting in their easy chair, if they're using their hands because they're angry, if they're keeping them low and calm because they're sad. You only get half the story on the phone. It's much too easy to lie.

"Are you going to answer it?" says Tony. He is always on his phone, taking calls, checking messages, leaving messages, texting, always texting someone. I'm sure it seems absurd to him that someone wouldn't at least check to see who is calling. I should at least examine it, pretend like I care it's ringing. I pull it out.

Alice. Again.

I look up at them, and they are expectant, waiting. Tony even has his arms crossed. I'm not sure if the phone has ever rung before in front of them. Maybe they didn't even know I had one.

"I'm going to take this call," I say. "I'll just be a minute." I hear the words come out of my mouth and I can't seem to stop them; and anyway, it *feels* nice to take a call. I'm so important. I even squeeze my facial muscles together daintily, adding a touch of officiousness. And where do we take the calls?

We take them outside. I give them a gentle index finger and I walk out front. I smile at them through the plate glass, proffer a wave, and then turn my back to them.

"You've got two minutes, Alice," I say. "So start talking right now." This new I'm-taking-a-call version of me is so tough!

"You've really become so ill-mannered lately, dear. It isn't flattering. You're going to get those worry wrinkles."

"I've been busy." Across the street a willowy girl in high knee socks and a short plaid skirt glides by on a bicycle. Two men in white tank tops and shorts hanging out on the corner catcall her. One of them clutches his heart. The other keeps talking after she has passed, but then she's stopped at the light, waiting for it to turn. Without turning to look at them, she raises one arm in the air toward them and extends her middle finger.

"I'm sure," she says, dry as a pinch of sand. "As have I. Building relationships, developing contacts, making plans for the future. Your future. It's time to think about your future. Whatever may or may not have happened in the past, it's behind us. He's not coming back. So let's think of the good times and honor his memory, and, yes, I'll say it, I will be indelicate, let's make some money."

"Did you fuck him, Alice? Did you fuck my husband? I had always assumed you were a lesbian. That's what really threw me."

"I'm not sure why you're even asking," she says. "Why do you need to hear it from me?"

"Because I do," I say.

"We were collaborators, Jarvis. We came up with great ideas together, for his work, for his shows, for his identity. I was as much a part of his success as anyone else. More so. And don't let Davis tell you otherwise."

"You're such children," I say. "You'll fight over him forever."

"And what are you doing right now?" she says.

"I am *his wife*," I scream. I feel crazy. This is a whole new brand of it, and I have seen a lot of crazy over the past six years. I could jump up in the air and howl, I could pound my fists against the wall. I could tear my hair out. I could pass out. I could break something.

"Oh, but darling," she says, her voice as crisp as a moist, rosy apple falling from a tree in the English countryside, "I was his dealer."

I hang up the phone. I am never taking a call again.

I REMEMBER the two of them at the kitchen table, their heads close together, plotting his future. Eager breaths and bursts of information. I didn't pay attention. Maybe I should have.

LATER ON, when I am calmer, after Tony has rubbed my shoulders, and Scott has brought me water, and I have tried my hardest not to completely break down in the laundromat—a goddamn laundromat, that's where I'm living my life these days—Scott invites me over for dinner. A dinner party. This weekend.

"I'm terrible at dinner parties," I tell him. "I'm always saying the wrong thing."

"There is no wrong thing," he says. "There is only you being out in the world."

I think I am a little in love with Scott.

24.

At night, under the covers, a fan blowing next to me insistently, a chorus of whispers, I dream I'm the one in a coma. Martin sits next to me, awake, waiting for me to rise out of my permanent slumber. Inside I am fully alert, and I have so much to say to him, but more than anything there is the feeling that I need him to touch me. To embrace me even though I'm unable to hold him back. I will him to rise from his chair—I am screaming it in my head. *Come to me.* And finally he does, he comes to me, and lies next to me, just as I lie next to him whenever I see him. And I feel as if, just from the glide of his skin on mine, I will be able to speak soon, I will wake up out of my dream. The pull of his arms, the warmth of his breath on me, on my face. He holds me. He moans sadly. I'm almost there. I'm almost awake. And when I wake we'll be able to be together again.

But instead when I wake it is just me, alone in my bed. And it occurs to me that soon I won't be able to hold him ever again,

even in his supine state. I should go see him. I should get in
my goodbyes. Never again will I be able to hold my sleeping
husband. Never again will I be able to keep him close.

PHILO IS SITTING on a bench in front of the Beverly Home
when Missy drops me off and drives away, Blue Öyster Cult
pondering loudly through the windows, until finally it fades. I
slide Philo's hoe over and join him on the bench. Everything is
off-kilter with him. His shirt is buttoned incorrectly, his hair is
parted on the wrong side of his head, creating an odd wave, and
it's sticking straight up in the rear. He is dirty: the remains of
lunch crowd the corners of his mouth, and I can smell him,
he's probably soiled himself. His belt isn't buckled, either.
This is bullshit. Someone should be taking care of him.

"Hi, Philo." I take his hand. I clasp it in between both of
mine. "How are you today?"

He turns to me, and his eyes are unfocused, and then I see
him struggle to get a little control. I dive through the gray zone
of his irises into the dark center of his pupils. I throw myself in
there and try to help out. If I could just fix something, just one
sick man. If only I could help.

But his eyes return to a glazed state. A tiny disturbance on the
surface, like an asteroid hitting the moon, and then it's over.

I stand, and I try to pull him up with me, but he's not going
anywhere. A nursing assistant, young, with round cheeks and
hair split in two braids on either side of her head like a farm
girl, rounds the corner of the building, holding the hand of a
woman in a black dressing gown embroidered with a massive
array of dark-blue and purple flowers. I admire it for a moment.

It's a vibrant tapestry. Green stems intertwine. She's wearing a garden. The woman has long gray hair that falls elegantly to her shoulders and shines brilliantly in the sunlight against the dressing gown. For a moment the whole vision seems magical, and I wonder if she's got any special powers. But then the sunlight turns her face sour, her lips and jaw into a scowl, her eyes into a pinch. She's yelling at the nurse.

"You don't know me," she says. "You don't own me."

I wave them over, and they stroll toward me, the old woman crabbing the entire time. When they reach me, the woman looks me up and down, the preciseness of my outfit, I suppose, the neat clasp in my hair, and then demands, "Don't you know who I am?"

I ignore her.

"He needs some help," I say to the nurse. "He looks like he's been lost for a while."

"No, you know me. I know you do," the woman says. She stops scowling.

I feel my sympathy reserves running low. And I need to maintain a certain level if I'm going to spend any time here. I let go of Philo's hand, I pat down his hair. It's stiff and dry under my hands. It feels like it would crumble if I squeezed it too tightly.

The old woman bends her arms, raises her hands, and begins to squeeze her fists in the air. "Look. It's me."

"I have to go visit my husband," I say to the nurse. "Good luck."

I walk my Manhattan walk toward the front door, head up, legs bouncing, but in control, arms in gear. Don't stop, not for a second, or you'll never get out of here. A power walk past the powerless. I am young, I am energized, I am alive. This is just a quick visit. In and out. This is temporary. I am so over this.

I cruise through the home: no greeting for Linda at the front desk, just a quick nod; I scarcely touch the floor in the halls, I take one step where I might have taken two before; I duck a gaggle of old ladies leaving bingo in the cafeteria; I breathe short breaths through my mouth so that I don't have to smell anything. It's enough that this place is seeping through my pores.

How did I spend so many years in places like this? How did I waste so much time? How could I have been captivated for even a moment?

Everything is going to change in a week. This is my mantra as I climb the set of stairs that leads to Martin's floor. I pass the photographs in the hallways and they glow at me, as if they had been taken and developed yesterday. No time, no time, I've wasted enough of it.

I finally arrive at Martin's door and push it open with one hand, almost violently, as if I were karate-chopping my way inside. I stand in the doorway confidently, and then I see Martin. He's sitting straight up, a smile on his face, with the yellow cat curled up in his lap.

I scream so that the asteroids can hear me.

And then there is a thump of footsteps from either direction, and I am leaning against the door, pulling myself out and away from him even as I am inclined to rush toward him, too. I slump to the floor in the hallway, then curve my head around the corner, and there he is, still smiling. The first nurse, a ruddy older woman who has worked at the home for twenty years—*a lifer*, she always jokes—arrives with heavy breaths, and then Vaz. The other nurse walks into the room, and Vaz leans down next to me.

"What is it, Mrs. Miller?"

"Is he—alive?"

"Of course he's alive."

"I mean, is he awake?"

The other nurse walks back out of the room. She's carrying the cat, who is fighting her, thrusting his legs, which dangle in the air. She pulls him by the scruff and hisses at him. He hisses back.

"I'll get the cat out of here, Mrs. Miller. Was that the problem? We can keep him out from now on if you like."

I wave her away. I can't speak. I feel cold, no life left in me.

"She just thought he was awake is all," says Vaz. "I'll take care of her. No worries, miss." Vaz takes my hand. "Do you want to get up? Or do you want to stay here for a while?"

I pull my knees up and rest my head on them, and stay that way until I feel my heart beating normally again. When I look up, Vaz is still there, and the other nurse is gone. I have no idea how much time has passed. I only know I saw Martin awake, at last, for one last time.

"HE'S NOT AWAKE," says Vaz.

She had led me to an empty room, laid me out on a bed, covered me up to my chin in a stiff standard-issue blanket. She had turned out the light, and shut the curtains, and left me there, alone. I made humming noises, and then I slept. And then, after a while, she came back and woke me. We were quiet for a while, and now, at last, I can speak, I can ask her questions, and she can give me the information I need.

She continues: "The smile on his face—it's an involuntary reaction. Just like when he blinks sometimes, or tears form in the corners of his eyes, or the little noises that come out of his body. His brain isn't really responding to you, or to that damn cat. I'm cursing myself, that I talked you into that. I didn't know it was going to be like this. Too much drama."

I feel calmer, though I am still chilled. If I thought for a moment that I was making the wrong decision . . . I've just convinced myself to move forward, and now I'm wondering if I've moved too quickly.

"But what about how he was sitting up? How do you explain that?"

"Oh you thought he pulled himself up all by himself?" Vaz laughs. "I'm sorry, it's not funny. I can see you've got the true terror."

The sun is setting, and an errant ray pokes through the curtains and flashes in Vaz's face. She shades an eye with a hand. On her wedding finger she wears a simple but massive silver ring with a turquoise stone in it. I wonder if there's an inscription. I wonder if someone loves her that much.

"No, no." She laughs, then she stops herself. She knows she's supposed to be serious. I see her refocus herself, her lips tighten, her dark eyes smooth over, the chaos of merriment disappearing. "His parents were here. They raised the bed for him. They wanted to see him better, I think. I showed them how to do it, and then I left. That was this morning. I didn't know it would upset you so. I wouldn't have left him that way if I knew."

His parents were here?

I hear her say, "We're here to help." I'm not paying attention anymore, though. I'm thinking about his parents, about Meryl and Calvin, playing with their son like he was a doll.

"They've got good hearts, those people," says Vaz.

I say something, a murmur of information, just enough so she'll stop talking, stop explaining, stop nursing me. I'm not the one who needs help.

She's leaving anyway, getting off her shift. Did I need a car? Did I need anything else?

"No," I say. "I've got a ride home."

AT LAST, as the final shreds of daylight melt in the distance, Missy arrives. I make a dash from the lobby, dodging any remaining land mines. No more seniors on meltdown. No more haunted husbands. And for God's sake, don't let me run into my in-laws.

"Sweet Home Alabama" rocks out from the stereo. Missy has her hair down.

"You look pretty," I tell her, even though I can only see part of her face.

"There was a thing at Mira's school," she says.

I roll down the window. I see Vaz walking across the parking lot. She's changed out of her uniform and into baggy jeans, low on her hips, a pair of boxer shorts sticking out from the waist, an athletic jersey, and an oversized Mets jacket. There's a headband wrapped around her braids. She walks with a swagger, legs with purpose, with entitlement, arms casually swinging at her side, seemingly lazy, but there's the portent of power there. Sleeping giants encased in nylon. Vaz lifts one of her powerful arms and opens and closes her palm in the air.

"Who's that?" says Missy.

"Vaz. Martin's nurse," I say.

"He's hot," she says.

"It's a she," I say.

"No he is not," she says.

"Swear to God," I say.

We both laugh, but it's more like a bark. Sharp.

Missy pulls the car into reverse, pulls out of the driveway. "I wonder what that's like," she says. "Living half your life one way, and the other half the other way."

"One foot through the door, the other foot back out," I say.

"I bet it's hard," she says.

"I bet it's really hard, and then it's really easy. Like most things," I say.

I see signs for the BQE. Signs pointing home.

25.

When I walk out my front door—hair slicked down, an antique gold clip embedded with ruby flowers (a gift from Martin's mother) holding a loose strand in place, somber plum lipstick, pretty pink eye shadow, a new pink summer dress, with criss-cross straps and tiny posies in a neat pattern—I feel fresh and light and young. I allow myself to feel this way. I allow myself to feel pretty. I allow myself to be at my best.

I shopped all day. I spent money on vain and frivolous items. Years ago I didn't think clothes were frivolous. I used to have dreams about clothes, about what I would wear the next day, about clothes I wished I owned. Sometimes I would wake up early in the morning and start sewing.

But it has felt unnecessary for so long. Who would I look pretty for? And yet here I am, looking pretty for someone. Scott. It is one thing to seduce Mal by fulfilling his requests for a short skirt. I've got a closet full of short skirts. It is a far different thing to walk the streets of Williamsburg looking for the perfect item to please a man who loves all women. I had to take myself to a new level, or rather, back to an old, forgotten level. It is easy to have Scott look kindly on me. But how can I make him see I am more special than the rest of the women? Than his wife?

In the elevator I finger the crisp newness of the pleats of the skirt. Only one flier today: someone found a dog, a pit bull. There's a picture of her from the side. Her nipples hang down from her body. Oh, she's expecting, I think. I wonder if they know that. I take out a pen and write on the flier: "She's pregnant."

I look down at my cleavage. I rub the skin on my arms, soft, moisturized flesh. The elevator door opens and Alison is standing there, sans guitar.

"What's shaking?" she says. Did she just look me up and down?

"A dinner party," I say. I sound exceptionally giddy.

"Sounds fun. Bring me some leftovers," she says.

We switch positions: she enters, I exit. She brushes against me as she passes.

THREE YEARS INTO our marriage was when Martin started to ache at night. I hadn't seen it happen before, though he swore he'd had bouts of it over the years, more so before he met me. The aches struck him all over his body, little twitches in his muscles, in his joints, tiny spasms that shot through him and woke him up. A jerk of flesh. He would emit a small gasp as he awoke, and it would wake me up with him.

"It's like being bit by a snake," he told me. "And then the poison coils and recoils through my system. A sting and then a release."

"What can I do?" I would say. I would hold him, and he would twitch until the morning. And then the day would begin, the sun would boldly wash through our windows, and he would get up and paint, and I would get up and draw or sew. Sometimes I would go for long walks along the water and then come back and tell Martin what was going on out there: the stray dog I saw running around the lot off South First, barking at nothing; the anxious day laborers awaiting pickup who whistled at me; the smell of the sugar plant blasting in warm pockets as I passed; the unbearable noise of traffic thundering above on the Williamsburg Bridge. He liked that, when I translated the world for him.

Then in the afternoons I would sit quietly and steal worried looks at him as he painted. The effortless coiled power of his arms, the black bars of his tattoos, the stretch of his T-shirt across his chest. He was fine then, when he was painting. And even through dinner, or drinks with his friends. He would talk, he would laugh. He would pull me onto his lap, and make me tell stories about the day laborers, and call me *mami*. "We're turning her into a real Brooklyn girl," he'd say. Years after I'd moved in with him, he still wondered if I would have been happier riding out my youth across the water. I never thought of him as older unless he reminded me of it. And he wasn't that much older, he was just finished with his youth in a way that neither of us was sure that I was.

Then, at night, when all the noise and excitement of the evening had died down, and he was too worn out to look at his work any further, that's when he felt the disturbances under his skin. It went on for a few months. Some nights were better than others, and then suddenly they were all the same, uncomfortable, fitful, stressful. Poisonous.

"I need to leave," he told me finally. "I'm going to go to the cabin."

His parents owned a small cabin in Oregon, near the border with Washington, on the Snake River. His father used to take him there for getaway weekends when he was a child, and they would go fishing and hiking. They cooked potatoes and freshly caught fish in aluminum foil and drank cold root beer and talked about how if Martin really looked hard enough he was sure to see God everywhere he looked. It was a trade-off for Martin. He loved the outdoors and his father but had no connection to Jesus. He hid his punk-rock magazines in his sleeping bag and learned the power of holding one's tongue. The mixture of restraint and freedom had always defined him.

"It'll straighten me right up. I'll be a new man," he said.

What could I do to help my husband? I had to let him go for a while.

He had planned to leave me for only a month, taking with him his favorite brushes, a sketchbook, a few cameras, and a duffel bag full of T-shirts and two pairs of jeans. I remember sitting on the bed and watching him pack. I rolled the T-shirts for him like logs and handed them to him, one by one. I could not help but wonder if this was the last time I would see him, if he would find the solace of the cabin more to his liking, better for his work, more soothing to his aches. But I said nothing, even though I was sad, and I was angry, because I was terrified to say anything in either direction. If I tried to deny him, maybe he would go anyway, but then never come back. But I didn't want him to think I was pleased, either. So I kept myself in the middle, a silent protest. *I am helping you pack, but don't think I like it, not one bit.*

He said he was going for a month but it lasted much, much longer, as I suspected it would. The first week, I slept most of the day. I skipped my morning walks, because without Martin to report to they didn't seem as much fun. I would talk to Martin on the phone late at night—he would go into the main town and call me collect from a pay phone. The connection was so clear and quiet, and Martin's voice seemed stiller than usual, a smooth blue-green lake, the occasional stone skipping across it. He would tell me about the animals he saw near the cabin, and the exchanges he had with the locals. They remembered him from his youth, he told me, and he was delighted by that. They'd tell him stories about the flood from last spring, or how the new shopping mall development a few towns over was a complete disaster. A girl from the high school was going to an Ivy League school, she was always bright, and had spent her junior year in France. The Native Americans were petitioning to build a new casino. Martin reveled in all these stories. They were so different from the ones he and his friends shared in New York, the same tales of art-world backbiting and competitiveness mixed with the occasional triumph.

"This is reality," he would tell me. "This is how real people live."

I started to fear he would never return. And this drove me out of my bed and out into the world. I started taking my walks again, only this time I took one of Martin's cameras with me. When I got the prints, I spread them out before me on the kitchen table. The stray dog, barking against the city skyline.

The sugar-plant employees, showing up for work in the morning. Graffiti on construction. The pitted streets of the South Side. They weren't bad. They were pretty good. It was the same story as always, but I was telling it in a new way.

I reported to Martin my activities, and he listened to me, but I wasn't sure if he really heard me. To him, the stories sounded exactly the same. And he was so excited about his news. He had found a tavern—it sounded a bit like a strip club to me, but he was being vague about the details—and now he was getting to know the real men of the town, truly understanding their makeup. His enthusiasm surprised me a bit, I guess. I had always thought of him as genuine and confident and masculine. I didn't understand why he needed to reaffirm that part of him by hanging out with what sounded like a bunch of town drunks. He wasn't some fussy intellectual, nor was he like one of those Wall Street types I used to see coming into the bar where I worked. He was just simply Martin. He knew who he was. And he knew who *I* was. Together we didn't need to define ourselves through anyone else.

And yet there he was, drinking, bonding, singing, swooning with the men of this town. After the second week, he stopped calling regularly. I didn't bust him on it. I recognized the lure of the small town for him. I started to think about what my life would be like without him. He was burned out; I hadn't recognized it. I missed him terribly, and I hoped he wasn't burned out on me—we had only been together for five years—but if he was, I could only accept it and move on. It was what I was good at anyway, the moving-on part. Another person disconnects, pulls the plug from my emotional outlet. I didn't know how to fight for anything, I never learned how. My mother didn't fight for her life when she was dying, and my father didn't fight to keep our family together after she died. Who was left to teach me? How do we learn these things?

So I spent my time taking pictures and meeting up with friends—Martin's friends that I thought were mine, and a few friends from school and the bar—and carried on with my life. Two months passed, and in my brain there were the rumblings of a plan for the future. I could move back into the city. An old girlfriend from the bar, now an aspiring clothing designer, told me her roommate was getting married and moving to Brazil. There was a small room in the back of the apartment, and it would be all mine. I would have a home. I even went so far as to visit it: it was depressing, barely more than a closet. There was a twin mattress on the floor, a clothing rack next to it, stacks of shoes in the corner. The walls were made of dusty bricks. It smelled like sage.

"Beggars," I said. "And choosers."

I could be someone new, I thought. I don't want to, but I could do it.

But then a week later, I heard a rustle of keys at the front door, the press of metal against metal, and there he was. My husband had returned.

I ran to him, and then stopped myself. A suspicious child, contemplating candy from the stranger.

"Are you back or are you just visiting?"

"I'm back. And baby, do I have a story for you," he said.

THROUGH THE DOOR, outside, out front, and there's Davis. He's wearing a cowboy hat and a bright-blue shirt with a shiny star on the pocket and blue jeans and cowboy boots. He's cut his hair short around the neck. He looks wonderful, and I realize I missed him. Alice, she can fuck off. She's never been fun to be around. But Davis, he's a good time.

"Well, aren't you summertime on a stick?" he says.

"Hello, Davis," I say. I don't know what to do with him.

"I've been standing here trying to get the guts to come up and see you."

I hold my hands up in the air. "Don't worry. No deadly weapons."

"It's the guilt I'm worried about, sweetheart."

I push out some air through my mouth. I don't know if I have it in me to keep going on this way, making someone hurt.

I STOOD AND studied him, head at an angle, arms crossed. My husband looked different to me, but I couldn't tell if the changes were solely superficial. His hair was longer, and he hadn't shaved in a while, and he looked a little leaner, like he'd been sick with a lingering flu. I wondered if he had gotten lost in the woods and had been living on berries and leaves for a while. Maybe that's why he didn't call. Maybe he *couldn't* call.

"Come on, give us a hug," he said. "A hug won't kill you." He dropped his bag and walked toward me, and wrapped his taut arms around me. He was wearing a blue T-shirt, plain cotton, and it felt crisp against my bare arms. I knew all of his T-shirts intimately, I had them memorized, but this was new. He was so careful about his clothes, and here he was, in this nondescript shirt. There was nothing special about it. I knew I was being ridiculous—I was being distrustful of his clothes. But he'd been gone for so long, any little thing would have bothered me. Still I hugged him back, because he was still my husband, I still loved him, and he felt so good.

"That's better," he said. He kept one arm around my shoulders and turned me toward the living room, then marched me toward the black leather couch. "Now let's sit down together and I'll tell you everything that happened."

So we sat there, Martin on one end of the couch, feet stretched out, and me on the other, with my legs curled underneath me, just like always, only "always" felt like it had been years ago, and not merely two months.

Martin closed his eyes for a minute, then opened them. He apologized. "It's just nice to be home," he said.

"Is this your home still?" I said.

"Of course! It wasn't ever not my home. I'm sorry I was gone for so long. I just had to work everything out of my system. You are my wife, and I am your husband. And we are together." He leaned over and reached for my hand and stroked it in the way that I liked, top of the hand, down the inside of my index finger, and around the thumb, ending on my palm, which he tickled gently with the tips of his own fingers.

With a nod of my head I gave him permission to tell me his story. I hated that he had lived this separate life, that he'd had experiences without me, but I needed to know where he'd been, what he'd seen. I could decide whether to forgive him later.

"LET ME WALK you to your party," says Davis. "We can walk and talk. Pretty girl like you shouldn't be walking the dangerous streets of Brooklyn by herself, especially in a dress like that."

"Shut up, Davis," I say. He knows as well as anyone the streets of this part of Brooklyn are littered with recent college graduates, a decidedly danger-free population. But I let him walk with me anyway. I have some questions for him.

I let him chatter for a while first, let him get comfortable. He tells me the whole studio has been on vacation for a few weeks. He went home for a while to Memphis and stayed with his mother, who has been struggling with her health off and on for the past few years—heart problems, and most recently her doctor informed her that her arteries were hardening at an alarming rate. "It's all that southern cooking," he says, and he laughs, but it's not up to par with his usual jokes and he knows it.

Davis tells me also that he's met a new woman, another assistant (I roll my eyes silently), but she's older than his past girlfriends, and also, he says in an oddly proud fashion, she's American. Perhaps he thinks he's made progress.

"She knows how to put me in my place," he says. "She's got my number, that one."

I feel proud of him until he says, "And she's a redhead, and redheads, they drive me crazy." I don't know why that disappoints me. He's allowed to have desires.

We pass by a young woman with a blanket spread out on the ground, various wares for sale covering it: antique cameras, a few old copies of *Vogue*, a pair of high-heeled cork sandals. Davis stops in front of her, squats down close to the cameras, picks up one and examines it.

"Fifty bucks," says the woman. She's wearing sunglasses and sitting on a beach chair. An issue of *Us Weekly* rests in her lap.

"Davis, I have to go to dinner," I say.

"One minute," he says.

It's as if he's already forgotten everything that's happened between us. All it takes is a shiny toy to distract a man like Davis.

"THE ACHES NEVER got any better," said Martin. "So I started drinking at night, just so I could pass out and go to sleep."

That was unlike him. He was usually cautious about his drinking. He had always had the capacity for great discipline, something his father had taught him, even as Martin struggled to distinguish himself from his family.

"I couldn't sleep," he said sadly. "And I was so tired."

"You should have come back," I said. "We could have gotten help."

"I know, but . . . once I was there, I felt like I was supposed to be there. I felt like I had been embraced by this town. And then I started going to the Sheep—Sheepshead Tavern, but everyone calls it the Sheep—every night. I looked forward to seeing these guys. Hearing about their families. What their days were like." His voice picked up with excitement. "They let me take their pictures sometimes, and during the day, after I shook off the hangover, I was getting amazing work done. I shipped all the canvases. Wait till you see them, Jarvis. And at the Sheep, the dancers—"

"The strippers," I said. "Call it like it is, please. I'm not an idiot."

"Okay, they were in bikinis, sure. And heels. They swung around a pole sometimes. But they kept their tops on, and they weren't hookers. I didn't see any of that happening anyway.

And I got to know some of them. They let me backstage to shoot. I was like an older brother to them. They hadn't met too many artists before, a lot of them, let alone anyone from New York. They really were just hungry for exposure to the outside world. Anyway, honey, it was all about the guys there. The women were just a distraction."

He told me about Hugh, an older guy who always wore a fedora and used to teach poetry up in Bellingham. "Now he's just retired down there, puts out a chapbook every couple of years just because he has something he wants to say," said Martin, nodding. Hugh was a real drinker—got divorced because of it—and so he happily went to the Sheep every night. It sounded like Martin was closest with him, I suppose because they were both artists.

And there was Larry Jackson, who ran a tree farm. "There were a lot of guys who worked in logging," said Martin. And Bartlett, the town sheriff, a skinny, lonely guy who never drank, just kept a table in the corner and a watchful eye over everyone. No one was drinking and driving on his watch. Sometimes some of the older guys from the reservation would show up, but just for a quick drink. They kept to themselves.

There was also this little weasel of a guy, Tom O'Leary, who used to date one of the dancers, Patty, a sweet girl, just nineteen, with long red hair that ran straight down her back. He was supposed to have been a smart guy, had gone to school down in California, some sort of philosophy student. But then he'd signed himself up to go over to Desert Storm and had managed to get some shrapnel in his arm. Everyone in town respected him for his service, but the town joke was, "Still didn't make him tall."

"I guess now he feels like the world owes him something," said Martin. He was there from opening to close for months, sitting near the stage, drinking, staring at her. But then, the drunker he would get, he would start yelling things at her, it would brew up and bubble over, he just couldn't help himself. He'd call her a whore, he'd call her a slut, and then they'd kindly ask him to leave. The first week Martin was there, they kicked him out for good, Bartlett first leaning him against the wall with a nightstick, then roughly walking him out the door. He just couldn't keep his mouth shut. He was a ruined man.

Two days before Martin arrived back in Brooklyn, he went into town during the day to pick up some more supplies. (He had, at that point, no intention of coming back anytime soon, I noted.) He had skipped the Sheep the night before and had stayed up all through the night, painting dancers and loggers and old poets, all captured in the throes of a dark club and dim candlelight and an unending swirl of cigarette smoke. At the one café in town he ran into Bartlett. They sat together at a table out front, slugged back some coffee. Martin told him about his life in New York. "He asked me if I missed you," said Martin. He chuckled. I wasn't sure why that was funny.

Then Tom O'Leary pulled up in his mother's station wagon.

"What a runt," said Martin. "And he's got these thick glasses with huge black frames—way too big for his head. He kind of looked like a cartoon character. This tight little bundle of wires bouncing around under these big black glasses. He walks right up to us, asks us if he can join our table. Bartlett handled him fine, told him to sit right down. No harm done, I guess. And then he told us about what it was like over there, and that was pretty interesting. What the bombs looked like in the night sky, the way the sand was constantly blowing in his face, the language of the other soldiers, the way they talked so rough. He really is an articulate kid. But then he started getting into all the chemicals they pump into your system, and how he thought maybe it was rotting him up from the inside out. You don't know what to believe, Jarvis. I mean, the kid is nuts, right? But he sounded pretty convincing."

I rested my head back on the edge of the couch and studied him. He was so handsome. I was starting to forget about where he had been, what he had been doing. Now I just wanted to hear the end of his story. That was the way my love for him worked when he was still awake.

"Bartlett calms him down, tells him he needs to go to a doctor and tell him what's going on. 'There are different *kinds* of doctors, son,' he said. 'For all kinds of illnesses.' And Tom freaked out. 'I know that. You think I don't know that?' And Barlett's like, 'I know you do.' Finally they just ended up giving each other a big hug. It was too much." Martin shakes his head. "The thing is, honey, when you go away, you feel like you're done with your problems, and everyone else's problems around you, that's part of it too. But you stay anywhere long enough—I think it's two months, that's the going rate"—he laughs for a moment, then continues—"you realize there's problems there too. And as much as you want to stay out of it . . . well, you can't. If you've got any kind of humanity, you can't help but feel something for everyone."

That night, Martin headed back to the Sheep. He'd been up for a day, just wanted to take one quick drink to push him over the edge. He figured he'd sleep for a day, then start all over again. He was in a really unique place with his work, he told me, and he wanted to see where he could go with it.

"I needed to keep going. Do you understand?" he said. He squeezed my wrists lightly.

I nodded. All that remained from my resentment was a low-grade jealousy humming like a naked lightbulb in the background. I wished I could have been there when it was happening.

"I got a drink, sat at the back table, just watched everyone, trying to take it all in. Absorb it so I could sleep on it, then wake up and paint it right away. Some of the girls came over, tried to get me to buy them a drink. I think I bought Patty one, just to get them away from the table. She stayed, and we talked for a bit. She's a happy girl. She said she was saving up for school. Her sister was up in Seattle, she said they might share a place next year. So she could study art. She said knowing me, it had inspired her to explore her creative side. Can you believe it?"

My resentment cranked right up again. My husband, a sitting target for strippers. And he called himself a New Yorker.

"Martin, you don't think she was playing you?"

"Well, she didn't get anything out of me but a rum and coke," he snapped. "Look, she was a nice kid in a bad situation. Anyway, I bought her the drink, and then I went to hit the bathroom. There was a line out the door, so I went out back. Some of the guys did that, pissed out in the woods next to the parking lot. So I stood out there, stared up at the stars through the trees. Beautiful night. Clear sky. No city lights, so you can see a million stars in the sky. I really have got to take you to the cabin sometime."

"I'd like that," I said, but I knew it would never happen.

"All of a sudden, the sky just lit up. Shots of red and orange and yellow, big bursts of it. I stood there and stared. All you could do was stare. I was captivated. And there was a particular smell, sort of like gas, I guess, and a loud crack, crackling maybe. And then I heard screams. The women. They started, and they weren't stopping." Martin shook his head for a while. "Turns out that Tom O'Leary kid threw a couple of Molotov cocktails at the place. One went through the window, and it lit the front corner of the stage."

I put my hand over my mouth, my fingers pressed into my skin until it hurt. I let out a sad moan between my teeth.

"No one got hurt, don't worry. Some burns, nothing serious. But the place was so old and rickety—plus there was foam insulation everywhere—it burned down in no time at all. There was only a volunteer fire department in town and most of them were there and too drunk to do anything. So we all stood and watched it burn."

"Tom's in jail?"

"Tom's in a hospital. He's out of his fucking head." Martin shifted onto his hands and knees and started to crawl toward me. "I slept for a day. All of my aches are gone. And now I'm back. I'm here, my love. I'm all better now."

I TAKE DAVIS's arm, drag him toward the corner. "Come on, you big jerk," I say. He glances back, a forlorn look, almost pathetic, like he was a child staring at a box of puppies. "She'll be there when you come back," I tell him.

We walk arm in arm on Bedford for a block, forcing people passing us to separate and walk around us.

"I have to ask you something," I say. "And you have to tell me the truth."

"Whatever you want to know," says Davis. "Whatever we need to do to get this thing going between us again."

"How many others were there?" I say. "How many other women?"

I TOOK MY husband back that night. I took him between my arms and between my breasts and between my legs. He looked like a stranger, but he felt the same, felt me the same. I let him hold my arms down, and I let him force my nipples between his lips, and hold them tight, so tight. I let him squeeze my hips and lick the sides of them, and then up to my waist, both hands on the waist, holding me tight.

He stroked my arms, he stroked my hair. He whispered, "Were you waiting for me?" He took his hands and put them on my ass, both sides of me, he slid them down and around. "So soft," he said. He ran the backs of his hands along the insides of my thighs. He ran his thumbs on top of my clit, and then an index finger, and then slid his hand dead center underneath me, and cupped. "I want to feel it drip down," he said.

And I squirmed under him. I let him massage me, my ass with his one hand, my pussy with the other. And I ran, wet, all over him.

DAVIS STARTS TO laugh, but it's not an honest noise. "You were his love," he says.

"That's a nonanswer," I say.

"Look—what good is this going to do you?"

"Davis, why are you still trying to protect him after all this time? What does it matter?" I say.

"I'm not trying to protect him," he says. "I'm trying to protect you."

I SHOULD HAVE known when the paintings showed up a week later. Martin was secretive about them at first but then I insisted he show me. And there they were, all the girls. Many of them in pairs. Flesh against flesh. There were some of the men, too, and I knew who they were immediately. Poor Tom O'Leary, and his oversized glasses. But it was with the girls that Martin had taken the most care. The best colors, reds and oranges flush with sexuality, the best brushstrokes, the brightest eyes, the most energy. The men were old, and tired. The women were revered. Now when I think back to all of his paintings, it was the women he loved the most. And I never saw it. I believed everything he said, because I loved him.

WE STAND IN front of Scott's apartment building, and Davis opens his mouth a few times, and then closes it, and I am looking at him, but not through him, I can see in his eyes that he's almost there, he almost wants to tell me something.

"It might hurt me," I say. "But I need to know. So I can move on." I raise my hands up high to his face and clasp his cheeks. "I'm stuck, Davis. I've been stuck for so long. This is going to help me let go. I think I can do it. But you've got to help me."

Behind us an ice cream truck drives by, its speakers wheezing out a gentle song of summer on repeat.

And then Davis begins to speak.

"It was both of us at first," says Davis. "I was . . . complicit."

He tells me that there had been so many women before me, and then we were married, so he stopped for a while. And when he started up again, he called Davis and asked if he wanted in, and Davis had said no—"Even I know better than that," he says. "Also, I really do care about you, sugar"—and had tried to convince him not to do it, but Martin had no interest in listening.

Davis grinds his hands together. "There is no explanation I can offer you, only that when he felt those aches, it was like it was calling him. He could paint, and he could love you, and he could get a million shows, but none of it was enough to make him feel better. There was still something dark in there, this dark spot that made him fuck up."

I think of Mal, the lines of cocaine laid out before us on the kitchen table that his wife probably bought. And all of the ways we had grinded against each other, with our hands and our mouths and our dirty, dirty words. I had felt it, too, that dark hole, sealed up for a moment inside of me, only to breathe again as soon as we were done. And I felt it now, breathing so heavy inside of me. I felt a choke in my chest. It was gasping for air, for my air.

26.

Scott lives in one of the new buildings near the Bedford L, a slender, sleek building with substantial glass fronts to each apartment. I admire it before I enter. Most of the buildings sprouting up in the neighborhood are standard issue, at least from the exterior: bricks and concrete, small windows, tiny balconies with room only for plants. They've been going up so fast—everywhere I look, it seems. But the architect of this building took a bit more care than the rest, imbued it with some originality, at least from the outside looking in.

Upstairs, narrow halls, no posters, no signs of life, just an efficient and clean new building. But then Scott opens the door and there is a home in there, a fully embracing home: tangerine walls and hardwood floors and bookshelves and a huge couch, deep red and warm and plush, and there are the baby toys, and baby seats, and a baby swing, and there is the smell of tomatoes and cilantro and other spices, and there is music, jazz, a clarinet, coming through speakers, and there is laughter coming from the corner, and a baby squeals, another baby laughs, and at my feet a cat rubs up against me.

"Jarvis, you're a picture," says Scott. He's got a bottle of wine in one hand, and a glass in the other. He presses his lips to my cheek, holds it for a count. He must love me, I think, even though it's wrong, I'm wrong.

There's Elizabeth, bouncing Nina, and another couple with a baby, a tall blond man, cradling an infant dressed in red, and a tiny Asian woman who is laughing boisterously, almost hysterically. She wipes her eyes. "You're killing me," she says. She lets out another laugh. "Too much."

Introductions all around (Paul and Patty Lund, friends from college; he's a lawyer, she works in publishing), a glass of wine in my hand, the sound of an industrial fan—"The air conditioner blew a week ago," explains Elizabeth. "New buildings." And then she shrugs—is drowned out by all of the voices, rising louder. Scotty forces appetizers on me. Tapenade, the rich taste of olive sinks into my tongue. Sweet, soft cheeses. There are some dried apricots. A baguette Scott keeps slicing every few minutes, silently, smoothly, replenishing the plate.

It is all so seamless, this life. If you just let it be.

DURING THE FEAST—cold gazpacho, a mozzarella salad, risotto, pork roasted in cracked pepper and lemon, and more wine, always more wine—I ask lots of questions. I make them tell me about their new apartments and their jobs and what their hometowns were like and what books they are reading and what movies they've seen and where they're going on vacation and where they just went on vacation, and I know I am diverting attention from me by asking all these questions, I know it, but I have learned by now, nothing kills a buzz like a guy in a coma. Finally I ask them about their love stories, how they met, how they knew they were the ones, and I'm fully intent on asking what their weddings were like, what kind of cake they served, what kind of dress the women wore, how drunk the men got at their bachelor parties, and if anything scandalous happened at the wedding, the best man and the maid of honor getting caught screwing in the bathroom, when Patty turns to me, takes a long look at the gold band on my left hand, and says, "What about your love story?"

I WORE YELLOW to my wedding, because Martin always liked me in yellow. We were married in a church uptown, because Martin's parents always liked pretending there was hope for our souls. My father was the only member of my family who attended the wedding. He walked me down the aisle, weeping like a rainstorm, but he never made it to the party at our loft. We walked to Times Square after the wedding, and I think we lost him somewhere in midtown. I pictured him in an Irish pub, sinking into the pints and the cigarettes, thinking he'd have just one, but it was never just one with him. I only cried a little when I realized he was gone. Martin assured me he would show up eventually, but he never did. I guess I'm grateful now that he didn't make it.

"I DON'T HAVE a love story," I say.

"Oh, forgive me but you have the best love story of all," says Elizabeth. She taps the table with her finger. "You need to tell your story." Whatever restraint she might have of her natural aggressive instincts had completely disappeared with the consumption of wine.

"She doesn't have to tell the story if she doesn't want to," says Scott.

And suddenly I am pink all over my body, the lobes of my ears, the slope of my neck, the thrust of my nipples, my belly, my thighs, my toes. Why am I always looking for a hero? And why does it feel so good when I find one?

"I just mean, that's love. That's a love that we don't know." Elizabeth, with the golden hair that falls to the shoulders. Elizabeth, with the full, juicy life: a powerful job, a warm and generous man, a baby who coos when you touch her cheeks. Elizabeth, with everything I could ever dream of wanting. Elizabeth thinks I know something she doesn't.

She motions around the room, at Paul, at Patty, at Scott, at Nina. "Our love is easy," she says.

"Love is never easy," says Scott.

"I know what she's saying," I say. I will give you this, Elizabeth, for opening your home to me, for sharing your husband with me even though you don't know the half of it. "What she's really saying is that my love is hard. And she's right."

CARROT-CAKE CUPCAKES, iced coffee—"More coffee for my wife, please," says Scott, but he doesn't know I'm the one who really needs sobering up—and then the baby starts to fuss, and no amount of wheedling will calm her down.

Scott invites me to help put Nina down for the night. I look at Elizabeth and she throws her hands at me. "She's all yours." As I walk with Scott I hear her say, "He's just so good with her."

Scott lays Nina on her changing table and she squirms for a second, but then he pulls her dress over her head, and she begins to giggle and smile. "She loves being naked," he explains. "Every night, this is her favorite part." She stretches all around her, chitchats nonsense with her father. Her belly is so round and smooth.

"She's precious," I say. I feel tears coming on, I don't know where they come from, I only know I can't stop them.

"A gift," he says. He expertly changes her diaper, wraps her in a short-sleeved onesie. "Guess what time it is?" he croons. "It's bedtime." He picks her up, rubs her back with his hand. She reaches out toward me, she touches my face, a tiny hand on a tiny tear. He carries her toward the crib, and she opens her mouth, waits, and then lets out a howl.

"That's right, cry it out. Just don't do it for too long," he says. He tucks her gently under a blanket, and lays another across her middle. She flips herself at an angle. "She does this thing where she turns herself completely around at night. Like she starts off with her head at one end, and then when we come in, in the morning, her head is at the other end. I don't know how she does it—" He has turned and sees my face now.

"Oh, honey, no." He hugs me. "Are you okay?"

"I wanted this too, you know," I say. "I thought I was going to have this. A life." I feel like you should be mine, that's what I'm thinking, but I could never say it out loud.

Nina howls, fists in the air.

"I wish I could help you," he says. He lets me go. "I don't know what to do. I—we just thought inviting you out, getting you out of the house, it would help. I didn't mean to upset you. We're not rubbing our lives in your face. Not that there's anything wrong with your life."

"Not that there's anything wrong with my life. Right," I say.

"Cut it out," he says. He puts his hands on my shoulders.

I move my hands up to his, and I hold them, and pull them off my shoulders. I don't let go. And then I don't even know I'm doing it—I'm not numb, it's more that I'm not in control—but I do it, I move his hands up to my breasts. He keeps them there, for just a second, maybe he's not in control, too, but then he drops them, and backs away. A ripe stain of red covers me, inside and out.

"Jarvis, no." He shakes his head.

"I'm sorry. I just feel close to you. I don't know what I'm doing. I don't know how to be anymore." I'm mortified.

Elizabeth pokes her head around the door. "I was going to make more coffee. Do you want any?" She's still a little drunk and her cheeks are pink. She looks Scotty in the eye, and he looks right back, and I watch them exchanging information without saying a thing, the way you do when someone is your partner—oh, I *ache* for that—and I know it is time for me to leave, and never come back.

THE STREETS ARE full of partially dressed kids—short skirts, thin T-shirts—smoking, drunk, stumbling. Everyone is sweating, that end-of-summer sheen. I can see them glistening. Bedford is the worst. Bedford is packed. Where are they all going? Where have they been?

I stop at the Polish liquor store. I buy an expensive bottle of chardonnay, already chilled. I'm going to tie one on. Tight.

I am horrified at myself. I didn't realize that the sum of my parts equaled this person. I thought there was enough good in me to combat the bad, but now I can see that's not true. I don't want to give up the battle to be alive and whole, but I'm not sure if I deserve it right now, deserve that life.

I push through the crowds. I turn off Bedford onto Eighth, down to where it's quieter, though I can still hear the buzz behind me. Past a group of smokers, huddling outside a pub, past a kid with a skateboard trying to sweet-talk a girl, past a large man in a sweat-stained knit shirt talking on a cell phone in Russian, loud and excited; past all that, up ahead, I see a glow of light.

Maybe it's some sort of divine intervention, I think. I snort. Like anyone divine is paying attention to me.

The lights become tips of candles as I get closer, the candles are held by huddled people. They're standing in front of my building, to the side of the front door. Some of them are holding signs. Now *this* is a happening, I think. I look up at the signs, and I see the same thing on all of them: there are photos of Martin, and he's sitting up, holding the yellow cat, and he's smiling. There are words on the signs, angry words about life and death, but they don't form sentences in my head, they just float around Martin's heads, all of them, until finally I feel my legs and arms release, and all I see is dark.

27.

I wake with a deadening thump in my head, and a sharp line of pain in my back, and then I remember the protesters outside my building. My heart seizes and releases, and the push of adrenaline forces me upright. The room I'm in looks a bit like my living room—it's the same shape, and there's the crumbling industrial ceiling and the high windows facing the empty lot across the street—but it's somehow different. There are a dozen hanging plants, and a thick, furry rug, and a pale, pink, patterned couch that looks about thirty years old. And then there's the futon I'm sitting on, the frame handmade, I'm guessing. The wooden slats are uneven. I rub my back. It had poked me as I slept, I suppose. And then there's the noise, filtering in from the street below. I realize I'm in my own building, but about three or four floors down from my apartment.

Alison walks in from the other room, wearing only a long T-shirt that says "Ladyfest East 2000" on it. She's holding a mug, the paper end of a tea bag hanging over the edge. She sits down on the couch, pulls her legs up underneath her, the shirt bunching up at her upper thighs. She bends her knees, stretches the shirt down over them, and she suddenly looks young to me, with her dreadlocks split into two pigtails, and her toes wiggling. She asks me how I'm feeling, and her voice is tender, and concerned. I know I should probably join her on the couch, but I'm a little scared in new territory.

"My head hurts a little," I say. "Did I bump it?"

"I don't know. Oh shit, I should have checked for a concussion. I just thought you needed to sleep it off. I found you outside when I was coming home. All these freaky protesters were standing around trying to decide what to do. I started yelling at them, 'You don't leave a woman lying on the street.' Fucking freaks." She pulls a cigarette from a pack lying on a small glass side table and lights it. "Like, seriously dude? I don't know what you did, but unless you killed someone or something, no one deserves that."

"They think I'm a murderer," I say. "Or a murderer in training anyway."

I tell Alison about Martin. She widens her eyes, she nods, she smokes. I'm out of her frame of reference, I think. But then she says, "How many crosses does one person need to bear? They really need to leave you alone." Sympathy is as good as understanding.

I thank her. I join her on the couch, the futon creaking as I rise. She offers me a sip of her tea. I tell her I'd prefer a cigarette right about now. She takes one from the pack, lights it for me, hands it to me.

"So what are you going to do?"

I feel myself spiraling into something dangerous for a moment. I could just go back to my apartment and get under those covers and hide myself for the next six years, the next twenty years, hide myself until I die or Martin dies; whoever goes first, wins. But that's not the answer Alison is looking for, and I am energized by her boldness, and her comfort with herself.

"Proceed as planned." The words click out of my mouth. No stay for this execution.

I get up, I walk to the window, and look downstairs, one flight. The protesters are still visible in the dark, huddled near the front entryway, and people pass them on the street without a second glance. Across the street, a man, backpack dropped between his legs, shoots them with a digital camera. He laughs as he clicks; the flash is on repeat. "Excellent," he says. "Beautiful."

"Is that legal? For them to be there?" I say.

"It's not legal if they hurt you," she says.

"No, I think I just passed out," I say. I rub my head, search for the bump. "I hope I don't have a concussion."

"Let me check," she says. "I think it's something with the pupils. If they're big, you're in trouble. Come here, closer to the light." She taps the couch.

I sit next to her. She moves closer to me, so close I can feel her breath on me, and I can smell her, too, and she smells like cigarettes and some sort of honey scent, and I can see the way her lashes curl up at the ends naturally, and how her eyebrows are so light they're almost invisible, and that there are a few gray hairs mixed in with the blond hairs at her temples.

"You're fine," she says. "If your head still hurts tomorrow, you should seriously go to a doctor, though." She gently pats my cheek, and I jerk back.

"Are you okay?"

"I'm fine. Sorry. It's just that I—you know, I really am straight."

Her mouth opens, and her nostrils flash me, and then she starts to laugh, loud. I have to admire the beauty of it, the way it fills the apartment, even as I realize I am about to be embarrassed in a new and terrifying way.

"Oh honey, you are so not my type." She flops back and starts laughing again, until she starts to hold her stomach. "That's rich." She sits up, pulls out another cigarette, and continues to laugh. She has to light several matches before she can successfully ignite her cigarette, the breath from her mouth extinguishing each successive flame. She looks at me, shakes her head, then considers me one more time before she speaks. I think she's deciding how much shit she's going to give me.

"I like girls who like girls," she says. "Not girls who are slumming until they find a husband. Not girls who are experimenting, who saw some fucking porn movie once and think we all have bikini waxes and do each other with strap-ons. And definitely not girls who are just looking for attention. Which I think is your category. You're one of those girls who just needs to be loved. It probably works most of the time, right? Guys fall for you like that." She snaps her fingers. "Nice legs, pretty face, those *cheekbones*." The way she says "cheekbones" rips a small hole in my belly. "You come off smart, quick on your feet. But still kind of fragile, or, what's the word—malleable? You want to know how people are looking at you, you want them to know you can be what they want you to be."

"I'm not some sort of shape-shifter," I spit. "I'm a whole person. I'm real."

"Right. And yet you were about two seconds away from making out with me, even though you're straight as six o'clock."

I blush.

"We all need love. Don't hate yourself. I don't hate you."

"I'm just really lonely," I say. "And I wasn't going to make out with you."

She starts to feel bad, I can tell. "I'm sorry. It's hard being single in New York," she says.

"At least you're single," I say. "I'm in nowhere land. I can't have my old life back, but I can't move forward, either. I'm trapped."

Alison takes a drag of her cigarette, fiddles with a pigtail, regards me with calm eyes. I wonder if she's looking at my cheekbones.

"Right now I'm even trapped in my own home." A final plea. I didn't need her to love me; I just wanted her to like me.

"You're going to be okay," she says. Softer, at last. She starts to tell me all of the dumb things she's done because of love. It's easier because she doesn't know me. She tells me about loans she gave that were never repaid, and times she was crueler than she intended because she didn't know how else to communicate her pain, and how many songs she had written that had never been heard by their intended ears, because no one ever comes to her shows, at least not the right people. And this part she says with such weight, I can only imagine how heavy her heart must feel inside of her right now.

"I will come to your shows," I say. "And you don't even have to write a song about me."

"Don't worry, I won't, breeder."

"I don't need to be a part of anyone's art again," I say, but of course that can't be true, can it? If I'm not a part of someone's art, who am I?

28.

In the morning there are bruises and a headache, and when I look outside my window, there are protesters, maybe a handful more than the day before. No candles, but still, those horrible signs. A gauntlet of humanity.

I shower, fingering the bruises as I wash. I look through my closet, hoping to find some armor. I decide to dress all in white, white T-shirt, white pants, white flip-flops. I'll seal myself with innocence.

I call Missy. I know it's early, I know it's her day off. "But I really need a ride from a friend," I say. And she says, "Well, you called the right number then, girl."

As I sit and wait, dressed in white, a snake of anxiety slides through my body. I am going to have to stand up and fight for something I never wanted to fight for in the first place. A fight for death.

. . .

DOWNSTAIRS, AT THE front door, I stand, my head tilted to the side, and stare at the protesters, and they stare back, all the while yelling at me. They're mostly middle-aged, mainly women, with a few spitting men. All of the women could be someone's mother, they have that look about them: tidy, tailored, not an insane hair out of place. Some of them are even wearing suits. "Dress pretty for the protest, ladies," I can almost hear someone instructing them. The men are attired like elementary school teachers during first period, button-down shirts without creases or wrinkles, neat khakis, comfortable loafers. I imagine by the end of the day they'll be a rumpled mess, though. Their eyes are all so fierce and focused; they have the squint of a commander, his eyes pressed into the periscope, a Russian submarine approaching.

Why do they have to yell? They're not cursing, though they might as well be. I'm a killer, they're telling me. I have to admire them for their firm belief in something. They know exactly what's right for them, and they are unwavering in their principles. I wish I could say the same for myself. Still, I have to hate them. They're trying to control me.

I hear a honk and I see Missy across the street. Her mouth is hanging open, her eyes are wide.

You are a submarine, I think. *Now act like one.*

I push open the door, and try to pass them, and their voices push together in a chorus. A sea of Martin posters bounces furiously; his high tide.

"You don't even know me," I say to them. "So why don't you just leave me alone?"

"We know exactly who you are," says one man. He has pink stripes in his crisp shirt, but the gentility ends there. I see a glint of gray in his blue eyes, and his skin is an unhealthy yellow. He steps forward from the crowd and leans in close to me. There's a line of unhinged stubble around his chin. "Life is not a game, young lady. It is not yours to give and take away."

The snake recoils inside of me. I can feel his tongue preparing to strike, ill-advised, but then Missy honks again, and I rush past him toward her car.

"What the eff is going on here?" says Missy as I jump into her backseat. Mira's in the front seat, and Missy's got one hand over her eyes.

"Just go," I say.

"Are you okay?" she says.

"I'm all right. I think I hit my head on a Christian last night, though," I say.

She curses under her breath. "Ain't no Christians I know that act like that," says Missy. She pulls her hand from Mira and drives away.

"It's his parents. Martin's parents don't want me to do what I"— I look at Mira, who has turned to stare at the protesters— "what I was planning to do. And instead of taking it up with me directly, they pretended they would go along." I feel a burn of anger, as if someone had lit a match to a trail of gasoline. "And now they've ambushed me." I slap my hand against the window. "No respect," I yell. And then, quieter, "Sorry." I don't want to scare anyone.

"Mira, sit back in your seat right now."

"It's not nice to stare at crazy people," I say. I keep my hand flat against the window, steady myself. "His parents have been

here for a week. I'm going to try and find them at the home.
They've been going in the mornings."

"Did you call the cops?"

"I haven't done anything yet. I don't know what kind of situation I'm in here. I mean, who are these people? Where do they come from? I don't even know them, but they think they can tell me what to do. Or what not to do."

"It's disgraceful," says Missy. She's driving quickly. "This is a private matter that they're making public. And this is *our* neighborhood, not theirs. They can't just bring their crazy-ass signs wherever they want." She is quiet and then she slams her hands on the steering wheel. "There are children in this neighborhood."

"I really am sorry," I say, and I am sad and soft. It's my fault.

"Don't you apologize. Don't you apologize for a damn thing. I don't ever want to hear you being sorry for this." She cruises through a yellow light. The streets are empty this early. She drives with authority. She owns the roads. "You did not make this happen." She wraps her headset around her ear and takes her cell phone from where it rests on the front seat, flips it open, and hands it to Mira. "Dial your cousin Freddy for me, baby, okay?"

Mira scrolls slowly through the phone. "Can I play Ms. Pac Man on it when you're done?" she says. "Please."

"Later," says Missy.

She hands her the phone, and as soon as there is a "Yo" on the other end, Missy begins to speak rapidly in Spanish, and does not stop, even after we arrive, except to tell me, "We'll be here when you get back. And remember: no apologies."

I have so many other things I have to apologize for, I want to tell her. But now is not the time.

. . .

THE NURSING HOME is getting blurrier: the nurse, the bingo game in the cafeteria, the smells, the colors, like a film in fast-forward. Flecks of light and motion, but nothing is clear except my feet, my legs, my arms, propelling me forward. I take two stairs at a time up to Martin's ward. I am a speed demon. No, not a demon.

When I hit the photos, I stop. The old woman in the glorious blue nightgown is standing there, staring at the vision of old New York. She sees me and says, "You. You know me."

"I don't," I say.

"These are my photos."

"You're Sylvie Porter," I say.

"See? You know me."

"I guess I do," I say.

I have to give respect to the artist. I stand with her, and we look at the photos. The cat is glowing a bright yellow. It's impossible, but I feel heat from them.

"That cat," I say.

"You know the cat, too," she says.

"What about it? What do I know?"

"I can't explain it. He just . . ." She waves her hand. "Appeared."

"In the photos?" I say.

"No. I don't know. I can't remember things sometimes. My head." She knocks a fist against her head. "I think he was there that day. Sometimes I think he was, sometimes I think he wasn't. But he's here now, anyway. And there's nothing we can do about it."

A chubby nurse comes running up through the stairwell.

"There you are," she says. "She's a crafty one," she says to me. "But I always know where to find you. Here with your photographs." She puts an arm around Sylvie. "Always trying to hide when you have to take your medication. Don't you know we're just trying to help you?"

"You don't know me," she hisses, but she doesn't put up a fight. They walk off together, off to a far-off ward of insane people. I've got some religious zealots back at my place you can take, too, I think.

I continue down the hall, and I can see Martin's door is open. I wonder if they're up to more tricks. I see Vaz, and she makes a move toward me, swiftly.

"I don't think you want to go in there."

"I can go wherever I like," I say. "I'm paying the bills around here." I push past her, and move to the doorway. Inside, Calvin and Meryl have their heads down. They're holding hands with a suited man who has slick dark hair and an older man who looks like a minister. It looks like they found their own armor this morning.

Calvin notices me first.

"Jarvis." He nods at me. "You're welcome to come pray with us." His eyes are full of tears, and when Meryl looks up, I can see she's been crying, too.

"I'll pass, thank you," I say.

They slowly drop their hands.

"This is Martin's wife."

I look at Martin. His bed has been put at an angle again, and he's sitting up, eyes open, glazed over. There is nothing there. He can't hear your prayers. Don't you know that?

"I'm Representative Bill Lincoln," says the man in the suit. He really does have a fine head of hair. "No relation," he says.

"To whom?" I say. I slit my eyes at him.

"I'm Reverend Lament," says the older man, but he makes no move toward me.

"I would like to talk to my in-laws for a moment," I say. "Privately."

"This is a matter that involves all of us," says Reverend Lament. "We are all concerned when it comes to Martin's life." He has a voice like a car hitting gravel on an old country road. And ordinarily I would like to listen to that voice, and I would even want to consider his words, but he's so incredibly wrong that I can barely contain myself.

"But you don't—you didn't even know him," I say desperately. "Please help me out here. Just . . . let us talk for a moment. Come on, Calvin."

I look at both of them, I turn, I meet their eyes, and I can see that underneath whatever spiritual haze they've worked themselves into—or have been worked into—they want to talk to me, they want to work it out. They know what's right. I know they do.

But then the politician starts talking quickly, something about a lawsuit, and the preacher starts preaching, and then Meryl and Calvin retreat from me. They've gone too far. Wheels. Motion.

And so I start to yell, because I don't know what else to do.

EVENTUALLY WE ARE all ejected from the home. There are security guards I never knew existed, I am humiliated to discover. But we cannot stop yelling, none of us, except for Meryl, who is silent and staring. Her hands fly up once to cover her ears. By the end we are speaking in our own personal tongues. As we walk to the parking lot, the preacher says to me, "This isn't over, Jarvis. But don't worry. I'll be praying for you."

Missy honks her horn.

I get in the car. "Get me the"—I look at Mira—"get me the *eff* out of here."

We drive in complete silence all the way home, except for the sound of Mira's video game on the cell phone. She occasionally howls when she loses. Once she says, "Oh darn it."

Missy drives slowly. That's fine by me. I'm dreading another walk of shame. We do a loop around McCarren Park. I see the farmers' market and think of Scott and his family, searching for the elusive red, ripe tomatoes. Searching for perfection.

Missy's phone rings and she talks for a minute, then snaps it closed.

"Let's get you home," she says. She turns down Wythe Street, and the blocks click off. I can feel the snake sliding around inside of me. The car slides up next to my building. There's not a protester in sight, but there's Freddy on the corner, smoking a cigarette with two other men. They all raise their thick arms together and puff in unison, as if they had choreographed it.

"What happened?" I said.

"We just couldn't have that going on in our neighborhood," says Missy. "And that's all you need to know."

"You know what? You're absolutely right. I don't want to know," I say.

I reach out from behind the seat and squeeze her shoulders. I thank her. I tell her I love her. I tell her that she's my hero, too.

29.

I sleep for a day. Even though it's quiet on the streets beneath my house, I'm still afraid to face the world. So much unfinished business.

Under the sheets, I dream of Sylvie Porter. She's dressed as I was the other day, all white, a white T-shirt and pants, but she's barefoot. Her long white hair is all around her shoulders. The yellow cat is with her, sitting on her lap, and she's stroking him. It seems like she's looking at me through my dream, staring me in the eyes. I have a feeling of great comfort. The snake that's been terrorizing me has disappeared from my body. Finally, she speaks. "It's only art," she says, and I wake up, laughing.

I throw off the covers and lie for the moment. I am trying to figure out what this is all about. I am trying to understand.

I get up from bed, and go to Martin's studio and start pulling out paintings. I spread the series he did of his parents against one wall. They're chilling, and they make me sad. So many icons that hold so much weight for them, but in Martin's vision, they're rendered meaningless, simply accessories.

I pull out the paintings of me and Davis and Alice as angels, and spread them against the wall on the other side of the room. We are about as young and powerful as we can be in these paintings. We were his fiercest allies and lovers. These paintings are love notes to us.

I reveal one more. Two strippers from Sheepshead Tavern, leaning into each other over a bar, arms intertwined, feeding each other the straws from their drinks. Their breasts encased in cheap bathing suits, small and high and firm.

And now I study an NYU student, legs crossed, a notebook in front of her, sitting amidst the garbage of Washington Square Park. She is smiling at an imaginary camera. The perfect picture of youth.

There are hundreds more. I could make Davis give them all back to me. I could surround myself with his art, but isn't that what I've been doing already? For *years*?

I loved him for his art. I loved being a part of it. But when I break it down, when I break him down, who was he besides an artist? And who was I to him? Nothing more than a part of a palette. That's not how I felt when he was alive, but that's how I'm starting to feel. Enough. It's unfair to the memory of our marriage. And I deserve more. This must end. Soon.

30.

It's laundry day. My three men, the ones who started all of this for me, are probably never coming back, but I decide to walk over there anyway. I'm carrying a small bag of clothes, the white clothes I soiled with nervous energy just a few days before. I want to wear them again, though. I want to protect myself in white.

The large pink crane near Bedford is still folded, inactive, waiting for the word to go. A few "Sold" signs spot some smaller buildings nearby. This whole neighborhood is being bought and sold every day. Everything is up for grabs now.

An ice cream truck rings the same sickly sweet song over and over again.

A tall slender boy in a striped Charlie Brown T-shirt skateboards by me in the bike lane, and a short girl in cutoff jeans plugs along behind, trying to catch up to him. I almost stick my foot out to trip him. How do you compete with six more inches of leg? The odds are stacked against her.

I toss my bag around in my hands as I walk. This feels like my neighborhood. This *is* my neighborhood, as much as it is theirs.

I feel loose and easy. It could be temporary, this feeling. I accept that. It's all subject to change at any moment. The variables—about two dozen well-funded religious fanatics—are not in my favor. But I'm learning to enjoy a good mood when I can take it. I think I'm almost jaunty. I feel like I have wings, like I could fly over Williamsburg and see all the beautiful young people, with their expensive clothes and lifestyles, and the Hassids hiding behind their robes, and the Polish girls with their long blond hair and thick accents, and the Puerto Rican families, boisterous and tightly linked, and the artists, the old loyalists just stretching their arms, getting ready for a day in their studios—this gorgeous mix of people, who, unlike the buildings around them, are not for sale.

I breathe it in. This is my neighborhood.

I stop for an iced coffee at a café on Bedford. There are beautiful sweets under a glass counter, tiny cupcakes with thick chocolate swirls on the frosting, and tarts, the fruit glazed and juicy, shining, and cups of chocolate mousse topped with fresh white whipped cream.

"Can I have"—I point eagerly—"one of those, and one of those, and one of those?" One for each of my kept men.

NO MAL AT the laundromat. No Scotty either. I'm not surprised, though I was hoping my offerings of love would somehow conjure them up for me. But there's Tony's bag. He's probably in back again. What does he do back there all the time? Pando must have some really good weed. Maybe I need some.

I giddily drop my bag and the sweets and slide back across the laundromat's slippery, gleaming floor. The machines whirl in the same direction. Whites, colors, denim. Sheets and pillow covers. Beach towels. Tank tops and shorts. Socks. Panties. An unending cartwheel.

I enter into another world at the end of the washers and driers, like Lucy looking for Tumnus. I pass the extra laundry carts, and a laundry-detergent vending machine, buckets of cleaning supplies, and a bunch of tennis shoes lying lazily on the floor. It's dusty and dark back here, so unlike the front of the store, which reeks of newness. I hit the industrial double doors and push—hard, they're heavy—and peek through.

"Tony? Are you here?" There are boxes everywhere, and not much else. I see an office at the rear, the door slightly ajar, a slice of dim light. I wonder if I'm going to bust in on their drug deal. What if they knife me? How exciting! I'm willing to take that risk. I walk to the door and push it wide open.

I see the back of Tony first, his dark hair mussed just so, a nicely tailored cotton shirt, and . . . no pants. Pando is facing me, on his knees, sucking off Tony. I start to laugh, I can't help myself. And then I clap my hand over my mouth. Of course it's not funny. Except that it's hilarious. Pando opens his eyes, and they widen, and he starts to choke a bit. Ah, I've thown him off.

"I'm so sorry," I say. "Oh God." I close the door, and stand there for a moment, mouth open, and I check myself. *Am* I surprised? I walk back through the weird jungle terrain of the laundromat. I'm still laughing. I can't decide if this is an appropriate response, but I don't know what one would be. I start to pack up my bag, but then I decide to stay. This'll be good. And it will be so nice to witness someone else's discomfort right now.

A few minutes later, Tony surfaces, sans Pando, and slaps himself down on the couch across from me. The music changes from techno to some sort of creaky industrial noise, and then finally some salsa music.

"Salsa, huh? He likes his Latin lovers." I try so hard not to laugh, but here it comes again.

"Shut up," he says. His tan skin is glowing, that fresh blowjob glow. That's why he's always looked so sexy.

"You got some 'splainin' to do, Tony."

"Well, you got some 'splainin' yourself." He stretches his arms out across the back of the couch, taps his feet, his legs follow. "I'm not the only one who's been fucking around, Mrs. Miller."

A sting on my cheeks. It's pink, I just know it.

He leans forward, close to me. "You know he left his wife, right?"

"Where did he go?"

Is he waiting for me at home right now?

"He left her for his agent. She got him a book deal, and then he moved in with her. He finally got his apartment in the city."

I'm stunned, and then I'm not. He was the sneakiest of all, now I know.

"A book deal for what?" I say. "He's never even written anything."

"Looks like he was ready to talk about his dad." Tony looks around, then leans forward, raises his eyebrows, and whispers, "He said he got six figures." He settles back into his seat and raises his hands in the air. "And now, his marriage is over." He slaps his palms to his legs.

"And what about yours?"

"Me? What, you think I'm going to leave my wife for Pando?" He turns toward the front counter, and I look, too. Pando's staring intently at the *New York Post*. "He just loves Page Six, that kid," says Tony. "No, I ain't going anywhere. I love my wife. I mean, it's rough, she works all the time. End of the night, you think she has any time for me? I listen to all her bullshit, but what about my *Law and Order* audition, you think she wants to hear about that?"

"I can see how that might be a problem," I say.

"Who knows? Maybe my time's running out."

"Enjoy it while it lasts. Enjoy everything while it lasts."

"Exactly." He sits back again, a satisfied smile on his face. Who am I to begrudge a little satisfaction?

I hand him the bag of treats and then head to a washing machine. I dump in my whites. Hot water, as hot as it can go.

When I return, Tony has already torn through the cupcake and is devouring the fruit tart. He calls Pando over, hands him the chocolate mousse. Pando sits down with his newspaper and elegantly scoops the mousse into his mouth. I sip my coffee. We sit like that, contentedly.

AFTER MY LAUNDRY is done—delicate dry—and after I have given Tony a huge hug, and Pando a peck on the check, I walk to the door.

"So what are you going to do, Jarvis?" says Tony.

"Funny. Everyone keeps asking me that," I say.

"Well, you know—make a move," he says.

"I will," I say. I put a hand on the door and it pulls open behind me. It's Scotty, breathless, childless.

He pulls me outside, into the intersection of the raging sun and humidity. He starts to speak, but I stop him. "I'm so glad you're here," I say. "I wanted to talk to you."

I touch his shoulders, and then I drop my hands. I remember I'm not allowed to touch. "I'm so sorry for everything."

"Oh, it's fine. I mean, my wife hates you, but it's fine. We decided you probably should get some counseling or something. You know, later."

"I just feel so terrible," I say.

"I understand, it's fine," he says. Spits it out of his mouth. He must really hate me. I must have really messed this one up.

"But look," he says, "there's no way you've seen the news in the last hour, have you?"

31.

I run through the streets, and I know I look like a madwoman. No one runs through the streets of Williamsburg: they stroll. But there's no time for that now. Because there they are, just as Scotty told me. A hundred protesters. A news crew. And Martin's parents, the priest, and the politician. Like a bad joke. Two grieving parents, a priest, and a politician walk into a bar.

A reporter has his microphone out, and Bill Lincoln, standing erect, this time in a somber gray suit, is sweeping his hand toward the sky. Next to him, the reverend nods. And then there's Calvin and Meryl, poor Calvin and Meryl, standing there, the hints of grimaces on their faces. (I notice Meryl is wearing the worst lipstick ever and another one of her goddamn vests. If we still speak to each other when we're through this, I'm taking her shopping.)

The posters of Martin are waving strong again, held by people of all different ages, though mostly white. There's a group on the corner praying by a mass of candles. I hear some chanting, some cheering. Bill Lincoln leans in closer to the microphone. The preacher clasps his hands and closes his eyes, bends his head down.

Scotty and Tony are suddenly next to me.

"Holy crap," says Tony.

Several protesters are holding signs that say "Death Without Dignity," and the words are circled in red, and there is a slash through them. I zone in on that, the word "Dignity" battering upside my head. They are wearing all white, these protesters, and I think: You are pretending. *You are pretending.* I narrow my eyes and my jaw stiffens. Inside, deep inside of me, a pot of water boils at a million degrees.

"Dignity. They don't know anything about dignity," I say. My voice is already hoarse even though I haven't even started screaming yet, but soon I will be. I will scream.

"You should go home," says Scotty. He puts his arm around me. "You don't need to see this."

"I can't go home," I say, and that's it, my voice is levels higher and louder than usual. I wave my hands at the mess of people blocking my front door. "I can't get in my building."

My arms and legs feel like puppet limbs, easily collapsible. And yet my spine is erect with anger.

"Where do I go?"

I look at Meryl and Calvin across the mess of people and noise, and they look back at me. I put my hands in a plea toward them. I just can't imagine this is what they wanted. But I get nothing back from them, they squint, they turn away, and it's as if I were never there. They've deadened themselves to me.

The politician says something loudly, and the whole crowd roars. Members of what looks to be a boy's choir, dressed in matching dark suits, arrange themselves on the sidewalk, right where Alison should be strumming her guitar. This isn't a fucking party, I want to tell them. This is my life.

"Calvin!" I'm screaming. "Meryl!" These are proud people, who lead good, solid, private lives. "Don't you want to go home?" I want to say to them. I don't feel like begging anymore, though. They've been lying to me for weeks. I hadn't thought they would be capable of betrayal, these people who claim to lead such pure lives. But I can't be angry with them, I cannot be angry at someone who loves the same as I do. I want them to put an end to this, though. Right now. Only they can stop it, if it can be stopped at all.

And then I hear, "Darling, this is a fine mess you've got going on here." It's Davis. He's sweating, he must have been running, too. He is wearing the dumbest hat ever, a mesh trucker hat with a bikini-clad girl, nipples protruding fiercely through her pink polka-dot top, printed across it, and it's just ridiculous, a man his age, when is he going to grow up already? And it makes me laugh, only I realize it's coming out like a howl. I grab him and he holds me. I could cry, but I'm pissed off, too, so instead I just feel something recoil and coil inside me, the sensation that something is about to explode. I have become the incendiary device.

"Martin sure as shit wouldn't have wanted this," says Davis. He takes one step forward, pauses, but just for a second—Davis is always certain of what he's doing, even if he knows it's wrong. He grabs my hand and we walk toward the crowd. I look back. Scotty's uncertain, but Tony's in, he's game for anything, and he gives Scotty a shove in his back, and then quickly, they are with us, walking as a force toward the front door.

There's about half a block that's clear between us and the protesters and the media, the frenzied mess outside my front door; the air between us feels thick and muggy, pregnant with moisture, almost electric, and we push through it slowly. I hear Davis cursing under his breath. I wonder if he should take that hat off. It's not going to look nice on camera. Great. As if I weren't already a murderer, now I'm hanging out with white trash, too.

And then suddenly we're there, we're facing them, these young men and women, these old men and women; a few of them have red tape across their lips—Oh, how that red is glaring at me!—with "Life" written across it in black Magic Marker; and all of them are holding signs, some of them again with those awful pictures of my comatose husband tricked up to look alive, and many others with messages, some of hate, some of hope, though it all feels like hate to me.

Wife, do your job. Take care of your husband.

Put God first, not yourself.

Heaven for him, hell for you.

Then, I don't know who starts it—I feel like it could have been Davis, that he tried to push through first—but there is a thrust of shoulders and elbows, arms and fists everywhere, all around me, a swell of anger and heat and flesh.

Davis is in the thick of it, and so is Tony, and Scotty is next to me, his bulky arm around me, pushing me through to the door. "Don't turn around," he's saying. "Keep going, don't look back." There are so many arms, though, so many angry bodies, writhing planks in a wall, and we are moving so slowly, it seems like we won't get through.

Dark utterances of hate whispered in my ear.

Murderer, Sinner, Killer.

Tony is now in front of us, and then Davis, too. They push, we all push, against the wall. I feel a scratch of nails against my arm, a rip of blood pulses from my skin. I reach out and scratch back.

Davis and Tony are shoving so hard, and I hear Davis roaring a dangerous, wild noise, and a few people back off, I can see they're scared, they should be.

Davis's fist in someone's face.

I yell for Davis, he yells back. I can't see Tony, and suddenly he's back in view, calmly dispensing with some people, one body, then two, a few more, polite shoves, and Tony's saying something under his breath to them that seems to be working, and then we're at the doorway. I pull out my keys, and Scotty says, "You may want to hurry," and I drop them because I didn't realize it, but my whole body is shaking. Scotty bends and picks up the keys, and my hands are still shaking, and he says, "Just point," and I do, and he slides that key in so easily, I love him all over again. Tony and Davis are right behind us, we hustle ourselves in, and Scotty locks that door tight. Davis slams his hand up against the glass door, then turns up his middle finger at the crowd.

"Davis, enough!" I say.

We get in the elevator. Someone's missing a cat. Please recycle. A new piece of graffiti: a bright pink heart with a gun next to it.

Inside, in my apartment, where it's safe, the noise from the street below is still raging. The boys' choir commences something religious and they sound awful. Right-wingers have no soul.

I look at my friends, cut and bruised and bleeding. I rush to them with damp washcloths. While I rummage through a cabinet for antiseptic and bandages, they talk, still charged, shuffling like horses at the gate before a race. Davis introduces himself to the other two men, they all shake hands, and this makes me laugh. I hand them bandages, and Scotty points to my arm, to a deep scratch from a sharpened fingernail. I imagine it was a housewife from New Jersey, that it was the most exciting thing that had ever happened to her, and she needed to work some of her issues out on my arm.

I forgive you, I think. I just wish she would forgive me.

The phone rings and I pick it up. It's a reporter, he's calling for a quote. You want to know how I feel? How the fuck would you feel? I want to scream, but I don't. Instead I hang up the phone, and then take it off the hook. There is a recorded message, and then a buzzing noise, and then eventually it fades away.

I hear Davis say, "They got my hat."

They did you a favor, I think.

Sirens start to filter in through the window, and Scotty looks out. "It's clearing out down there," he says. "I'll head back in a bit."

"I'm sorry," I say, and I am. He's going to have to explain this somehow to his wife.

"I'm sorry for you," he says. He walks over to me and hugs me, but not for too long. "You're going to be safe up here now. But I don't know if I would leave for a while."

"I'll hang out with you, sweetheart," says Davis. "We'll get a pizza delivered. It'll be fun. A little slumber party."

I had fought through the outside world just to get back where I started, in this loft, surrounded by memories of Martin. Only this time, it was different. This time I wasn't alone. I don't know how I got here, but I wasn't alone anymore.

"For as long as you need," says Davis.

What I need could last forever. The trap of forever.

I walk to the window. The protesters are scuttling away, little dark beetles of doom and gloom. I spot a few journalists huddled around the front door, but a police officer walks over to them and they move away. I watch as Meryl and Calvin talk in a huddle with the preacher and the politician. This is what they wanted, I think. They wanted to terrify me so that I would go away, and they could have their precious empty body all to themselves. So they can fill him—fill it—with whatever they like, with whatever memories, whatever visions, whatever is left of themselves. I understand them completely.

I thank my friends, I embrace them, and then I pick up the phone.

32.

Missy meets me near the subway.

She tells me she drove by the protest before she picked me up. "It's sick," she says. "It is making me physically ill. Like I could pull this car over and hurl right now."

"Just take me to Martin," I say.

"Where's their dignity? Let a man die in peace."

"Missy, I'm as guilty as they are. I kept him alive for six years."

She starts to say something, and stops herself. She makes a humming noise. She turns on the radio. "Tell me who you are" blasts from it. "I can just about remember who I am."

I STOP AT the front desk. It's Linda M.

"Linda, may I ask you a question?"

"Sure, Mrs. Miller." She seems startled.

"What does the 'M' stand for?"

"The 'M'?"

I point to her nameplate. "I've always wondered."

"Macklin," she says.

"Ah. That's a nice name."

"I married into it," she says.

"Me too," I say.

I pat my hands quietly on the counter. I wish her well, and she does the same.

I start the long walk to Martin's room. Philo is standing at the tip of the entryway into the cafeteria. He's holding his hoe. Someone has tidied him up. His shirt is tucked in, his hair is combed, his belt is buckled. He's smiling.

"Having a good day, Philo?"

"My roses look great today. Real winners. You want to see?"

I start to say no, but I find myself unable to turn him down. It's nice to see him happy. I take his arm and we walk out the cafeteria door, to the garden. Indeed, the roses are in spirited form, high and proud, spiraling up toward the sun. Reds and pinks and oranges, some in full bloom, others still in buds.

"They're just lovely," I say. "You should be proud of yourself."

He looks shyly at me. "Thank you, young lady. It's what I do best."

"I can see that."

"What's your name?"

"Jarvis Miller," I say.

"Why are you here?"

"My husband is here."

He shakes his head. "Too young."

"I know," I say. "It's a shame."

"That's okay," he says cheerfully. "You can come visit me, too."

"I will," I say. "I will come by and say hello next time I'm here. I am always happy to look at your roses."

I take his arm again and walk him back inside. He tips an imaginary hat to me. I accept it. I accept his love.

As we enter the cafeteria, I see Vaz, decked out in her Mets jacket, arriving for her shift. I wave, and she stops. She asks me to join her for coffee, and I agree.

We sit quietly in a corner and sip sour-tasting coffee. She pulls off her jacket, stretches her arms. "It's been a nuthouse here," she says. "More than usual."

She tells me that reporters have been trailing through the hospital for the past few days. "And that creepy priest, and that politician. I don't like those men."

"Now they're all at my house," I say. "It's a big party."

Vaz looks down at her coffee, contemplates her fingers wrapped around it. Her fingernails are short and so clean they shine.

"I can't talk about this anymore," I say.

"There's been too much talking, you're right," she says.

"I need to go see my husband." I get up from the table. "Please don't disturb us."

THE PHOTOS JUST look like photos now. The cat is just a cat in a picture, the abnormal glow has disappeared.

It's just art, I think.

I PUSH THE door open, and there he is, sitting erect. The cat is there, too. He's purring. I lock the door. I know his parents will show up eventually, but I've got some time.

Lower the light, close the curtains. It's dark, but I can still see everything clearly. I release the back of the bed, and lower Martin down gently.

The cat readjusts himself, makes a cranky noise. I shush him.

I sit next to Martin and stroke his arm. I touch his face. There's stubble. They haven't been taking care of you like I do, I think. His eyes are wide open. I look deeply in there, waiting for some response. I still want to believe he's in there. But now, more than ever, I know he's not.

I think about the night we met, how he stayed until the bar was closed, long after Davis had left him there in the midst of all the music and cigarette smoke and drunks, how he had sat through all of that quietly at the bar, waiting for the moment he could walk me home to my squalid basement apartment (which he eyed so warily and sadly, already likely planning my rescue even then) and give me a gentle kiss goodnight on my cheek. He walked off smiling, my phone number scrawled in eyeliner on a cocktail napkin clutched in his hand.

I think about him, so strong and young, packing up my belongings into a double-parked borrowed van, hustling a heavy trunk up the stairs, sweating, and me touching his sweaty forehead and kissing him on his lips and cheek, and the taste of the sweat, and the taste of his lips, and me wanting to kiss him forever for the way he hefted that trunk into the van, and him stopping me and saying, "We'll be able to kiss as much as we want as soon as we get you home."

I think about the way he looked the last time I saw him awake. He was already on the ladder, and he was wearing a white T-shirt and an old pair of Levi's and black Converse tennis shoes because he preferred the classics. Because he was a classic man; when he was awake and alive, he was a classic. And the sunlight was thick around him, and he was happy, because he was busy, he had made a lot of progress that week, and on that day, I could tell he felt very full. He looked back over his shoulder, a paintbrush in his hand, and said, "Bring me back some good stories, baby."

He was the best thing I ever did with my life. But my life can't end here.

"Move over," I say to the cat, and he pads down to the end of the bed, near Martin's feet.

I need to sleep with my husband, one last time. I pull back the covers, and lay next to him. Pull the covers over us, pull him close. He's light, like a child. He's worn down to nothing. There's no strength left in his body. The cat purrs like thunder at the foot of the bed. Asteroids crash. Stars form and re-form. The sky is moving and changing and we don't even know it, although I know it, I know what's going on out there.

I close my eyes and sleep.

I DREAM OF nothing. It's a blank slate in there. Not empty. Just clear.

.   .   .

WHEN I WAKE, I am cold. But the air around me is warm. The cat is lying across the two of us. Watching me. Eyes wide open.

I am icy. But it's not me, it's not the air, it's not the cat. It's Martin. He's cold to the touch.

I stay there, calm, my arms wrapped around him, feeling my warmth beat against his chill, and then, at last, there's a knock at the door, and then two hands begin to pound. I take one last moment of quiet with my husband, until I have to let the outside in.

EPILOGUE

I put one foot down on the trail and the other one follows. Behind me, Alice is making noise about her Prada shoes, and the dirt, and the sting of cool air.

"I thought you grew up in the countryside," I say.

"Yes, and I left the countryside for a reason," she says.

Davis tells her to shut up, and she curses at him.

Tony grabs my arm and says, "Are you sure you want to do this?"

"Of course I do," I say. "This is what he would have wanted."

"No, I just meant, with *them*." He jerks his hand back.

"Yes, well, he would have wanted them here, too," I say. "I didn't make the rules, I'm just enforcing them." I kick a stone and watch it tumble down the trail.

. . .

MARTIN'S MEMORIAL SERVICE was six weeks ago at the Swiss Institute in SoHo. Artists flew in from all over the world, there were hundreds of people there. I let Davis and Alice pick a few of their favorite paintings to hang, and then I selected the rest: the angel paintings of the three of us, the paintings of Martin's parents, and—just to prove to myself that I had forgiven him—a handful of stripper paintings, including one of Bartlett, sitting in the back of the bar, quietly smoking a cigarette, while the red glare of the stage beckons him.

Martin's father came. Meryl stayed at home in Seattle. "She's not been well," he told me, and I didn't pursue it, simply told him to send my regards.

THE LAST TIME I saw them was in Martin's room at the Beverly Home, minutes after I woke up next to Martin's corpse. I had heard the knock at the door, I had counted under my breath to sixty—*one minute, just one more minute with my husband*—and then I rose from the bed and walked to the door. I put my hand on the door, and I could feel them through the door, Martin's parents, feel their worry, feel their pain, little rivulets winding their way through the wood from their chests to my fingertips. I slid my hand to the doorknob. I heard Vaz say, "I'm coming, I'm coming," and then there was a rustle of keys. "Hold on," she said. "I'm finding it." But I knew she was taking her time— she had every key to every door memorized—and I expressed some sort of noise, something like a laugh, and I know it wasn't funny, none of it, but I just needed to laugh for a second. I was just testing to make sure I was going to be okay. And I was.

I took a step back and opened the door, and then I took another step back to let Meryl and Calvin into the room. I thought I had left lots of room for them, but looking back, I don't think my limbs were working correctly; I know my arms were all calm and loose down the sides of my body.

"Move," said Meryl, and then Calvin put his hands on my shoulders—he was strong, just as Martin used to be—and he shifted me over, easily, just pushed me aside. And I would have moved, but I appreciated the help.

Meryl was at the bed already, her arms wrapped around him. "Oh Martin, oh my baby," she said, and there were chokes of air.

Just breathe, I thought. *It's going to be all right.*

Calvin stood behind her and reached out to her back, and shoulders, and hair, and it was gentle, he was supporting her. He did not cry. The Miller men, stoic till the end.

"He just died," I said, and it was true. I had done nothing, but let him go inside of me. "He was ready," I said. "We held on too long."

Meryl turned and looked at me over her shoulder. Her eyes were narrowed, and massive tears pushed through the corners. I knew she didn't care what I said, she only cared that her son was dead. It had been so long since we had all been in the same room alone together, I had forgotten something very simple: that he was their child. I could only hope that they would someday remember that I was his wife.

"That's enough, Jarvis," said Calvin sharply.

And he was right, of course. The time to make a point was past. There was no argument left to win.

Then I left them there, Meryl moaning and stroking Martin's head, Calvin gripping her, whispering in her ear. I left them there, to mourn their child.

And after the nurses and the doctors and the preachers and the politicians and the lawyers and the reporters came and went from his room, and from our lives, all that was left was a piece of paper that said "Died of natural causes"—evidence that Martin had somehow made his own choice. And while I was already well on my way, that piece of paper, I believed, was what Calvin and Meryl needed to move on.

I WATCHED CALVIN walk around the room, looking at his son's work, stopping and nodding in front of the paintings of him and his wife. One by one, Martin's friends walked up to him and told him how much they had loved his son. How much he had influenced and inspired them. How sad they were that he was gone. Even though I had assumed they had let him go a long time ago, it seems as if there were more people than just me who were still hanging on to his memory. Not like me, not so it took over their lives as it did mine, but still he had haunted them in small ways, the loss of their friend and his talent. Maybe just the thought of him wasting away in that room.

Calvin came over to me, the remnants of tears on his cheeks, and said, "I didn't know he knew so many people. I just met someone from Berlin, and another gentleman from Zurich. They flew in just for this."

"Yes," I said. "He was loved."

Calvin whispered a quiet apology in my ear for the things that were said and done. "I was torn," he said. "I felt a great divide within me, but I had to go with what I knew to be right."

"You were right," I said. "And so was I."

I touched the side of his arms lightly with my hands until we found ourselves in an embrace. It wasn't like hugging Martin, but it was enough for me.

THERE ARE BRIGHT yellow flowers in great bunches everywhere, dotting the trail, and off in the distance near the hummocks, a skyline of yellow lining the highest points in view. There are tiny purple flowers, too, and thistles, mixed in with the brown earth near our feet. I take care not to crush them, these brand-new lives. And then there are hunks of rocks, covered with moss in leaf formations, the outlines of what once was, and what will be. The air is dry and cool, and the sky is a rich turquoise, mixed with pregnant humps of perfect, white clouds.

We round a corner and there's the mountain, our first clear view. It's dark brown and blue and perfectly sedate. The clouds and sky form a magnificent backdrop: the colors, together, in their purest form.

"I read in the paper this morning that there's been some activity in the mountain," says Davis. He's excited by it. He's always loved explosions.

"Oh, that's just brilliant," says Alice. "If we die, I'm going to kill you, Jarvis."

I readjust my backpack, heavy with the canister. Tony offers to carry it, but I decline.

"We're not going to die," I say.

. . .

I GAVE ALICE and Davis the paintings of themselves that night.
And the next day I shipped the paintings of Martin's parents to
their home in Seattle. Calvin and Meryl promptly put most of
the paintings up for sale—I imagine they have one or two hanging in their living room, though they'll never really understand
them—and with the proceeds contributed to a new wing for
their church, a day school for religious education, which they
named after Martin.

When I heard that, I started selling some of my own: every
painting in the NYU series, and every Sheepshead Tavern
painting, and a few others I found suspect, of young women,
unfamiliar faces from a past life. I couldn't have them in my
possession anymore. And then I called my lawyer and formed a
foundation to give grants to emerging artists. I may just sell
some more and start an after-school arts program for the kids
in the neighborhood.

Because I still believe in art. I believe in the power of colors,
that each color has a different meaning and weight and sub-
stance, that colors are a force of nature, of the real and the
imagined. I believe in texture, that the way a rough piece
of wood feels means as much as the smoothness of iron or
the bumps of dried paint on a canvas, but they all mean
something different. I believe in the light coming out from
a photograph, just as I believe in the painted representation
with no light at all of the same moment in time. I believe
they are all true and they are all lies, and they are all important to me. None of what has happened will ever change any
of that.

. . .

WE SKIP OVER small creeks: rays of sunlight swimming around with brown leaves, delicate dragonflies, their bodies electric blue, crazily hovering. Bushes with slender leaves like spider legs frame the creeks.

"It wasn't like this ten years ago," I say. "There weren't any bugs. Or all this foliage. So much green." This is what excites me, this new growth.

Alice and Davis have quieted down in the rear. I do believe they're finally enjoying the view.

I'M LETTING DAVIS and Alice divvy up the rest of the work. There will be no calendars for college kids, no marketing of the Martin Miller mystique. But he'll have his photo show at MoMA and the retrospective at Alice's gallery. And then there's the book, which I finally agreed to, with the provision that the proceeds from it go to fund the grants program. And Davis gets to curate everything, because Davis is my friend, and because Davis never fucked my husband.

And now I'm just trying to learn how to fill my days. I drive around with Missy once a week, and flip the radio dial and listen to Missy bitch about Freddy. And I baby-sit Mira on Saturdays, so Missy can have some time to herself. We ride the train in to Chelsea and I drag her to galleries. Sometimes I take Mira shopping, and Missy yells at me when we return, bags in hand, and I ignore her. How can I not dress her up?

And Scotty meets me for coffee now every Tuesday. He lets me bounce his daughter on my knee. Everything she sees is brand-new to her, and I love watching her eyes widen at shiny things. Scotty's wife still hates me, but I pleaded temporary insanity, so she's agreed to let me come to another dinner party sometime. Maybe next year. Not soon, I suspect.

Mostly I've been hanging out with Tony. His wife saw some racy text messages from Pando and kicked him out, so he's been sleeping on my couch. I told him he could stay as long as he wants. The company's nice.

Pando came over once and the two of them made me dinner. "You just sit right back and relax," they told me, and so I did.

Outside, on Bedford Avenue, the pink crane finally unfurled, a giant middle finger to the residents of Williamsburg.

AS WE WALK farther east, closer to the mountain, the foliage starts to thin and there are only hummocks and rocks, with some flowers creeping in. The small subtle approach of a takeover. Give it another ten years, they'll win this war.

I wish Calvin and Meryl had agreed to come, but they didn't approve of Martin's cremation, nor my decision to scatter his ashes at Mount St. Helens. I called them yesterday when we arrived to try to convince them one last time. Meryl told me, "We've already said our goodbyes, dear."

"So where are we going to do this already?" says Alice. We ignore her.

We move faster, every turn taking us closer to a more spectacular view of the mountain, until finally we are dead center in front of it. It is terrifying in its size. I feel a small quiet warmth in me.

Tony whistles, low and long. "It's like a painting," he says.

I glare at Alice, defy her to question the simplicity of his statement, but she says nothing.

"It is just like a painting," says Davis.

"Then we'll do it right here," I say.

I take off my backpack and remove the canister that contains Martin's ashes.

"Stand back, everyone," I say, and then I let it blow.

Acknowledgments

The photos and introduction from Richard Avedon's *In the American West* were a direct source of inspiration for some of the photos and techniques described in the book. I first encountered these brilliant photos as a teen, and have been haunted by them ever since.

Dr. Alex Haynes kindly educated me on matters involving coma victims and their families.

A big thank-you to Sunil Thambidurai and Que Thanh Luu, for generously providing me with a lovely home in Seattle.

For their support and friendship, I am grateful to Wendy McClure, Cinde Boutwell, Kerri Mahoney, Bernie Boscoe, Whitney Pastorek, Kristin McGonigle, Sarah Balcomb, Kevin Sampsell, Lauren Cerand, Hana Schank, Stephen Byler, Sally Kim, and Neal Pollack.

A special thanks to my agent, Doug Stewart, for his wisdom and gentle guidance, and to the tenacious Megan Lynch, my amazing friend and editor, who believed in me first.

With love, as always, to my family.